HOME

*Our scars remind us
the past was real.*

Keren Hughes

ISBN 978-1-912768-09-7

Published 2018
Published by Black Velvet Seductions Publishing

HOME Copyright 2018 Keren Hughes
Cover design Copyright 2018 Jessica Greeley

Author's Note: This story is part two of a duet. To fully understand the characters, you should read SAFE *first*.

HOME is Drew's story *after* meeting Elise in SAFE. The beginning is set six months later and is still told in dual point of view. We find out more about his past and what makes him who he is.

Find someone who makes you realise three things;
One, that home is not a place, but a feeling.
Two, that time is not measured by a clock, but by moments.
And three, that heartbeats are not heard, but felt and shared
~ Author Unknown ~

Acknowledgements

I never know where to start saying thank you to people. There are so many people who have inspired me along my journey so far as an author and I'm always frightened of forgetting to thank them personally.

To everyone who took a chance on me; whether that's new readers or people who have read my books since the beginning; thank you for picking up my books, for enjoying the characters and their stories. I always say, when I am writing a book, it's mine. But when that book is published, it's yours. It no longer belongs solely to me, it belongs to everyone.

To my nan; I owe you a debt of gratitude for all that you have done for me over the years and for what you continue to do for me. You've always been the mother I wanted, the mother I deserved, and so I don't really see you as my grandmother. You're my mum. I love you dearly. So, to you, I say *diolch yn fawr*.

To my son; Calum, you are the greatest thing in my life. You are my life. I don't know whether I'd be me without you. You're my light in the darkness, my anchor when I feel adrift at sea. You'll always be my heart. Thank you for always being you.

To the real Drew; Andy, one day, you will find your own Elise. She'll be just what you need to finally knock down those walls around your heart. You're an amazing guy and if only you would allow yourself to open up to the possibility of love … take it from a woman who knows how hard it is to put yourself back out there after you've been hurt. A woman who doesn't know how to put her heart back on the line because she doesn't want to have to pick up the pieces again. Take it from someone who knows how wonderful being loved can feel … one day, you'll meet someone who will see your scars and love you regardless. Don't forget, it's our scars that remind us the past was real.

To the book community; readers, authors, bloggers … thank you to everyone who helps raise each other up instead of tearing each other down. I am proud to be part of such a close-knit community. Every day I am reminded why I keep doing this job. There are times when I've wanted to quit, but so many of you have reminded me of my love for the written word. Thank you for standing side by side with me.

To the "Boss Man" Richard Savage; Thank you for taking a chance on publishing SAFE and now HOME. I am loving being part of the BVS family. Thank you for helping me get my books out into the world. I look forward to working together for years to come!

To my cover designer, Jessica; Thank you for making this cover for Drew. This is one of my favourite covers. I love the guy you chose and those eyes! *swoon* Thank you for making the Jagged Scars Duet look fab!

To Amy Brock-McNew; Thank you for my blurb. You made me cry, because it was absolutely perfect! Thank you so much for helping a gal out. I hate writing blurbs!

Lastly, but by no means least; Thank you to YOU for picking up a copy of HOME. I hope you enjoy Drew's story. This story wasn't one I intended to write. I normally write stand-alone contemporary romances. But the real-life Drew asked me if he was getting his own story. The idea kept knocking around my head and I decided to give it a shot. I hope I did it justice and that you love learning more about our Drew's background.

Prologue

Broken. Battered. Bruised. Neglected by the people that should have loved me the most. They say a parent's love for a child is unconditional. They say a parent is a protector, there to nurture their children. Pity the same couldn't be said about mine. My mother lacked the supposedly natural maternal instincts; my father was too wrapped up in himself to be paternal. Neither one of them was any use to anybody. They only ever cared about themselves. Chasing their next high, selling everything we owned of any value so that they could pay off their dealer … that was their life. My life? Well it was … not a 'normal' childhood. It was—to me—at the time. I didn't know any better. It's only now as a grown man that I can accept that things weren't right back then.

Love was something I knew nothing of. It was a foreign concept to me. I never received it, so how could I learn to show it to anyone else? What I thought of as love turned out to be toxic, so I've gone about my life without opening my heart. I've used travel as a coping mechanism for the longest time. As soon as I was old enough to leave school, I got a job and started saving every spare penny I could. I didn't want to become anything like my parents. I've always wanted better for myself. I pushed myself to excel at school. Studied hard, stayed away from parties where there would be drink and drugs. I didn't want to turn out to be some washed-up junkie, so I made the best of everything offered to me.

Becoming a paramedic was the one thing I really wanted to do when I grew up. I'd always wanted to help people. I knew without a doubt that I wanted to try and make a difference in the lives of others. It was my way of trying to make up for my parents wasting their lives. I thought it was my job to try and make amends for what they had done. Who I was making amends to, I wasn't sure, I just felt like I had to do something. Those two people were the biggest waste of space, nothing but a big black void that sucked the life out of everything around them.

When my parents abandoned me, I felt lost. I had nobody to guide me. I ended up in care until social services could track down my maternal grandparents. My father had forced my mother to stop speaking to her parents somewhere along the way and I had grown up not knowing them. They took me in when I was fifteen and it was a very bumpy road for a while there. I wasn't a bad kid—I don't think—it's just that I wasn't used to rules and curfews, love and affection. I was used to having to do everything for myself. I always fed myself, even if it was just stale bread and a can of out of date soup. My damn parents never had much in the way of food in the house. I couldn't go to a food bank because then people would know what I was. What my parents were. As for clothes, that's a laugh. I used to have to go to the cashpoint for my mother; she got to a point where she couldn't even remember her own pin number, her brain was that drug-addled. I'd draw out what little benefits she got, I'd pay the bills, try to put a little food in the cupboards, but clothes were things I took from the lost property box at school or bought with what little of my mother's money I was able to set aside. I remember thinking it was better to have uniform for school than it was to eat because I didn't want people looking at me in ratty clothes and making fun of me or, worse still, the teachers catching wind of there being trouble at home. As much as I detested my parents, I didn't want to end up in the system, so I did all I could to get by. I ate dinner at school every day; that was something my mother's benefits afforded me—free school meals.

As it turned out, being in the system wasn't something I could avoid. The day my parents overdosed was the day I could no longer hide what was going on.

Questions about my life began on that fateful day and, where I'd once kept everything bottled up, I felt I could finally unburden myself on those who were intent on helping me. It took a few days to track down my mother's parents because they lived in another county to us and I hadn't known anything useful about them to tell social services. They finally found them and placed me in their care. The foster family I'd had had been nice enough. In fact, they couldn't do enough for me. I just didn't know what to do because that wasn't what I was used to. Clean clothes, clean bedding, food in the cupboards, hot running water … I wasn't used to any of those things. People who cared where I was, what I was doing … I wasn't used to that either. It was all so alien to me.

When I moved in with Edie and Albert—or Pops, as he liked to be called—I was so out of my depth. I didn't have to go and withdraw my mother's money to pay the bills and make sure we had electric so I could wash my clothes. I didn't have to go to bed hungry; I could eat until I was fit to burst. Edie and Pops were so openly affectionate towards me and each other, it was unusual for me to see such a happy couple that weren't wasted, jonesing for their next fix. Edie wasn't gaunt in the face like Miriam had been. I could see a light in her eyes that had never been present in Miriam's. She was a very naturally maternal woman. Pops was gruff, strict, made sure I knew to be home by curfew—not that I had many friends to hang out with anyway, I just used to tell them I did so they didn't have to pity me—but he was loving and had the energy of a man ten years younger.

I learned about love from Edie and Pops. I finally knew what it was supposed to mean. I just still hadn't felt it. Yes, I'd felt familial love for my grandparents, but that's not the same, not even remotely. I wasn't sure I was ready to love anyone anyway. I was still so young and had so much of my life ahead of me. I could really work towards my goal of becoming a paramedic now that I had a stable environment that was conducive to studying. Edie and Pops gave me everything they could, but, as soon as I left school, I attended college and got myself a job so that I could pay my own way. They never would take a penny from me; they told me to put it aside for when I really needed it. So that's what I did. I worked my ass off, really busted my balls studying and working. Then, when I finally got my diploma for higher education in paramedic sciences, I found I had to bust my balls even harder so that I could get an advanced driving qualification. Pops paid for me to have driving lessons when I turned eighteen. We'd argued about it of course—I'd wanted to pay my own way—but he and Edie wouldn't hear of it. So I studied hard for my theory and practiced often with Pops so I could pass my practical test. Driving an ambulance is totally different. For a start, you get taught evasive manoeuvres. That bit was fun though, I will admit.

When I decided I wanted more than to be a paramedic—I wanted to pursue search and rescue, maybe water rescue—Edie and Pops were there for me every step of the way. But that's not to say it was easy. I still didn't trust people easily and I didn't have many friends outside of work colleagues. I worked my ass off to learn what I needed to so that I could join the search and rescue team. I spent a while with water rescue after that. All the time, I was putting money aside for my future.

Pops and Edie helped me get a deposit together for an apartment of my own. It was a modest, two-bedroom place in a new build that wasn't far from their home. They also bought me a car when I turned twenty-one. I splurged and bought myself a motorbike. Edie was worried for my safety, but Pops told her the same thing I did—having learned everything on that advanced driving course, I'd be okay. I still wasn't used to being cared about, even after all the years Pops and Edie had been in my life. They were the only two people I let close. Until Elise Swanson. But she broke my heart, so I put my apartment up for rent while I took the first of what would be many trips overseas. Travelling became a crutch I leaned on heavily. I could be by myself—which is how I liked things—and I got to see some incredible sights.

My life was finally turning itself around. My hard work was paying off. I had two people who acted like my parents. I had a great job and was finally opening myself up to being friends with some of the other lads on the job.

That's one thing the job makes you do—you learn to trust and rely on your partner. It's a necessity in a job like mine. That's how I met Danny, Luke and Seb. They even came travelling with me sometimes.

I'd just started working at a new hospital and became friends with one of the nurses, Sam, when she said she wanted to set me up on a blind date. I kept saying no. I didn't want a relationship and random hook-ups were only good for so much. I didn't want to hurt her friend, knowing I didn't know how to give anyone my heart.

The walls around my heart were so tall. You couldn't climb over them, you couldn't dig a way underneath them. Impenetrable. That's what they were. I had to be bulletproof. What was the use in loving someone when they'd fuck you over one day, one way or another? I mean, my own parents were the prime example of that. When they were still alive, they beat me for spending money on the bills instead of letting them have more for their habit. They neglected me to the point where I retreated into myself to protect my sanity. They broke me. I thought that my life was slowly piecing me back together, that I was finally on the right track; but I still didn't have time for a woman.

Sam had other ideas. She showed me a picture of her friend. That red hair was what caught my attention first. My mind flashed back to red hair splayed over my pillow, smelling like shampoo and something that was impossible to name. Drawing my eyes back to the picture on Sam's phone, I looked over every inch of the woman. She was beautiful, the purest kind of beauty. Red hair, blue eyes, creamy skin … more tattoos than I remembered, but I was sure it was her. I asked Sam her name and, when she told me, that was when my heart beat for the first time in years.

I walked into the bar and saw her immediately. She was everything I remembered and more. That smile as she saw me—it was shy and endearing. A range of emotions flitted across her face and the instant our gazes locked my heart beat for the second time in years. All those old feelings rushed to the surface. Her blue eyes shone brightly and her lips were painted a soft pink. She looked gorgeous in black leggings and a purple tunic style top. As beautiful as she ever was; just the sight of her had my heart beating a little faster.

I knew in that moment, just as I know today, Elise Swanson was going to become my home.

Chapter One

Drew

I've been looking forward to tonight for the last two weeks. I haven't spent time with my wife, just the two of us, in too long. In reality it's only been a couple of weeks or so, but it feels so much longer. Work has been hectic and, with a six-month-old baby, an eleven year old son and Elise returning to work—even if it is only part-time—we haven't had any alone time. When we had Cassie, we promised each other that we'd still have 'date nights' so that we had some time as Drew and Elise, not just mummy and daddy. I love our children and I love our life, but I also like it when we get Sam and Karl to babysit so we can go to the cinema or for a meal. So many people make the mistake of not making time solely for each other and it leads to marital problems, hence why Elise and I made the promise.

Elise has been diagnosed with mild postnatal depression. It hasn't affected her bond with Cassie, but it has impacted life in general. She loves our daughter just as much as I do and she is the best mum I've ever seen, but there are times when she feels depressed and I make sure to help her the best way I know how. Counselling has helped and, though she didn't want to at first, she's accepted taking medication until the doctor says she doesn't need it anymore.

Elise is such an amazing woman and it's hard for me to see her feeling so down at times. She suffers from anxiety, so that doesn't help the situation either. She feels like she isn't a good enough wife or a good enough mum. I need her to know that she's wrong. I need her to know how much she means to me, to our family.

The deep purple wraparound dress she's wearing looks incredible. I rake my eyes over her body, from her head to her painted toenails. She has a great figure—not supermodel stick thin, she's curvy in all the right places with voluptuous breasts. The dress accentuates her cleavage, but not to a trashy level, in fact, she looks divine. My cock twitches in my boxers and I suddenly don't feel as hungry as I did moments ago—well, not for food anyway.

I'm pretty sure I'm looking at her the way a man on death row looks at his last meal, salivating and making a fool of myself. Suddenly I'm picturing what she's wearing underneath the dress, impatiently awaiting the moment I get to strip it from her and make love to her. I thought our sex life might diminish slightly after Cassie was born, but I was wrong. She's as insatiable as she has always been and the salacious grin across her face right now proves she's having similar thoughts to me.

"My eyes are up here, Drew," she says softly.

"Hmm…" is all I can manage to respond.

My gaze locks with hers and I see a twinkle of mirth in her beautiful blue eyes.

"Does my bum look big in this?" she asks as she twirls on the spot.

"Don't be daft. You look … incredible."

Why is it every woman is obsessed with their bum looking big in something?

"You don't scrub up too badly yourself, Mr Wright," she says, as she makes her way towards me.

I stand and pull her into my arms. The material of her dress feels so soft and silky, but it's nothing in comparison to the feel of her naked flesh against me. I feel like a hormonal teenage boy right now.

People say we're just in 'the honeymoon period' and it'll wear off soon, the newness of it will rub off and we'll be left like every other couple out there. But I know in my heart we aren't like that. I'm going to feel this way about her forever. I feel it soul deep.

Leaning down, I slant my mouth over her soft, full lips. It's a sweet kiss, soft, gentle, our tongues dancing rhythmically. My cock stirs to life and I break away before I sweep her off her feet and carry her to our bedroom, lock the door and never leave.

"Hey, it's a good job LipSense is kiss-proof," she says with a touch of sass as she pulls a compact mirror from her small clutch to double check and reapply her lip gloss.

What is it with women and their cosmetics? Personally, I like seeing lipstick marks around my cock, but I guess that's not what it's about.

Checking the time, I grab my car keys and turn to my beautiful wife. "We'll miss our reservation if we don't get a move on."

"Two seconds," she says as she taps something out on her phone. No doubt it's a text to Sam to make sure Cassie is okay.

Tonight is the first night Cassie will be staying elsewhere overnight. We haven't left her with anyone except for a couple of hours here and there. We're both nervous, but I trust Sam implicitly.

Putting her phone in her clutch, Elise walks to the front door, putting an extra sway in her step to tempt me, knowing I love her sexy ass.

I take her hand and walk out to the car. A smile spreads across my face as I imagine her surprise at what I have in store for our anniversary tonight.

***

The private room at Olive Garden looks beautiful. It's draped in golds and reds with plush comfortable seating and a table set for two. There's a bucket with a bottle on ice and a waiter standing to one side, ready to pour our first glass.

Elise's eyes light up as she turns to look at me. From the smile on her face, I can tell she likes my surprise.

On the drive to the restaurant I didn't tell her where we were going, and she knew better than to keep pestering me for an answer. She knows I'm stubborn and I wouldn't tell her and risk ruining our evening.

She sits across from me and I see her eyes shine in the candlelight. Her hair looks lustrous as it falls over her shoulders in long red curls. She really is breathtaking.

"This is so beautiful," she remarks, as the waiter takes the bottle and pours us both a glass of champagne.

"Not as beautiful as you."

A blush creeps across her chest at the simple compliment. She's still not used to being told how beautiful she is, even after how long we've been together.

We order our food and, when it arrives, it tastes divine, but I can't help wanting to rush so that we can get home faster. I know it's our first night without both kids and that I should slow down and savour the moment, so I sit and watch Elise as she talks about the food and the atmosphere here.

I feel a shiver run through me as Elise runs her foot up the inside of my leg. My cock twitches once in response and it's all I can do not to scoop her up caveman-style, throw some money on the table and race back to my car.

She runs her foot up to my thigh and I groan involuntarily. As her foot reaches my groin, I have to hold myself back from clearing the table in one fell swoop and taking her right here, right now.

Her eyes twinkle mischievously as her foot flexes against my semi-hard cock. She knows just what she's doing and the delight is evident on her face. I want to move back out of her reach just to see what she'll do, but I can't tear myself away from her touch. My lips can form no words, only soft moans.

Her foot shifts abruptly as the waiter re-enters the room. A slight blush spreads across her face as if she's been caught. Her eyes dance with silent laughter and I discreetly rearrange myself under the cover of the table.

***

We can't get home fast enough for my liking. I've had a great evening, but now I need my wife naked beneath me. For once, we don't have to lock the bedroom door to stop Caleb accidentally walking in on us. There's no need to turn the baby monitor on to keep tabs on Cassie.

The house is silent as we open the door. I tell Elise to take a seat in the lounge while I fix us a drink. After pouring her a glass of rosé, I back out of the room with a smile on my face.

Hurrying up the stairs, I pull the bag out of its hiding space, glad that she hasn't found it. I start placing things where I need them to be. I make sure the iPod is connected to the Bluetooth speaker and turn the volume so that it's playing softly in the background. I light some candles and scatter rose petals across the bed and the floor. Walking out of the bedroom door, I sprinkle a few more petals from the doorway and down the stairs.

As I walk into the lounge I look at my wife and my heart beats faster in my ribcage, so fast it feels like it's trying to break free from its constraints. Her red hair spills over her cleavage and her lips part on a sigh.

She places her wine on the coffee table as she sees me approach. Her eyes assess me like she's trying to figure what my game is.

"Time for an early night, sweetheart," I tell her in a gentle tone, but one that brooks no arguments.

Elise stands and gives me a soft kiss, but I pull away before she can do much more. I take her hand in mine and walk to the bottom of the staircase.

A soft sigh escapes her as she sees the rose petals. I urge her up the stairs ahead of me. The soft music plays through the bedroom door and I can hear Curtis Stigers singing 'You're All That Matters To Me'.

I open the door for Elise and watch her face light up as she sees the room before her. I've been planning tonight since I swapped shifts with Danny so that I could have the night with my wife.

"Drew, this is—"

She doesn't get to finish her sentence because I slant my mouth over hers and gently probe her lips with my tongue, seeking access to deepen our kiss. Goosebumps break out on my skin and I feel the hairs at the nape of my neck stand on end. One touch from her still makes me feel giddy. One touch sets my very soul on fire. I know that we were made for each other and that this is the life I was meant to live. Before Elise came along, my life was more of an existence. But now? Now I am truly alive and I want to make the most of every nano-second of it.

Breaking our kiss, I take her hand and lead her to the bed. I turn her to face me and gently edge her back until the backs of her knees hit the bed and she sits on reflex. I move to remove her shoes; holding her leg in my hand, I place a trail of kisses from her ankle to her knee. She shudders under my touch and I smile to myself.

As I kneel at her feet, I move her dress to one side to kiss further up her legs and am shocked to find that she's wearing no panties, the little minx. I can't help the growl that escapes me and the light laughter coming from her means she knows exactly what she's doing to me. My cock twitches to life and I undo my zipper because it's straining to be free. I slide my palm down over my shaft to appease the ache, but it only fuels me more when Elise lies back on the bed, her legs spread, showing me her glistening pink pussy.

I look up at my wife sprawled out on our bed and wonder how the fuck I got this lucky. I don't know what I ever did to deserve her, but I'm damn sure I'm going to make her as happy as she makes me, every day for the rest of our lives.

Sliding my hands up her thighs, I feel her legs quiver under my light touch. I'm not big headed when I say I know what effect I have on her.

A long sigh escapes Elise as I make my move, licking her once. Hands come to my hair and I move to lick her in languid strokes. She whispers a string of expletives as she writhes on the bed.

Palming my cock again, I find no relief. It's begging to be inside her. But I can't give in to those urges. I need to see her fall apart from my touch first. I slip a finger inside her and Elise arches her back off the bed. Her warmth is too inviting, so I slip a second finger inside her and feel her buck against my hand, matching my rhythm. Her hands in my hair pull my mouth closer to her, silently pleading with me to give her what she needs. I've never been one to say no when it comes to this woman, so I finally give in and move to suck her clit.

"Fuck, Drew…I…"

She doesn't need to say more for me to know what's coming. Her walls tighten around my fingers and I increase the pace of them inside her.

"Baby, I'm…I'm going to…"

Hooking my fingers to hit that sweet spot over and over, my baby comes so hard that her legs quake either side of me and her body shudders. I withdraw my fingers and lick her once more, slowly.

Standing over her, I watch her come up to her elbows on the bed. She watches me as I remove my trousers and pull off my shirt. When I'm naked, I take my shaft in my hand and see her pupils dilate as she watches my every move. I jerk my hand up and down a couple of times, pre-cum glistening on the tip. I can't wait any longer to be inside her. It's a primal urge, screaming at me.

Elise stands and pulls her dress over her head. She undoes her bra— the only underwear she was wearing—and discards it on the floor. But, just when I think she's going to lie back down, she grabs a pillow to put under her bad knee and kneels at the foot of the bed.

What my baby wants, my baby gets, so I lie down in front of her and open my legs for her to kneel between.

As she grips my shaft in her hand, I can't help the groan that escapes my lips, or the involuntary smile that graces them. Leaning up on my elbows, I see a wicked gleam in Elise's eyes as her tongue darts out to lick the pre-cum from my tip. Her tongue swirls and a delicious feeling spreads throughout me.

Her hand and mouth work in tandem, bringing an almost euphoric feeling with them. She takes me deep in the back of her throat and I moan loudly as she gently cups my balls. I feel a tightening sensation and know I am not far from my own climax. I'm torn between the need to be inside her and the need to come down the back of her throat. My body betrays my mind as she grips me firmly and her mouth moves up and down over me. Moments later, I feel myself come in hot spurts down her throat, coating her tongue. Her name is like a prayer and a curse on my tongue as I shout it out into the night.

As she licks the tip of me clean, she smiles that salacious grin of hers. I help her onto the bed and lay her beside me.

We're wrapped around each other in a tangle of limbs. I'm sated, yet not nearly sated enough. I'll need a few minutes to be ready to go again. Real life isn't like you see on television or read about in romance novels; I can't just be ready at the click of my fingers, much as I wish I could. But, in this moment I don't care. I'm lying here with my beautiful wife in my arms, knowing there's nowhere on earth I'd rather be.

Tracing circles on her back with one hand, I cup the other to her cheek and draw her in for kiss. What's meant to be a soft, sweet kiss turns into more. Elise's mouth claims mine in a fiery, passionate kiss. I feel like she's all I need to breathe and, for a moment, I feel dizzy, hypnotised by the power she wields. It's only when I lose myself completely in Elise that I find myself. The emptiness inside me fades and disappears. She fills the empty parts of me and breathes new life into them. It's in moments like this that I understand what it means to have a soulmate. Her soul calls to mine—maybe because we've both had so much hurt in our lives and our souls recognise that in each other. It sings its siren song and I am powerless to resist it. But I find that I wouldn't *want* to resist it, even if I could.

***

After a night of making love to my wife time and time again—including around three a.m. when she woke me and stirred the desire flooding my veins—I wake up in her arms. I catch a glimpse of sunlight shining down on her face and I take a moment to appreciate her natural beauty. She's relaxed in sleep and looks peaceful. For once, she won't be woken by Cassie and I don't need to be at work until this evening. Moving to cup her breast in my hand, I run my thumb over her newly pierced nipple. I was shocked when she had it done a few weeks ago but now I love it. Almost as much as I love her tongue piercing. Her breathing changes and I know I'm drawing her from her slumber. Maybe I'm a selfish prick and should have left her to sleep for once, but I'm hard and horny. Plus, she woke me at three this morning, so it's only fair to get my payback.

Leaning down, I trace circles around her nipple piercing with my tongue. I feel her gently tug my hair to bring my face up to hers. The look in her eyes says she doesn't mind being woken so rudely and I'm guessing she wants to make the most of our kid-free time.

I claim her lips with mine and gently coax them open with the tip of my tongue. The kiss starts soft and sweet, but Elise soon deepens it. It's passionate, intense and breathtaking.

A soft hand gently takes hold of my cock, the contact making me gasp and shudder. I feel like a teenager being touched for the first time. As I harden, she grips me more firmly and rubs her finger over the tip, smearing the pre-cum that glistens there.

Her kiss is more fervent and I can feel my heart pounding. I roll us so that she is beneath me. I want so much to be buried inside her—it's like an ingrained need. Sex isn't just sex with us, it's making love. Whether it's a 'quickie' or something more, it's always done with all the love my heart has feared feeling for so long. I kiss my way along her jawline to her ear where I nip her gently and carry on kissing down to the hollow of her throat before moving further down to the swell of her cleavage. I take one taut nipple in my mouth whilst I brush my thumb over the one with the piercing. Feeling Elise's hand in my hair—her silent plea for me to bite her just the way she likes—I gently bite her nipple. The moan it elicits makes my cock ache. Slipping a finger between her folds, I find her wet and ready for me. I've never asked why, but she likes being bitten, sometimes I've even left her with a sort of bruise or lovebite.

Gently I push one finger inside her, making her arch her back slightly off the bed. I know I've hit the spot when she moans loudly, so I add a second finger and hit the spot with a touch more force.

"Drew…" she says on a sigh.

"Yes, baby?"

"Harder."

Just that one word from her makes my pulse spike. I work her harder and faster, sucking and biting her nipple before crashing my mouth to hers. Feeling her walls tighten around my fingers, I know what's going to happen. I rub my thumb over her clit and within moments, she's coming in waves.

Positioning myself over her, I see her watch as I lick the essence

of her from me. There's something about me doing that which makes
her horny as hell. I feel the wicked grin spread across my face and see
it reflected in hers.

Her soft hand reaches down to guide me into her. She's impatient
this morning, but then so am I.

I push into her, wanting to hold back and make her wait, but at the
same time not wanting to wait a moment longer myself. It's inexplicable
how she feels around me. The best word is intoxicating. I'll never stop
wanting her and never get enough of her.

Chapter Two

Elise

Last night was amazing. I love it when we get a night to ourselves, our 'date night.' That's not to say I don't love our life the way it is as mummy and daddy, but it's nice to get some time where we're just Drew and Elise. I got a little emotional when it came to leaving Cassie with Sam. Not because she's not capable of looking after her—I know full well she is—it's just that with Cassie only being six months old, I feel bad about leaving her with anyone. I was the same when Caleb was born; maybe it's separation anxiety, I don't know. Drew tells me it's just a natural part of parenthood, the inherent worry. Of course, Cassie was fine. I didn't think she'd be anything but. But it was nice picking her up this morning and holding her warm little body against mine. Inhaling her sweet baby scent made me relax; I let go of the tension in my body and held my little girl until she fell back to sleep.

Life hasn't been easy since Cassie came along. I don't blame her for it in any way, but postnatal depression isn't something I wanted to end up with. I had it with Caleb, so it wasn't all that much of a surprise when the doctor diagnosed it again. I'm doing my best every day not to let it get the better of me. Drew has helped more than he knows, just being here for me every day, as much as work allows. In the first weeks after Cassie arrived, he took paternity leave and was around 24/7. It took some getting used to when he went back to work, what with his shift patterns, but we're managing well now.

Drew really is the best dad my children could wish for. He does the school run with Caleb, helps with his homework, takes him over the park to play football—all the things dads do with their sons. He also does night feeds with Cassie and lets me lie in so I can get as much rest as possible. I couldn't love him more for all that he does for us and for the wonderful husband he is. Sometimes I wonder if I tell him often enough how much I love him. At times, when the postnatal depression makes me feel at my lowest, I wonder why he loves me so much and why he stays. His way of reassuring me is to hold me in his arms, stroke my hair and tell me how much he loves me. In reality, I know he cares, I know how much he loves me; there are just times I question why.

Since the doctor put me on the medication to help with the effects of the PND, I have had fewer episodes like that. I feel more like myself again. Any kind of depression isn't easy, but with someone like Drew on my side, I know I can get through it. With him beside me, I feel like I can do anything.

Work takes my mind off my issues, but I'm only back part-time due to Cassie being just six months old. I didn't intend to go back to work so soon, but as a lot of it is a job I can do from home I don't have to leave Cassie with a nanny or put her in daycare—I can still be there for her myself—so I don't have to feel guilty. My assistant Amanda has been working out of the office. We keep in contact via email and phone and she has access to my online diary to help me keep track of event bookings. We've been getting increasingly busier as the business has got off the ground. Whether it's from our advertising or word-of-mouth from people that have used our services, business has boomed and I couldn't be happier that Memories Made is really taking shape.

Life with Drew over the last few years has been amazing. We've gone from strength to strength, even with my new doubts casting shadows over us. Anybody would think we're teenagers in the first flushes of a new love. Or maybe they think we're in the 'honeymoon period' or something. But we both know that isn't the case. I couldn't ask for a more loving, devoted husband.

It's the time of year where the hospital Drew works for starts to arrange their Christmas Ball and this year they've asked me to organise everything. It's a big job, but, between Amanda and myself, I'm sure we'll give them an event to remember. Hopefully, they'll enjoy it so much that they'll ask us to organise it again next year and the year after and so on. It would be amazing to have their repeat custom. Maybe the hospital trust could even end up asking us to organise balls for other hospitals in the local PCT. Maybe I'm getting a bit ahead of myself, but it sure would be fantastic.

Drew has the day off so he's looking after Cassie while Amanda drives us to a couple of venues to scope out for the ball. This year, the hospital has decided on a masquerade ball and there are a couple of beautiful options for where to hold it.

"This place is stunning," Amanda remarks as we pull up outside our first venue, Westbury Park Manor House.

"It's breathtaking," I say as I get out of the car, making sure to take my walking stick with me.

"The outside certainly has the 'wow factor'—I just hope the inside lives up to expectations. It looked fantastic on the internet, but there's nothing better than seeing it in real life."

Amanda turns around in the car park, looking out over the grounds and up at the imposing building.

This isn't just dependent on the venue though, it depends whether it falls into the price bracket that the hospital has given us to work with. There's so much more than just the venue to organise—we need to think of decorations, whether we can have an open bar, all sorts of things that need attention to detail. I have my notepad and pen ready to take notes and my digital camera ready to take some photos.

I take a few quick snaps of the grounds and the outside of the building. Amanda poses in front of the camera and pulls some funny faces; she's such a hoot, that girl. She always has a smile on her face and a pleasant disposition. I like taking her to meet potential clients because she seems to wrap them around her little finger.

"Good morning, ladies. My name is Pryce and I have been asked to show you around the halls," an attractive, slightly older man says as he approaches us.

Amanda's eyes are out on stalks; they look like they will fall out of her head if she isn't careful. I can see why—he has a look of Jason Isaacs about him. Tall, dark hair, good physique … he'd definitely be droolworthy if I wasn't a married woman.

"Good morning, Pryce," I say as I extend my hand to shake his. "I'm Elise, owner of Memories Made. This is my assistant, Amanda."

They shake hands too and I can swear I see sparks between the two of them.

Pryce walks us to the halls, stopping to allow me to take photos as we go. As we enter the main hall, I almost stop breathing. The room is incredible. It looks way out of our price range, but I'm still eager to see if we can negotiate a deal. I take out my notebook and pen, cursing myself silently for not buying a Dictaphone so I can transcribe my notes later.

Pryce tells us the décor can be changed to fit our theme and I scribble away as he talks. Amanda stands next to him, utterly transfixed by the room. It's momentarily taken her attentions away from Pryce.

Smiling to myself, I ask Pryce if we can go to the office to talk figures. He leads the way and, once we are seated, he asks if we'd like a drink.

Once I have a steaming mug of coffee in front of me, I ask the questions on my list. I'm stunned that the price is so reasonable, but glad that it is. This year's masquerade ball will be donating funds raised from ticket sales to the air ambulance, a charity, it would seem, that's close to Pryce's heart. He remarks how they saved his sister's life and how grateful he is, so he'd like to do anything he can to help us out.

We leave for the second venue, but only because it would be rude to cancel. In the back of my mind, I want to have it here and Amanda agrees.

After paying a visit to the second place, I make some notes and take photos, but, although it is beautiful, neither myself nor Amanda feel the same vibe about it as we did when we were at Westbury Park Manor House. Ultimately it isn't up to us as I must convey our findings to Emma Greyling, the person responsible for organizing this ball. She works for the hospital and would normally find the venue and make the arrangements herself, but as I helped them out with a Christmas Ball before, she contacted me again. She was so pleased with how it turned out that she wanted to retain my services again and I was only too happy to help.

Emma and I exchange emails and I send her the photos and notes I took from each place. She also prefers Westbury Park Manor House, so that's a relief. Amanda smiles a near face-splitting smile when I tell her we're going ahead and booking it there. I can't help but wonder whether it's because of the place itself or because of Pryce. It's most likely both.

I fire off an email to Pryce, letting him know that we would love to do business with them and his reply is enthusiastic. I'm wondering if he digs Amanda in the same way she does him.

Pulling up outside my house, Amanda drops me off and drives away with a wave. Drew greets me with a smile and a soft kiss as I enter the kitchen to make coffee. We talk about the venue and I show him the photos I took. He pulls a drawer open and takes a small box out before handing it over to me.

"What's this?"

"Open it and find out."

"It's not Christmas yet, why am I opening a gift?" I ask as I stare down at the box in my hand.

"Just do it," Drew replies with a smile and a wink.

I unwrap the box carefully and take off the lid to reveal a Dictaphone.

Pulling Drew in for a hug, I thank him for his thoughtful gesture.

"You keep saying you need one and yet you never seem to get around to buying one. So, this is to make life easier for you."

I capture his soft, full lips with mine and kiss him gently. He wraps his arms around my waist and pulls me closer to deepen the kiss. I allow him to take control and I squeal as he lifts me off my feet and places me carefully on the kitchen counter in front of him. He nestles between my legs and I cross my ankles behind him. Moments later, his hands are in my hair, drawing me closer to kiss me once more. I don't allow myself to think, I just give myself over to my husband. I kiss him with every ounce of love inside of me. He may not know it, but Drew pieced me back together. He gave me the missing piece of the jigsaw puzzle when he came back into my life.

Breaking our kiss, Drew lifts me down gently and I stand on the floor once more. He takes my hand in his and pulls me toward the staircase.

"Where's Cassie?" I ask as I hesitate at the foot of the stairs.

"Fast asleep. I put her down about ten minutes before you got home."

I follow as Drew walks upstairs to our room. Closing the door behind me, I turn to face him only to bump into him. He cages me between him and the door and leans in to kiss me, his tongue dueling with mine for control. His hand traces the bottom of my blouse and I shiver as he makes contact with my stomach. The butterflies take flight and I relish in the sensation Drew's touch elicits.

Taking my hand in his, Drew momentarily breaks our heated kiss and pulls me in the direction of our bed. He stands before me and begins to undo the buttons of my blouse. In a flash, he discards the purple material and brings both hands to cup my breasts. I moan as he runs his thumb over my piercing before unzipping my skirt and letting it pool at my feet. His hands are back on me in an instant, roaming my body and setting each place he touches on fire. If there's one thing I can say, my libido hasn't lessened since giving birth to Cassie.

Lying me back gently on the bed, Drew hooks his thumbs in my panties and peels them down my legs. Then he unhooks my bra, leaving me lying there exposed. I feel his gaze roam my body and I've never felt more alive.

***

Cassie is awake and hungry, so I make her bottle as Drew coos over her and keeps her occupied. We head into the lounge, where I take a seat on the sofa and Drew passes Cassie over to me. Looking down at my daughter, I see the innocence in her beautiful hazel eyes and I'm transfixed by her. She's the most beautiful little girl in the whole world—in my eyes at least—and I love her with all my heart. Nothing means more to me than family.

I didn't have the greatest upbringing myself. Well, that's an understatement really. My family were no real family to me. There's no love lost between me and them. What's that old saying? You can't lose what you never had. Well, I am determined that my children will have a better life afforded to them than that. While there is breath in my body, there is love in my heart.

Chapter Three

Drew

Watching my wife feed our daughter is a beautiful sight to behold. They are the picture of love and adoration. The only thing better to watch is my whole family together; Elise, Caleb and Cassie. They are everything to me. I don't know what I did before they came into my life and transformed it in the blink of an eye. Elise's face glows with the happiness of motherhood; something natural, something that makes her even more beautiful to me.

For a moment—the time it takes in between heartbeats—I am taken back to when I was a child.

My mother is looking at me as though I disgust her. My cheek still stings and my eyes hold unshed tears. I've learned not to cry around her or my father because it only makes them angrier. I'm pretty sure if I looked in the mirror, I would see a glowing red handprint on my face. I really angered her this time. I took longer to get her next fix than I should have done. I'd been over the park with my friends and hadn't realised the time until it was too late. I pedaled my bike as fast as my legs could go, but it wasn't fast enough.

Walking into the house half an hour later than I should have, I try to play it off as the clock in the house must be wrong. Anything to try and deflect her anger from me. But for once she seems coherent. Probably because her last fix is wearing off. She's not always so lucid on a come-down, but there are times when she can seem almost normal to anyone on the outside looking in.

She snatches the small, clear bag out of my grasp and empties the contents onto a mirror. I watch as she separates it into neat lines before snorting one up each nostril and hands the rest to my father.

I want to run to my room and lock the door behind me, but I'm tired and hungry. I'm still rooted to the spot where she slapped me, my feet feel heavy, like something is holding me in place.

My father waves a hand in my direction, dismissing me without speaking. I make my way to the kitchen and pull open the cupboards, hoping to find sustenance, but knowing I'll find fuck all in there. As I've grown older, I've learned to have my own hiding spaces, so I tiptoe quietly up the stairs so as not to disturb my parents.

Once I'm in my room, I pull the carpet up in the corner before taking hold of the floorboard and wiggling it out of place. It may not be the most hygienic hiding space, but it's one of the only places I know my parents won't check. As a growing thirteen-year-old, I need to eat more than I did when I was younger and there's never enough in the cupboards, even though I try to squirrel away some of my parent's' benefits for food. I try to make sure they have something in the cupboards for themselves, but most of the time they're too out of it to remember to eat. You can see it in how gaunt my mother's face has become. Her skin is sallow and her eyes are dull.

I remember a time when my mother was beautiful. I'm not sure if it's a memory or just the way I see her in old photos. There are albums with photos of my parents looking normal, healthy, happy—especially their wedding photos—but there's not much point in looking through them because it only serves to make me sad. I'm sad that life has come to this. I've wondered for years whether they ever meant to have me and why they bothered. It's not like they're good parents. But they're the only parents I have, so I do what I can to help us get by.

People might ask why I fetch their drugs, why I don't just tell them I won't be a part of it and that, if they want them, they should get them themselves. But the thing people don't understand is that without the drugs they are worse. When they are going through withdrawals, I get beaten more often. It's like that's when they remember I'm there. So I enable them the way I do because it hurts me to see them in pain going through withdrawals, but also because I know what they'll do to me. Is that selfish of me? If I'm being honest, yes, I am selfish. I would rather they were off their faces and oblivious to my existence because that way I'm safer. The amount of times I've been beaten, the number of bones I've broken…it's safer to give them what they want.

Pulling the box out of the hole under the floorboard, I place it on my bed. I open the lid and grab a can of beans and some bread. I can't chance going downstairs to warm the beans or toast the bread, so I use the tin opener in my bedside drawer to open the can before grabbing a spoon. I settle against my headboard and eat the cold baked beans and slightly stale bread. I know I'll *have to get some more shopping in soon, but I can't risk taking too much of their money. Most of the time, they are too out of it to notice if I take just a little. But it depends how much their next fix costs. They can't always use the same dealer because they are known on our estate as people that don't pay their debts. There's always someone knocking on the door demanding money.*

"Drew, sweetie… Drew…"

I am pulled from my reverie by Elise's gentle voice. She looks at me and the love she has for me is evident on her face.

"Sorry, I was miles away," I reply, shaking my head to clear the fog that resides there.

I've told Elise things about my past, but not in full technicolour detail. She had a hard enough past of her own without me burdening her with more shit in her life. She'll never have to meet them, so she doesn't have to worry about what her in-laws are—or rather, 'were'—like. She knows they weren't good to me. I know that's an understatement, but I can't bring myself to tell her to just what extent they hurt me. Edie and Pops were the only parental figures I ever had in my life and they were all I needed. Unfortunately, they passed away before Elise could meet them. They didn't get to meet their great-grandchildren and that is something that saddens me. Edie would have lavished our two children with love and affection, something she was famous for. And Pops would have told them great stories from the war, just like he did with me. He was famous amongst my friends as the greatest storyteller.

"I was just thinking that we could do something before your shift tonight. Maybe we could go to the park, take a football for you and Caleb to have a kick around. What do you think?"

"Yeah, sounds good," I reply, trying to muster some enthusiasm.

Thinking about my parents always makes me melancholy. But I mentally shake it off because Elise needs me in the present. She once told me that it doesn't serve any purpose to live in the past. She was talking about both of our pasts, knowing we've both had it rough in different ways. Her words were wise. It really doesn't do us any good to live in the past because we miss what's going on in the present. Before our wedding day, I made her a vow that I will do my utmost to keep; I will live for today and all the tomorrows yet to come. We have a bright future ahead of us and, as she said, we should make the most of it. We must find a way to give our children everything we missed out on.

Making new memories every day is the only way forward. Once you've hit rock bottom, the only way is up. And we really are going up.

When we get to the park, Caleb grabs the football from the boot of the car.

"I hate that you have to work Saturdays, Dad," he says as he kicks it towards me.

"I know, buddy, it sucks. But I don't work every Saturday. I'm not on shift next weekend at all," I say as I dribble the ball between my feet.

"We should have a movie night," he says enthusiastically.

"What should we watch?" I ask, already knowing his answer.

"IT," he replies, completely taking me by surprise. "Gotcha!" he adds with a laugh.

"You little monkey."

I forget the ball and chase after him. Tackling him to the ground, I make him roar with laughter.

"Behave, boys, behave, or else you won't get an ice cream when the van comes this way," Elise shouts at us.

We get up, brush the grass off ourselves and make our way back to where I left the ball.

"So, what film shall we really watch?"

"*Logan.*"

"Again?"

"Yeah. We can get some popcorn and sweets. We could even build a fort in the lounge so we can chill out."

If we've watched that film once, we must have watched it a hundred times. I laugh at the thought of having to endure it again.

"Why do you like that film so much anyway?"

"Because of Laura, of course! She badass and I love that she can talk but *chooses* not to."

"Language!" Elise chastens.

"Oops, sorry mum. It just slipped out. I promise I won't say it again."

I don't think badass is swearing—although, a boy of his age probably shouldn't say 'ass',—but I don't say anything, knowing it's not a good idea to disagree with Elise in front of Caleb.

Kicking the ball around tires us both out and we're glad when the ice cream van pulls up just a little way from us. I nudge Caleb and we both get up from the ground where we've collapsed, exhausted. We make our way over and then traipse back to the girls with ice creams in hand. Caleb made sure we got sauces of all flavours and a flake in each of our cones. The kid could eat his weight in ice cream and not put on a pound; I don't know where it goes, but we joke he must have hollow legs.

Sitting back on the grass, we eat in relative peace and quiet. Cassie wakes up and Elise takes her out of the pushchair, bringing her to lie in her arms. Caleb passes her a bottle from the changing bag and Elise thanks him before removing the lid and giving Cassie a little milk.

I watch her, my attention rapt on the visible bond between mother and daughter. Elise is such a great mum and it warms my heart to see her so in love with our little girl.

When Elise first announced that she was pregnant, I was scared, excited, anxious ... a whole myriad of emotions. It wasn't going to be easy for her to come off the tablets she takes for the problems with her spine and the nerve in her leg, but I knew she'd rather do that than continue with her medication and have our child be born with a possible addiction to it.

I was excited to find out if we were going to have a son or daughter. I won't lie, I was silently hoping for a daughter. I thought it would be good to have a son and daughter and I got my wish. Caleb was so excited to have a little sister and now he's utterly devoted to her. Anything he can do to help, he does without hesitation. He never grumbles when he's asked to do something. He makes the two of us so proud.

After we've packed the pushchair and stuff back into the boot of the car, we all buckle up for the ride home. Caleb sits with his eyes glued to Cassie, wanting to be alert if she wakes.

Pulling up at the house, Cassie doesn't stir as I carry her car seat into the lounge. Elise goes to the kitchen to make a cup of coffee and Caleb sits watching over his sister. I smile to myself as I walk into the kitchen and wrap my arms around my wife. Inhaling her scent, I lean my head on her shoulder. She turns in my arms and places a chaste kiss against my lips. I move to deepen the kiss but she pulls back slightly.

"Go and get some rest," she says as she turns back to her coffee.

"I'm good, don't worry."

I pull her back for a kiss and this time she doesn't stop me as I deepen the kiss. Our tongues collide and glide effortlessly together. My cock stirs to life and I grind my pelvis so that Elise can feel the effect she has on me. She moans quietly, trying her hardest to contain it. The children are only in the other room, so it's not the best time for us to be getting hot and heavy. I can't help stealing one more kiss before adjusting myself and pulling back, trying to keep my hands to myself.

"Go and get some sleep. You'll be kicking yourself later if you don't."

I mumble my disappointment and pout like a child before turning on my heel and making my way to the bottom of the stairs.

"Night, Dad," Caleb says, as he hears the bottom step creak under my weight.

"See you later, buddy."

I head to our bedroom and discard my clothes before sliding under the covers. My cock is still semi-hard as I recall our lingering kiss, my wife's soft lips pressed against mine. Closing my eyes, I imagine Elise naked and almost feel the weight of her lying on top of me. I groan as I palm my cock and jerk my hand twice with a firm grip. It does absolutely nothing to dispel my fantasy or help me fall asleep of course, but I can't help it.

Deciding I need to do something about my erection before falling asleep, I lie on my back and pull the covers slightly higher. I know Caleb won't come up to disturb me while I'm meant to be sleeping—he never does when he knows I'm on shift later—but I still move to cover myself in case.

Closing my eyes, I go back to imagining my naked wife. My vision of her feels almost tangible, like she's here in the room with me. Her soft lips open and her tongue darts out to lick me from base to tip. I swear the moist warmth feels real as she takes the tip into her mouth. She does that thing I love with her tongue bar before swallowing me deeper. I feel myself hit the back of her throat and almost come too soon. She pulls back slightly and takes her time with me. Her hand wraps around the base of my cock while the other cups my balls. The touch of her skin sends an electrical current through my body, leaving a deep warmth settling in my bones.

I feel a tingling sensation in my balls as my wife's tongue swirls around my throbbing cock. The tightening that follows lets me know I'm not far from my climax. I want to hold it back for longer, selfishly wanting Elise to myself for a little while longer. I know she's not really here, but it doesn't hurt to pretend.

Her hand works me faster and her mouth moves in sync. It's only mere moments before I come in hot spurts down her throat. She swallows and then licks the tip of me clean before pulling away, leaving me cold.

Looking down to see how much of a mess I made when I came over myself, I see lustrous red hair and have to blink twice to reaffirm I'm not hallucinating. She really is here. No wonder the warmth felt so real and the orgasm was so explosive.

Heading towards our bedroom door, Elise throws me a wink over her shoulder as she opens the door.

"Sleep well," she whispers.

I smile at her before snuggling into the covers, that warmth still present in my bones. The last thing I have in my mind before slumber takes over is those baby blue eyes that sparkled wickedly as she closed the bedroom door behind her.

Chapter Four

Elise

I'd made sure Caleb was okay with a sleeping Cassie, telling him I'd be back in five minutes before sneaking upstairs and opening our bedroom door. I crept in as quietly as I could and knelt next to the bed. Drew's eyes were closed but I knew he wasn't asleep, I could see the duvet resting over his hand which I assumed gripped his cock. As I pulled the duvet back, I saw I was, in fact, correct, so I licked the length of him that I could get to with his hand in the way. His hand moved, so my left hand took its place as I took the tip of him in my mouth, and reached my right hand to cup his balls.

His orgasm didn't take long to build and was explosive as it spurted hot and thick down my throat. I'd swallowed and licked the tip of him clean before pulling back and standing to make my way to the door. Drew's moans had me wanting to climb into bed with him and wait for him to be ready for round two. Even now, I can feel the heat and moisture in my panties. Frustrated doesn't cover it, but at least Drew will fall into a deep sleep and get some rest before work this evening.

My heart still racing, I walk back downstairs and into the lounge. The sight in front of me brings a smile to my lips. My handsome boy is holding his baby sister close and humming to her.

Caleb looks up at me with a sweet smile. He adores his little sister so much and it fills my heart with pride.

As Cassie sleeps, I set about sterilizing her bottles and doing the laundry. Once that's all done, I start prepping the meatballs and tagliatelle for tea. Drew's still not up and about, so he must have fallen into a deep sleep after all. I have my iPod plugged into the dock, playing quietly as I work. Caleb comes in for a drink and says that Cassie is still fast asleep. He has the baby monitor in his hand so that he can hear if she wakes.

After pouring himself a drink, he stands next to me and leans up for a kiss. I smile as he walks back to the lounge. I couldn't have wished for a better son. He amazes me every day.

Sometimes I feel guilty, like my disability made him have to grow up sooner. He's had to help me a lot over the years and, although he's always done it with a smile and no arguments, I find myself wondering what it would be like for us if I wasn't disabled. There are so many things I can no longer do. Once upon a time, as an able-bodied mum, I could take him to the park to kick a football around. I could take him to places like Jump Nation, where I now rely on Sam and Karl to take him if Drew isn't able to. Theme parks and days out are a thing of the past now, for me at least. We still take him out, but only Drew can go on roller-coasters with him or have a kick-around over the park. The guilt overwhelms me sometimes and I have to deal with it all internally so that Caleb doesn't see me upset. There are times I've cried myself to sleep at night but, thankfully, those nights have been fewer and further between since Drew came along.

"Something smells good," Drew says, his voice husky with the remnants of sleep.

I turn to him and smile as I look over his toned body. He's only wearing a pair of low-slung jogging bottoms. He's in great shape and I can't help but stare down at the prominent V shape that disappears under the waistband of his bottoms.

Drew clears his throat, alerting me that I've been caught staring. I catch his eyes but don't miss the coy smile on his lips.

He walks to me and stands so there is scarcely any room between us. He wraps his arms around me and draws me in for a kiss. It's tender and loving and I almost melt in a puddle at his feet. This man holding me in his embrace has quite literally swept me off my feet. He came along when I didn't know I needed anyone. But, once he was in my life, it was clear that there was nowhere else either of us was meant to be.

"These meatballs will burn if you don't let me tend to them," I say as I break our kiss and turn back to the stove.

"Would that be such a bad thing?" he asks as he strokes his hands gently up and down my arms, down my sides to my hips and rests them there.

"Yes. We'd have to go hungry," I try to disguise my laughter as a cough but fail miserably.

I go back to cooking as Drew pulls up a stool at the kitchen island. As I put the finishing touches to our meal, he just sits and sings along to the song on my iPod. I must admit, he has a great voice. I love the fact that he likes my favourite band. Not many men do. Or not many I know, at least. I've been told many times that Lady Antebellum is a girly group. My ex didn't like them at all, so I was shocked when Drew told me that 'Need You Now' was his favourite song. It also happens to be one of my favourites. There's something about Charles Kelley's voice that I love. I can't wait to see them live next month with Drew and Caleb.

"Is tea ready yet? I'm starving!"

"Nearly, honey. Is your sister okay?"

"Yes, Mum, she's still sleeping."

"Good. Can you set the table please?"

He moves around the kitchen, collecting cutlery and glasses to place on the table.

I serve tea and the three of us sit down to eat before Drew has to go to work. I love nothing more than sitting here as a family, eating and chatting to my two favourite boys. Looking at Drew, I wish he didn't have to go to work tonight. But at least we're having a movie night next weekend; we'll all get to be together.

As Drew gets ready for work, Cassie begins to stir. I take her from the Moses basket and settle down with her in my arms. Caleb passes me a bottle and she begins to drink it greedily, which is typical of my baby girl.

"It's time I was getting off, baby," a voice penetrates my thoughts.

"Be safe. I hope it's an easy shift for you."

I always worry about him going into work. I guess there's risk involved in many jobs, but, as a paramedic, he never knows what each shift will bring. My anxiety gets the better of me sometimes, but I try not to show him that. I try to do things to take my mind off it.

Watching him give his son a hug, I smile and then lift my lips to meet his as he leans in for a kiss. He places a gentle kiss on Cassie's head, grabs his keys and walks to the front door.

Turning back, he smiles at the three of us.

"I love you, baby," he says as he looks at me. "Caleb, be good for Mum and I'll see you tomorrow. Love you, buddy."

"Love you too," Caleb and I reply in unison.

We're still laughing as Drew walks out of the door.

Chapter Five

Drew

"Control to two-zero-zero-six, come in." The radio crackles to life.

"Two-zero-zero-six to Control, receiving," I respond as I stand at the back of the ambulance with Danny.

"Ambulance required at 63, Park Road. Young child on balcony outside, unattended. Fire service en route."

"Shit!" Danny says as he gets behind the wheel.

"Two-zero-zero-six to Control, show us attending," I respond as I close the back doors and jump in.

We make our way through the traffic with the lights on and siren going. A child alone on a balcony? Why on earth would they be unattended? I'm glad the fire service is on the way too; they have equipment to deal with these types of situation. I've never attended one myself; it could be tricky.

Danny and I pull up outside the address in record time. It's as I climb out of the ambulance that I see why this is so dangerous. There's a toddler—he can't be over the age of three—on the balcony, alone, and what's worse is there seems to be some damage to the balcony, which could be hazardous if the child wanders across to their right a little too far.

It's clear Danny has spotted the same thing I have when he curses and grabs the bag from the ambulance.

We don't want to do anything to alert the child to our presence, it wouldn't prove helpful. In fact, it could prove quite the opposite. So, we make our way to the maisonette and knock on the front door. Nobody answers, so I bang a little louder. Still no reply.

The fire crew is on scene and a fireman is at my side.

"We've knocked twice. No answer. What should we do?" Danny asks.

The fireman raps on the door once. With no answer and no time to waste, he uses his Halligan to force entry into the home. He leads the way and Danny and I follow.

The scene before me defies belief. The room is a mess. No carpet, stuff piled up everywhere, hazards for a child just about everywhere I look. What really shocks me is the two people in the room. One is a man who is lying on a couch, drug paraphernalia spread on a coffee table next to him. He's passed out and it isn't any wonder by the looks of the empty plastic bag on the table. The other is a woman who looks to be in her twenties. She's sitting in an armchair and looks like she's high as well. Her skin is sallow and her eyes are closed. If it wasn't for the rise and fall of her chest, I might believe she was dead.

I'm suddenly not in the room anymore.

Mum and dad are high again. I know the signs now. They've told me never to touch any of their stuff as it isn't for children, but I don't think it's suitable for adults either. I might only be seven years old, but I know way more than I should at my age.

Dad is passed out on the couch along the back wall of the lounge; a small, clear plastic bag is on his lap. There's a spoon on the table, a needle a lighter too. There are small traces of white powder on the table and dad's dirty jeans.

I look at Mum and she is in no better state. She's in the reclining armchair and she has it resting back. Her hair is greasy and matted, it's plastered to her face, but she isn't alert enough to care—not that she would care anyway, that's just the way things are these days. Her skin is pale and, as I put a hand to her cheek, she feels cold but slightly sweaty. With her eyes closed, she looks like she could just be asleep, but I know better than that.

With both of them in such a state, it's up to me to find food for myself tonight. I know they won't bother to feed themselves, never mind me. I walk into the kitchen and immediately notice the sticky residue on the floor. My shoes stick to it, tracking the brown stuff wherever I place my feet. Pulling the fridge open, I see bare shelves. It should surprise me, but it doesn't. Turning to the cupboards, I search for anything I can eat. All I see is a box of cereal, so I take the box from the shelf and try to find a clean bowl.

Observing the plates, bowls and everything else mounted on the working surface, I know there's no point searching for anything that might be clean. Instead, I pull out a chair and sit down with the box. I take a handful of cereal and eat it dry. It tastes stale, but my rumbling tummy tells me to just eat it anyway.

I stand up and shuffle my way with sticky shoes into the lounge. My once beautiful mother looks far too skinny. Food isn't a priority for her these days. My dad couldn't be accused of being a handsome man, not anymore. He's tall and skinny like my mother; his clothes hang off his frame. He used to be a better dad, or so I thought. He'd take me to the park and play football, but what I didn't know then was that he just used it as a cover to go out and meet the person who was selling him drugs.

Sitting in the other armchair, I watch my parents as they lie there doing nothing. I don't want to be in the same room as them, especially if they wake up angry, but I want to be sure they are both still breathing.

I would call an ambulance, but the last time I did that my dad got so angry that he gave me a beating. I was covered in bruises and the teachers at school had wanted to know where I had got them from. Only a few of them were visible, so I got away with telling them that I was play-fighting with friends. I don't really have any friends outside of school—and even if I did I wouldn't invite them home with me—but the teachers seemed to buy my story.

Sitting here, I want to call an ambulance and make my parents go to hospital. I want them to stop taking drugs, get some help. But I know that they would refuse help and I would definitely be given another beating to rival the last time.

"Drew. DREW!" Danny sounds exasperated as he pulls me out of my own head.

"Shit, sorry," I mumble as I kick myself into action.

I walk to the French doors that open onto the balcony. As quietly as I can, I open one. The last thing I want to do is startle the child. Seeing the fire engine below, I wonder what precautions they have in place in case the child falls due to the structural damage. But there's no time for assessing what they are doing, I need to concentrate on my job.

I hear Danny in the main room trying to rouse the parents, but I know he probably won't get far.

Walking slowly and quietly, I look at the boy sitting at the edge of the balcony, with a dirty blue blanket in his hands. He's only dressed in a romper suit that won't provide much protection from the cold or the rain that is just starting to fall. I kneel next to him and offer a smile as he looks up at me with innocent green eyes. They remind me of my own, with flecks of gold in them.

"Hey, buddy. I'm Drew. What's your name?"

"Logan." His sweet voice has me thinking of Caleb.

I momentarily wonder how his parents could do this to him. How could they be strung out and not know that their child could be in danger? All too easily if they are anything like my parents.

"Hi, Logan, nice to meet you. What have you got there?" I ask, as I edge myself slightly closer.

"Blankie. Teddy fell. Can't get him."

I briefly look through the railings and see a teddy on the ground below.

"That's okay, buddy. See those nice men down there," I say, gesturing to the firemen, "They can get your teddy. Do you want to come with me and we'll go and find him?"

Those innocent eyes lock onto mine and I feel a myriad of emotions for this poor child.

Before I can say anything else, Logan jumps up and runs towards where the balcony is damaged. He trips over his blanket as he runs, and I spring into action, catching him at the last moment before he can slip through the crack.

My heart races in my chest, pounding my rib cage like it wants to break free. There's a lump in my throat and it feels like I can't swallow.

With Logan safely ensconced in my arms, I walk into the lounge and close the door behind me. Looking around the room, I see the fireman who opened the door for us. His face is a mixture of emotions—relief being the most prominent. I'm sure he sees the same look mirrored on my face.

Danny has managed to rouse the mother a little, but she doesn't really seem coherent. The father is still passed out. I want to get this kid the fuck out of here. I want to break into a run and never look back. Every fibre of my being is screaming to protect this boy. But I can't do anything of the sort. Instead, I put him down on the empty armchair and check him over for any injuries. There's a bit of a scrape on his knee where he fell over his blanket, but other than that he looks okay. He's dirty from head to toe, like he hasn't been bathed for a week or more. His nappy is sagging, and I know it needs changing. His romper suit is filthy and has holes in it. It also doesn't seem to fit right, like it's a size too small.

"He has a teddy down there on the ground outside. Could someone get it for him?" I ask the fireman.

He nods and disappears.

I pick Logan up and walk out of the lounge. Once I find which room is his, I put him on the bed as I go in search of something cleaner for him to wear. I grab a t-shirt and jeans from his chest of drawers—they may only just be able to be called that as they aren't really in any fit shape. I see a hoodie with Sonic the Hedgehog on, so I make a grab for that too.

We return to the lounge together and I rummage around for a clean nappy. Thankfully, there are a couple in the bottom of a pack in the corner of the room.

Walking back to Logan, I spot some baby wipes and get to work on changing his nappy and dressing him warmer. I don't know if it's breaking any rules to do this, but to be honest, I don't care about rules and regulations in this moment. All I care about is Logan.

Once he's changed, I notice the fireman standing to one side of the room. In his hands, he holds a brown teddy bear that isn't much cleaner than its owner.

"Teddy," Logan says and squirms in my arms as I try to use a baby wipe to clean his precious little face.

Seeing my struggle to contain him, the fireman brings the teddy to Logan.

"There you go, buddy. See, I told you the nice fireman would get him for you. What do you say to the nice man?"

"Thank you," he says, his 'th' sound coming out more like a 'ff'.

"That's a good boy," I say as he cuddles his teddy.

***

After the events of our first call-out, I am awash with emotions. My chest felt tight as the lady from social services came to take Logan into her care. I knew it was the way things went, but I didn't want to let him go. Such innocence needs to be protected and nurtured. My only hope is that whoever looks after him does a better job than his parents.

I don't know what will happen to them. We brought the woman in on our ambulance and requested a second for the man. Once we handed them over to the doctors, I found myself not caring what happens to them. They don't deserve to be given their son back, that's for sure. But, ultimately, that's not my choice.

I'm sitting on the back of the ambulance with my head in my hands. I tug my hair in frustration and let out a yell. Danny doesn't say anything as he cleans the ambulance behind me. It doesn't seem to have had the same effect on him, probably because he wasn't responsible for the little boy. He's not exactly full of the joys of spring either, but he doesn't seem as hacked off as I am. Or maybe he's better at hiding it. I'm not about to ask. The last thing I want to do is talk about what happened.

Before long we're on our next call-out and things seem to be a little harder to do. Just walking, my legs feel heavier and my heart seems to pound in my ears. Danny seems to notice and suggests I take the rest of the shift off, but I can't do that. Other patients will need assistance this evening and I refuse to let them down.

***

I turn my key in the door and push it open quietly. I close it behind me, put the bolt across and head into the kitchen. I grab a glass from the cupboard by the sink and run the tap for a few seconds before filling my glass. I gulp it straight back, wishing it was whiskey or something instead. I fill a second glass and turn the tap off. When I turn around I nearly drop the glass.

"Shit, sorry. Didn't mean to make you jump," Elise says sleepily.

My eyes rake over her. In her pyjamas, she looks beautiful, with a face free of makeup and her hair all over the place. Noticing me staring, she runs a hand through it.

"Sorry baby, did I wake you?" I ask as I cross the space between us.

I put my glass of water on the kitchen island and wrap my arms around my wife.

"No, Cassie only just went down. I was lying on the couch when you came in."

We're both silent for a moment and I'm sure she notices my slight awkwardness. She doesn't say anything, but she snuggles into me and holds me fast. Elise may not know it, but she and the children are my anchor when I feel like I'm drifting out at sea. They always keep me grounded and safe, just as I will them for the rest of their lives.

Tilting her head up to mine, Elise captures my lips in a sweet kiss. She's loving and tender with it. There's nothing sexual about it, just a kiss as the moonlight shines in through the kitchen window. She's the first to break the kiss, taking my hand and leading me towards the staircase. I follow behind her up the stairs. We walk into our room and I quietly close the door.

Elise turns to me and, without a word, she undresses me. She takes my hand once more and pulls me toward our en suite bathroom. She turns the shower on hot and pushes me in the direction of the spray of water, then quickly undresses and gets in with me.

I stand still for a moment and close my eyes. I feel her hands on me—if I hadn't had the day I have, I would be getting hard. As it is, my mind is still on little Logan.

Elise lathers the soap up all over me, then turns the shower head back to wash it all away. I return the gesture by soaping her up and rinsing her down. She looks glorious when she's naked and wet, the beads of water clinging to her breasts, begging to be licked off. But it seems she can sense my mind isn't fully here as she takes my hand and walks back into our room. She hands me a towel and I dry off while she does the same.

We climb under the covers and Elise hooks her one leg over me and snuggles her head against my chest as I lie on my back, closing my eyes.

***

Sleep didn't come easily last night. I kept tossing and turning, unable to switch my mind off. It's as if it was on a loop, acting as my own worst enemy. I would close my eyes and see Logan falling; only I was unable to save him. At some point in the night, I found myself sneaking into Caleb's room to check on him. I watched him as he slept—the steady rise and fall of his chest. When Cassie woke in the early hours, I told Elise to go back to sleep and I went to her instead. I sat in the chair in her bedroom, holding her close to my chest, rocking gently back and forth—I don't know whether that was to soothe her or myself, maybe both?! I inhaled her sweet baby scent and spoke in hushed tones, telling her I love her and will always protect her. I'd walk over hot coals for my children. They'll never know what it's like to go without or to grow up with parents that don't give a damn. On my life, I swear I will be a better father than mine ever was.

There's this fierce, all-consuming love within me. I feel it for Elise and our children. They make me a better man. I know that before Elise, I had used travelling the world as a coping mechanism, something to stop me from settling down, falling in love and getting my heart broken. But when Elise came back into my life, it was as if fate was telling me that it was time. Time to let go of my old insecurities, to allow someone beyond the walls I'd built around my heart and take a chance on love. I know that Elise won't hurt me because she loves me with every fibre of her being. She tells me every day how much I mean to her and it fills my heart with joy every time I hear her utter the words 'I love you'.

I'm up first this morning and all is quiet in the house, so I decide to jump in the shower. I turn it up hot and wait until steam billows around the room before stepping in. Getting in under the jets of water, I feel it beating down on my skin and I allow myself a few moments of just standing there.

After showering, I have a quick shave and throw on a pair of jogging bottoms. I head to the kitchen and find out the items I need to make a full cooked breakfast.

"Whatcha doin'?" a sweet little voice asks.

I turn and see my beautiful wife with Cassie in her arms.

"Hey, you."

I walk over and place a chaste kiss on her lips, leaving her smiling at me.

"I'm cooking breakfast, so why don't you go and get dressed because I'm taking you out after we've eaten."

"You are? Where?"

She flutters her eyelashes at me as though that will get me to answer. I don't. Instead, I look at her and smirk.

"That's for me to know, darlin'."

I make a shooing motion and she retreats from the room.

"Where are we going, Dad?" Caleb says, startling me.

"Hey, buddy, are you eavesdropping over there?"

A laugh bubbles out of him and he walks over to grab a bottle for Cassie and a juice for himself.

"Sorry, Dad. I brought Cassie downstairs for Mum. I thought you'd know I was there."

"Well, I'm not telling you where we're off to, you'll just have to wait and see."

I repeated my shooing motion, this time directed at him. He laughed and walked to the lounge.

Breakfast was lovely, even if I do say so myself. I'm not a bad cook; after all, I spent years as a single man, so I'd had to learn to cook or starve.

When the dishwasher is loaded, and everyone has their coats and shoes on, we get settled in the car and Caleb asks if we can listen to Panic! At the Disco. I put it on quietly so as not to disturb Cassie.

I follow the satnav, not being all that familiar with the route. As we pull into the car park, Elise asks where we are. I keep my lips closed and she leans over to kiss me, thinking she can persuade me to tell her.

I get out of the car and grab Cassie's pushchair from the boot.

Once I've clicked her car seat into place in the all-in-one travel system Elise insisted we buy, I grab her changing bag and the picnic hamper I stashed in the boot when they weren't looking. I pass the hamper to Caleb, telling him not to peek inside or he won't get his treat. His face lights up and he promises he won't look.

We walk to the ticket office and that's when Elise realises where we are. I'm glad the weather is so warm, otherwise today wouldn't have been a good idea.

Once we get situated on the train, Caleb can't sit still. Cassie is fast asleep, but Elise and Caleb are both looking at me, eyes full of excitement. Severn Valley Railway is somewhere Caleb has wanted to go for ages, but for one reason or another—usually the inclement weather—we haven't been until now.

I remember coming myself as a teenager with Edie and Pops. I didn't have the fascination or wonderment that younger kids might have had over it, but I had a good day nonetheless because my grandparents had packed a picnic hamper and we'd taken some silly photos of each other, making memories I should have made when I was younger. They made sure I had a good day, regardless of my age. Now it's my turn to make a special day for my wife and children. I know Cassie is too young to appreciate it, but I'm sure there'll be plenty of opportunities to bring her again.

The train takes off and Caleb stands to look out of the window, watching as we pass fields and trees, all looking beautiful on this unseasonably warm day.

I had worried Elise might have an anxiety attack if I told her where we were going, as she doesn't really like trains on the whole. Her anxiety makes it hard to do the simple things sometimes. I had decided simply not to tell her because then she didn't have time to get worked up. Before booking the tickets, I'd made sure she was okay with it and she explained she felt completely different because we weren't going to end up at a crowded train station. She said she's okay with the journey itself; it's the platforms that make her start to get panicky. Once I knew she was okay with it, I relaxed a little more.

***

As we pull into the drive, Elise wakes from her nap. Caleb and I had talked quietly on the way back so as not to disturb her or Cassie. He told me what a brilliant day he'd had and that he was glad that Elise had been able to have fun. He's so grown up for a boy his age. He worries about his mum's anxiety and disability and will do just about anything to make life easier for her. He makes me so damn proud and I know Elise is extremely proud of him too and grateful for all that he does. That's one of the reasons for a trip out like today. Not only to make memories as a family, but to give Caleb a surprise to show him how much he means to us.

We walk into the house and I settle Cassie in the Moses basket in the lounge. Elise puts her feet up because her ankles are a little swollen from our day out. Caleb asks if he can play on his Nintendo Switch, something we'd given him for his birthday and which he's currently addicted to. Finding myself without much to do, I stick the kettle on and grab a takeaway menu.

Chapter Six

Elise

Yesterday was a really good day. We took the children on a steam train on Severn Valley Railway. Drew had packed a picnic, so that was why he didn't let me in the kitchen while he was making breakfast. He hadn't allowed me to do anything, saying where we were going and what we were doing was a secret. It had come as a surprise that he wanted to go out, considering he's at work for the next two nights and I thought he'd have wanted a day to chill out and rest.

I'm not sure whether it had anything to do with the previous night. He'd come home looking despondent. So much so that I'd taken his hand and led him to the shower, then, when we'd got in bed, I just snuggled up next to him. He didn't say anything about work, in fact he didn't say much at all. It was late, and he needed sleep, so I snuggled my head into his chest, hooked my leg over his and we lay like that until I fell asleep. I'd woken up the next morning and he wasn't there, so I wasn't sure what he was doing. As it turned out, he'd been planning our day and cooking breakfast, but there was still an air of something around him that I couldn't quite place.

He'd kept a smile on his face all day. He'd played football with Caleb and a couple of other kids from the train when we made a stop. His actions said that he was just being himself, but I think there's more to it. Maybe I'm overthinking stuff, but when he's like this—which isn't all that often—it's usually because he's got something weighing on his mind. I feel like if I ask him about it, it'll force him to think about something he might not want to. But, if I wait, it could take a while for him to come to me—if it happens at all.

Drew and the kids are in the kitchen packing Caleb's lunch for school when I walk in. I make my way over to put the coffee machine on, bending to kiss Cassie on the top of her head as she sits in the highchair. She giggles and gets her hands tangled in my hair. Untangling myself, I flick the switch for my morning caffeine fix. I have lots to do today and need the boost. In fact, if I could have coffee in an IV drip, I probably would.

"Good morning, gorgeous," Drew says as he comes up behind me and slides his arms around my waist.

"Morning, baby."

I turn in his arms and snuggle into his chest. Inhaling his scent, I know he's been up for a while and had a shower; I can smell the body wash he uses, but also something uniquely him. I snuggle in against him further and he wraps his arms around me tighter.

"Come on Dad, we'll be late."

"Sorry, buddy," Drew says as he lets me out of his hold.

Caleb has a smirk on his face; he says he thinks our displays of affection are 'gross' and 'annoying' but if you ask him truthfully, he'll tell you that he loves the way his mum and dad love each other.

"Come and give me a hug, young man. You're never too old to hug your mother!" I tease.

He comes and wraps his arms around me and squeezes me tight.

"Love you, Mum. Have a good day at work."

"Have fun at school and don't forget to hand in your homework."

I tousle his hair and he pokes his tongue out at me, before running his fingers through his hair to make sure I haven't messed it up.

Drew and Caleb go out to the car, leaving just me and Cassie. I make myself a coffee and sit at the kitchen island next to her. She really is my beautiful little angel. She looks so much like her dad, especially having the same colour eyes with the same little flecks of gold. Hearing her babble away makes me smile. Sometimes I wonder what goes on inside that head of hers. I grab a banana from the fruit bowl and peel it for her. Just the smell of them makes me sick, but she loves them. I stand and grab a knife and one of her plastic bowls to put the pieces in. I give it to her and she gets stuck right in, mushing the pieces between her chubby little fingers.

Not long later, the sound of Drew's key in the lock makes me jump. I'd been so entranced watching our daughter that I'd forgotten he hadn't gone out to work and would be home after dropping Caleb at school.

"Hey, baby girl," he says as he sees Cassie with banana just about everywhere possible.

Her eyes light up when she sees Daddy. She starts babbling and waving her arms in the air.

"Looks like somebody needs a bath," he says as he comes around the island to give me a kiss.

"Her eyes lit up the moment you walked in, so I think she chooses Daddy to bath her."

"Oh, she does, does she?"

He tickles my ribs and I can't help the bubble of laughter that escapes me. As he leans down to nuzzle into my neck, I embrace the warmth of his lips on my bare skin. A shiver runs through me and I find myself wishing Cassie was asleep.

"I'll take this little madam for a bath while Mummy gets ready for work," Drew says, pulling away from me and leaving me feeling cold.

The two of them disappear and I take the opportunity to pour myself another coffee. I make my way upstairs to find an outfit for the day. Amanda and I have a couple of venues to see for some events that have just been booked with Memories Made.

I grab a quick shower in our en suite, blow-dry my hair and get a start on my makeup. I'm just stepping out of my towel when Drew walks into our room.

His eyes roam my curves and leave a burning trail wherever they go. He walks towards me, but it looks more like how a predator would walk, stalking his prey. Hooded eyes linger on my cleavage before moving to my face and locking onto my gaze.

I feel almost like I'm falling, but Drew's arm is behind me, lowering me to the bed.

"Where's Cassie?" I ask breathlessly.

"Happily playing in her playpen. The monitor is just there," he nods his head in the direction of the bedside table.

Silencing me with a breathtaking kiss, Drew fumbles with the button and zip of his jeans. I move to remove his t-shirt and he lifts his arms, so I can pull it off. As I throw it to one side, he discards his jeans and boxers.

As he stands before me, naked, I get a chance to run my hands over that delicious V that's usually hidden. His salacious grin is enough to make my knees weak. I don't really have long before I have to go to work, but I can't say no to this handsome, sexy man of mine. I find myself hoping that Amanda will be running a little late to pick me up.

His hands cup my breasts and I look down as he brushes his thumb over my piercing. Feeling him take my nipple in his warm mouth makes me gasp as it shoots a crackle of electricity through me. His gaze is intense as he looks up at me just before he nips my flesh between his teeth. My back arches off the bed and there's a pleasurable warmth beginning to build in my abdomen.

Soft, warm hands roam my body. I can feel the hunger and lust in his touch just as I feel it within me. He aligns his body with mine and without much warning, he pushes straight into me. His lips claim mine in a bruising kiss.

"Drew," I whisper as he licks slowly to the hollow of my throat.

He carries on down to the swell of my breasts as he pushes further into me. I can feel him deep inside me, but not just in a physical way—it's more than that. He's inside me even when our bodies are not joined. I carry him in my heart and soul.

I lift my hips to meet his and the warmth inside me starts to take over. Grabbing onto his shoulders, I dig my nails in with each thrust. His breathing is laboured and a moan escapes my lips as he pulls out slightly and plunges in deeper and faster. I move my hands to tug the hair at the nape of his neck.

His rhythmic movements become less so and I know he's about to lose all control. I move my hips faster, clench my inner walls tighter and it isn't long before we both reach our climax. It's nothing short of explosive.

I'm lying on my side next to Drew, tracing lazy circles on his chest as he lies beside me on his back. My breathing has finally returned to normal and I feel my eyelids drift closed. I'm sated, my limbs heavy and body tired.

Hearing a car horn blast outside makes me jump. Drew wraps my towel from earlier around his waist and goes to peek out of the curtains.

"It's Amanda," he says as he walks back to the bed, dropping the towel to the floor.

"You shouldn't do that."

"Do what?" The innocence in his tone is clearly fake.

"Stand before me looking incredible."

"Does that mean I don't always look incredible?"

I laugh and shake my head at him.

"You do, but more so when you're naked. How is it that I'm sated and yet I want you all over again?"

I really don't know how he does it to me. I can go from feeling 'completely fucked and exhausted' to 'horny as hell and ready for round two' in a matter of minutes, sometimes less.

"You don't have the time, baby."

Drew has the nerve to throw a wink my way before leaning down over me and slanting his lips over mine. It's a brutal kiss. Fiery, passionate, full of sexual charge. I know it will leave my lips swollen, but at this moment, I don't care. I kiss him with as much fervor and wrap my arms around his neck.

Amanda beeps her horn again just as Drew pinches my pierced nipple between his thumb and forefinger. I hiss in frustration, partly sexual and partly directed at Amanda for not taking her time getting here.

I look at the clock on the bedside table; we're going to be late if I don't get a wriggle on. I push Drew away and get up.

I dress hurriedly. Drew just laughs, and I huff in indignation as I button up my blouse for a second time because I did them incorrectly the first time I tried.

"You better have tea ready by the time I get home, husband. It's the least you can do, don't you think?" I tease as I grab my shoes and slip into them.

"Yes ma'am," he quips as he salutes me.

He has the nerve to stand there in only a pair of low-slung jeans. His body is putting me off my game and I really don't have time to waste.

The doorbell chimes and Drew laughs as he quickly grabs a t-shirt and pulls it on as he leaves the room.

"She was just drying her hair," I hear him say to a no doubt annoyed Amanda.

"Oh. I sounded the horn more than once."

"Sorry, I was with Cassie and didn't hear you."

His lie is smooth. He could have said he'd been in the shower but judging by the fact he doesn't look remotely like he's got damp hair or anything, his lie was a better one than mine would have been if the shoe was on the other foot.

"Come in Amanda, I'm sure she won't be a moment."

I hear the front door close and the click-clack of Amanda's heels on the floor in the hallway.

I make my way down the stairs, carefully holding both bannisters because of my leg. I've slipped on a couple of occasions and it's bloody painful afterwards.

"There she is," Amanda pipes up.

"Sorry, sorry. I was just finishing straightening my hair. I couldn't go out with it freshly blow-dried and messy, could I?"

"We'll be late." Her tone is more jovial than annoyed.

We both know I detest being late. Being on time is late to me. Wherever possible, I am always at least a few minutes early.

Grabbing my coat, I sling it over my arm with my handbag in hand. It's then that I realise I haven't kissed Cassie goodbye. I mention it to Drew, so he runs upstairs to grab her.

When he returns, I take her from him and hug her close to me. I kiss the top of her head and inhale her intoxicating sweet baby scent. I hand her back to Drew and lean in close to kiss him goodbye. Amanda averts her eyes and I giggle.

Knowing we really will be late if I don't get a move on, I reluctantly withdraw from the kiss.

"Lasagne would be nice for tea, husband," I mock as I walk out of the door.

"Then I guess I'll make spaghetti bolognese," he teases back.

"Love you."

I blow him a kiss and turn to walk to the car. I'm leaning a little more on my stick for stability since it isn't so long since Drew made me weak at the knees, but if Amanda notices, she doesn't point it out.

Once we're on the road to the first venue, Amanda informs me that the client had called and said they'll be meeting us there. They're quite a demanding couple and, in all honesty, I wish Amanda could take this appointment on her own now I know they'll be there.

As we pull up in the car park, I flick the visor down in front of the passenger seat, so I can check my makeup. Smoothing my hands down over my hair, I take a deep breath and hold onto it for a moment before expelling it.

Demanding couples like Mr and Mrs Brent can set off my anxiety, so I take a couple more soothing breaths before opening the car door.

It's important to get any event right, but especially so with this couple. They are spending a lot of money with us and everything must be 'just right'. It needs to meet their high expectations. It's their daughter's twenty-first birthday and, as it's a landmark birthday for her, they are being very hands-on in the planning. To be honest, I don't know why they got an event planner in; they seem more than capable of doing everything themselves and oversee every move we make anyway. But that's not something I'm willing to point out. Their cheque will bring our bank balance up nicely, so I slap on a smile and walk to the door. They're already here, but that shouldn't surprise me. Mrs Brent is looking at her watch and tapping her foot impatiently, which makes me look at my own watch. I see that we are in fact ten minutes earlier than Amanda had agreed to meet them, so I don't know why Mrs Brent is so impatient. I'd take a stab in the dark about it being the stick up her ass but wouldn't say that out loud. From the look on her face, I momentarily wonder if I did voice that thought, but from the plastic smile I see her force into place, I'm guessing I didn't speak a word.

***

Completely exhausted from spending time in the company of the nit-picking Mrs Brent, I want nothing more than to go home and crawl under my duvet. But Amanda drives us to the next venue anyway.

I make a remark about Mrs Brent's ever-present stick up her ass and Amanda laughs like I've told a dirty joke. Her laughter is infectious and we have a good giggle for a minute or two.

That's one of the things I like most about having Amanda as my assistant; she's laid back and knows how to have a laugh, but she's also serious when she needs to be and is a dedicated worker.

As we arrive at the second venue of the day, I do another quick makeup check and we're ready to go. We aren't impeded by overbearing parents, so this time should be easier. This venue is for another party, which is also being held this evening, a wedding anniversary for the client's mum and dad.

Amanda and I walk around inside, making sure everything is as it should be. We talk to the caterers and go over their menu to make sure they are catering for the vegetarians as well as providing a gluten-free option.

We come out of the kitchen and see the DJ starting to set up. He's been given a list of songs from the couple's era as well as some newer stuff for their children and grandchildren to dance to. I personally recommended him, so I know he'll do a good job.

The ringtone of a phone distracts me and I turn to see Amanda pulling her mobile from her bag. Seeing the name Pryce flash on her screen makes me wonder if there's a problem with the upcoming

Christmas Ball they're hosting for us.

Amanda's smile as she answers the phone is a professional one, but whatever he says on the other end causes her to blush, so I'm left to assume it's a personal call.

I walk over to the DJ to give her some space to talk without her boss eavesdropping.

By the time we are back on the road, Amanda has a face-splitting grin in place. I want to be nosy and ask her what it's all about, but I don't want to be intrusive. If she and Pryce are going on a date or something, I'm happy for her. He seemed nice and I know she couldn't keep her eyes off him when we visited Westbury Park Manor House.

"So…?"

Okay, I said I wouldn't be intrusive and I won't, but I'm nosy. What can I say?!

"So, what?" she says, all innocent and casual.

"Oh, come on, Mand, you know what I'm asking. Are you going to make me say the words?"

"Why should I make it easy for you?"

She turns and flashes me a grin before her eyes go back to the road ahead.

"You're no fun," I tease. "Are you going on a date with Pryce?"

"I might be."

"Is that what the phone call was about? Come on; give me something to work with."

"Maybe."

She shrugs, pretending to be nonchalant about it. Getting information from her is going to be like pulling teeth.

"Mand, we're friends, aren't we?"

"Yes, of course we are."

"Then tell your friend if you have a date!"

"Oh man! You just don't let up, do you?"

Anyone would think I've been giving her the Spanish Inquisition instead of asking a couple of simple questions. But Amanda loves to exaggerate.

"I'll give up when I get an answer."

"Okay, okay, I give in," she mocks. "We have our third date tonight."

Third? How did I not know they'd been out before? Amanda normally likes to have a good old girly gossip.

"Third date? Lucky you. He's handsome."

"He sure is. And he's a gentleman too. He's polite, well-mannered, opens the car door for me, pulls out my chair in restaurants. He's so sweet and has a loving, tender manner."

"Well, that's great. I really don't want to be nosy, I'm just happy for you is all."

"He's a good kisser too," she practically swoons.

"Hey, lady, eyes on the road if you want to make it to this date in one piece," I jest and burst out laughing.

"Sorry, he's just ... I don't know a word for it ... He's practically perfect."

"Nobody is perfect, not even Drew. He's amazing, sure, but perfect? Nuh-uh!"

"Well, Pryce is perfect for me. He doesn't seem to mind that I'm a little crazy and that I could talk for England."

"I take it back, any man that can put up with that must be perfect."

Amanda laughs. Her laughter is contagious and soon we are both fully on belly-laughing.

I lean over to turn the radio on after we've quietened down. I flick through the stations but there's nothing worth listening to, so I link up Amanda's iPod and scroll through her albums until I land on a favourite; *Need You Now.* I select the track *American Honey*. Amanda and I roll down our windows to soak in the gorgeous weather as we sing along.

Once we pull up at the house, I thank Amanda for driving us around. With my disability, I've never learned to drive, so it's a good thing that she does, considering our job requires plenty of travel, even if most of it is local.

She waves as she pulls out of the drive and I hear her turn up the volume of the music. I smile to myself, knowing she's out on a hot date tonight. Who knows, if it goes well, maybe one day we can arrange a double date for the four of us.

As I open the front door, I'm greeted by the aroma of coffee brewing in the kitchen. I walk in that direction, hoping my handsome husband will have a fresh cup ready for me.

"Hey beautiful," he says as he looks up from the kitchen island.

"Hey. Where's Cassie?"

"Upstairs taking a nap. Caleb is doing his homework in the lounge," he replies as he stands and walks towards me.

Wrapped in his warm embrace, I almost melt in his arms. I snuggle into his chest and bury my face in the crook of his neck. He smells fresh out of the shower; a hint of his body-wash lingers on his skin. There's also something about him that smells like home, like this is right where I'm meant to be.

***

By the time the weekend rolls around, we have more events booked through Memories Made and Amanda has another hot date with Pryce lined up.

I'm sitting at home wondering if I should do something I've been thinking over for a while. Drew and I have talked about it, but ultimately, although he can offer advice, he can't make the decision for me. It has to be me and only me. But what should I do?

Before I can overthink things, I grab my MacBook and click on Facebook. I found them ages ago but haven't had the nerve to get in touch and see if they are the right people. If they are, will they want to know me or not? I won't know unless I pluck up the nerve to make the first contact. I don't want to overthink it because they might not even be the family I am looking for.

I click on Sophie's profile and look at the 'About' section. I see her family listed: Jacob, Ricky, and Carole. There isn't a listing for Philip, but when I looked on the 192.com website, it listed him in their household ... or them in his ... whatever.

I open a new message and begin to type...

Hello Sophie,

My name is Elise and I am hoping you might be able to help me. I am looking for a man named Philip Andrews. I've seen that you are listed as a member of his family on another website, but he doesn't seem to have a Facebook account.

The reason I am looking for this man is because I believe he might be my father. I don't have much information to go on as my mother never told me much about him. I know he used to live nearby in Lye, also that he previously lived in Halesowen. He used to be a roadie for a group back in the 80s but I've forgotten what they were called. I was also told that he has two sisters and a brother, but I don't know their names except one; Isabelle.

He used to date my mother, Emily Swanson, in the early 80s and they had a daughter together, me.

I'm sorry to be getting in touch via you, but, as I couldn't find him on here, it was the next best thing.

If I've got the wrong person, I apologise. I hope you can understand my need to find him. I am 36 years old and have never met nor been in touch with my real father. I haven't been able to locate him until I did a recent search and found you.

Anyway, sorry if I'm rambling. If you could please get in touch and let me know if I have the right guy, I'd really appreciate it.

Many Thanks,

Elise Wright (née Swanson)

As I click 'Send,' I feel apprehensive. I'm not sure if I've done the wrong thing. But there's nothing to be done now except wait.

Drew gets home from work and I tell him I finally plucked up the courage to get in touch but that my anxiety is now beginning to take hold. He wraps me in his arms and we sit on the couch for what feels like hours. He doesn't even get changed after work or have his normal shower. He doesn't do anything except sit and hold me, tracing lazy circles at the base of my spine with one hand, talking in soothing tones about anything and nothing of importance.

Luckily, Caleb has gone to Josh's after school. Sam had asked if the boys could have a sleepover. And Cassie is sleeping in the Moses basket beside the couch. She doesn't even murmur, just sleeps peacefully until it's time for her feed.

I walk into the kitchen to grab a bottle I made earlier and a bowl of chicken, mashed potatoes and vegetables I had made for her dinner. I don't know how she finds it appetizing when it's all blended together like that, but she loves it.

When I walk back into the lounge, Drew is on the Mac, reading what I wrote to Sophie.

"There's nothing wrong with what you've written, baby. It makes sense, it's polite. What more did you need? It doesn't seem like there's anything else to say unless it is the right guy and he gets in touch."

"I don't know, I just feel weird having finally done it, you know?"

"I get that, baby. But you did what you felt needed doing. Not just for you, but for the sake of the children. They have a grandfather they've never known."

"Yeah, one they may never get to know either, depending on the outcome."

Drew takes the bottle from me and puts Cassie in her highchair. He positions it in front of the couch, so I can feed her easily.

I look at my daughter as I feed her. She really is beautiful. And so innocent. I never want her to experience anything like I did in my childhood. I want to protect both of my children from anything that would harm them. Caleb is in high school now and he's experiencing things that every child should. There will always be good and bad people in the world and I feel it's my job as a parent to protect them from the latter. I can't always be there to hold their hands. They need to learn from their own mistakes. But that doesn't mean I'll ever stop worrying. I wasn't protected by my parents, to say the least, but I know what to do and what not to do based on what my mother did wrong when I was growing up. The love she never showed me, the care and attention she never gave me—these are the things I give my children in abundance.

Once Cassie has finished eating, I take her from her highchair and place her on the floor with her jungle gym. She lies on her back and stares up at the stuffed animals that hang above her. Any day now, she'll be crawling around and running us ragged. I can't wait. I love nothing more than seeing my children blossom.

***

Drew put Cassie to bed, so now it's time for us to settle down with a movie and a bottle of wine. I open a bottle of rosé and Drew puts *The Holiday* in the DVD player. I love that movie; there's something about a good old chick flick that makes things seem infinitely better. As it's nearly Christmas, I love nothing more than Christmas films and songs on the radio. I have a couple of albums on my iPod with my favourite seasonal tracks on.

The film has just ended as I get a message notification on Facebook. I open the app on my phone and begin to read.

Handing the phone to Drew, I don't know whether to laugh or cry. Maybe screaming might be the better option.

It's not the message I was hoping for from Sophie. Instead, it's from Carole Andrews.

Elise,
I don't know what you're thinking, getting in touch with my

daughter. You've turned her world upside down; her brothers' lives will be too if she tells them what you told her. None of the children knew you existed.

Phil is your father, you found the right person. I just don't know why you got in touch with our daughter. What were you thinking? I get that you wanted to find your father, but now our family is in turmoil and it's your fault. Phil doesn't want anything to do with you. I'm sorry, but that's just the way it is. Your mother made it explicitly clear he was never to contact you. He only complied with her wishes. He stayed away and never tried to be involved in your life. Now he just wants to be left alone too. But you couldn't do that, could you?! You had to interfere in our lives. I don't know what you expected, and I don't know what else I can say.

Phil said if he changes his mind, he knows where to find you. Now please, leave my family in peace.

Carole.

I'm pretty gobsmacked at the message, to be honest. It seems like Drew is too from the look of fury on his face. He turns to me and smiles but his eyes remain sad. A feeling I don't know how to name washes over me and I stumble as I try to get up. I don't want to be here. I want to be anywhere besides here at this moment in time. It feels as though tiny shards of glass have splintered and lodged in my heart. I didn't expect them to lay out the welcome mat, but I didn't expect them to totally blow me off either. And as far as them not having told their children about me—I don't know what to think, say or do. I take my phone back and type out an angry response.

Carole,

You say I've turned your family's lives upside down, that I'm responsible for the pain they'll be feeling. I'm sorry to tell you that you're wrong. In fact, no, I'm not sorry at all. This is plain and simple for all to see. It's your fault—you and Phil. How can I be held responsible? I messaged you weeks ago and you never responded. So, I sent a message to Sophie because I wanted answers. I confess, in hindsight, getting in touch with her may have been a little insensitive on my part. However, I can't rectify that now. Sophie is a grown adult and I assumed you would have told her that I existed. So, when I messaged her, it wasn't me trying to be thoughtless on purpose.

But you're telling me I've turned your children's lives upside down? I don't think so. If you and Phil never told them they had an older sister, that's on YOU, not me.

I'm okay with Phil not wanting to know me. I didn't bother having any expectations about meeting him. I was realistic in my view when I told my husband that Phil most likely wouldn't want to know me. But I had to get in touch anyway, don't you get that? I needed to know for sure. If I hadn't, I would have spent the rest of my life wondering. At least now I know for certain.

My mother may or may not have told him not to contact me when I was younger, but I'm a grown woman now. Has he never wondered what I'm like? What it would be like to have a relationship with me? How has he never even told his other children that they have a sister? I won't pretend to understand his motives. Or yours for that matter. You are meant to be God-fearing Christians according to your Facebook profile. Well, this doesn't feel very Christian to me. I thought devout people were all about love and family etc. You know what, it doesn't even matter. As for Phil getting in touch if he changes his mind, I don't think so. I don't want to know, so tell him not to bother. Please don't message me again. It isn't likely to be received very well. As far as I am concerned, I have no father and that's fine by me.

Elise.

Drew reads my response before I hit 'Send.' He smiles at me, but again it doesn't quite reach his eyes. He's sad. For me and for our children. He knows I didn't hold out much hope, but there was a very thin slither. A fragile piece of me that is now broken because rejection from him only compounds the rejection I faced all my life at the hands of my mother.

I turn the Wi-Fi off my phone, so I won't get any more notifications tonight. Then I decide to block Carole instead. I feel slightly better knowing she won't be able to get in touch again.

I get changed into my pyjamas, climb into bed and huddle into the fetal position. Drew's arm comes around my waist as the first silent tear falls.

Chapter Seven

Drew

I wake with Elise still wrapped in my arms. She must have cried for nearly an hour last night. My heart aches for her. Her stepmother was callous—blaming Elise for turning their lives upside down—and that message really hurt her. Elise said she never had any expectations of them laying out a welcome mat in her honour, but I know that at least a small part of her held onto hope. What she hoped for, exactly, I don't know, but it was definitely for more than what she got.

Slipping from the bed quietly, I head downstairs to put the coffee machine on. I don't know whether she'll feel like eating, but I make her my blueberry pancakes anyway. I also make some porridge for the littlest member of the Wright family.

I arrange everything on a tray, carry it upstairs and open the bedroom door.

"Good morning beautiful," I say as I see Elise changing Cassie's nappy.

"Say good morning to Daddy," she says as she picks up our daughter.

"Actually, I meant both of you."

"Smells good, is that blueberry pancakes?"

"Mm-hm. I also brought banana porridge for Cassie."

I lay the tray on the bed and grab the seat we keep for Cassie upstairs. I settle her into it and sit in front of her with her breakfast. Her eyes widen as she takes her first mouthful.

Elise tucks into her pancakes with a contented sigh. She loves it when I cook for her. I'm glad she doesn't seem to be holding onto any negativity from last night. At least, not on the surface. I don't want to ask her about it in case it upsets her; I just hope she'll come to me if she needs to talk.

Sam calls and I hear Elise talking about Caleb coming back home. Then she says something about the messages last night. It makes sense she'd tell her best friend, but I hope it doesn't set the mood for the rest of the day. I don't want her thinking that upsetting her half-sister and half-brothers is on her. It really is as she said to Carole in the message; it's their own fault for not being honest with their children.

After feeding Cassie and getting her dressed, I take her downstairs and put her in her playpen while I brew some more coffee.

As if she knew exactly what I was doing, Elise appears in the doorway.

"Hey," she says as she walks over and makes a fuss of Cassie.

"When will Caleb be back?"

"Around lunchtime. Apparently, they are watching a film now, at the insistence of the boys."

I walk behind her and slip my arms around her waist. Nuzzling my head into the crook of her shoulder, I place a trail of light kisses along the line from her ear to her shoulder. She's wearing a soft, off the shoulder style jumper, so I kiss her exposed skin delicately.

Elise turns around, places both her arms around my neck and slants her lips softly over mine. She leads us in a soft and tender kiss, her tongue in perfect sync with mine. My heartbeat picks up pace, the swirling sensation in my stomach increases as my wife kisses me like I'm the very air she needs to breathe.

I'd say meeting her spun my world off its axis, but it didn't. In fact, it did quite the opposite; it made my world right itself. Together, we have everything we want and everything we never knew we needed. Our family is the most important thing in the world to me. After all, Elise and I know what it's like to come from broken homes; something we never want our children to know what it feels like first hand.

***

Elise has been a little distracted today and, whilst I don't blame her, I don't want her to dwell on the matter. The last thing I want is for it to feed into her depression, to burrow its way into her mind and refuse to leave.

I've done all I can to try and keep her mind occupied, but there's no telling when it will strike. Will I be here to calm her, or will I be at work, none the wiser to her pain? I can't not go to work, but my wife is my priority.

I've been thinking things over and wondering if a family holiday might be a good thing. It would be great to get away anyway, but the timing seems better now because it may distract Elise. But, then again, is it just stalling the inevitable? I can't prepare for what may or may not come; we'll just have to deal with it if it arises.

I'm just about to serve tea—my homemade chilli con carne—when Elise's phone chimes. She grabs it from the kitchen island and, as she reads the message, a myriad of emotions dance across her face.

"Sweetheart?" I say.

"Mm," is her only reply.

I wander over to her and she hands me the phone. I take it and start to read.

Hi Elise,

Sorry for the late reply, I've been struggling to stop crying long enough to compose this message.

First things first, yes, my dad is your dad!

I'm sorry that you've not known for so long. My family is a bit of a broken mess right now, as my brothers and I had no idea. Mum and Dad have kept you hidden from us. None of us knew you existed and the boys still don't.

I don't know what Dad wants to do, to be honest. I rang him straight away, and he was honest and open that he wouldn't have chosen to walk away from you. I don't want to put the blame on your mum in this situation, but Dad told me that she was the reason he stayed away. He said she told him never to try and contact her or you and he respected her wishes. He said your stepdad was crystal clear when it came to him wanting to adopt you—he told my dad to stay away because you had a dad now.

I happen to think that he should have fought harder for his daughter and I'm pissed as hell that he didn't tell the three of us that we had an older sister. I've always wanted a sister, having grown up with only brothers.

I told Dad that he has to tell Ricky and Jacob tonight. If he doesn't, I've warned him that I will. Mum wasn't happy I was giving them an ultimatum, but I said that it's tough shit and they need to do the right thing.

Until they tell my—or should I now say "our"—brothers, tonight,

I have no idea what they want to do about the situation!

I'm sorry you grew up without a dad. I know how hard it is if I'm completely honest, as he hasn't been the best of dads to me or the boys either.

Please can I ask, do you have a son and a daughter? Does my dad have grandchildren? Also, how did you find out about us as a family? I don't really understand.

Again, I'm sorry, I can't imagine how hard this is for you!

Sophie.

I look at Elise and see a tear escape her eye, so I wipe it with my thumb, but within seconds, it's been replaced by another. I wrap her in my arms and she nuzzles my neck softly as she cries. It wasn't a cruel message or anything, I think the tears are because now she has more information about the shitty situation. Her sister, Sophie, has got in touch—something that was totally unexpected at this point, especially after what Sophie's mother had said previously.

"Do I bother replying?" she asks quietly.

"You do what you feel is right, sweetheart. There's no pressure on you to reply to her."

"She asked about me having children. Why would she ask that? How would she know that if she didn't know anything about me?"

"I don't know, darling. That's something only Sophie can answer."

Elise dries her eyes and steps out of my embrace.

"Finish dishing up. Caleb must be starving. Don't plate anything up for me; I've lost my appetite."

"You have to eat something, Elise. It won't do you any good not to."

"I can't force myself to eat right now, Drew. Leave me something in the microwave that I can reheat if I get hungry later," she snaps.

"Elise…"

"No, Drew. Leave it. I need to think."

I bristle at her attitude, but I know that it's as a result of Sophie's message and thinking back to Carole's words from earlier. Her dad wants nothing to do with her; that's a big thing to have to come to terms with.

Plating up the chilli, I call Caleb from where he's playing on his Wii-U in the lounge. He sits at the kitchen island and I pass him some sliced and buttered baguette to go with his meal.

"What's up with Mum?" he asks in a hushed tone as he watches her walk to the lounge.

"She's a little upset, mate. Do me a favour and don't mention it to her, please?"

"Okay, Dad."

With that, he begins to tuck in. I sit at the island with him and eat my own meal before it gets cold. I did what Elise said and put a plate in the microwave for her.

She walks back in with Cassie in her arms, places her in the highchair and sits down to feed her. No words are spoken and the air almost vibrates with the deafening silence.

As soon as Caleb has finished eating, he asks to be excused and goes back to his game.

Elise gets up and loads the crockery into the dishwasher. There's still silence in the air, except for the noise of the plates and cutlery being placed ready to be washed. I take a deep breath and stand. I walk over to where my wife stands facing out of the kitchen window, slip my arms around her waist and rest my head on her shoulder. Nothing is said, but I feel her chest moving and realise that she is silently crying.

Cassie makes noises as if she's frustrated at being trapped in the highchair, so I turn to her and undo the harness keeping her in place. As I lift her into my arms, she quietens almost immediately. Elise turns to us, her eyes a little red and puffy.

"I'm sorry," she says, her voice sounding broken and weak.

"What for?"

"I didn't mean to snap. I just … well, I don't know … I got frustrated and upset. But I shouldn't take it out on you."

"That message came as a shock; I get it. Honestly. Do you want to talk about it?"

She nods, so I take Cassie into the lounge, put her in her playpen and ask Caleb to keep an eye on her.

I walk back into the kitchen and see Elise sitting with a mug of coffee and one on the island for me. I sit opposite her and reach to take her hands in mine.

"When I read Carole's message and blocked her from contacting me, I thought that was the end of it. Now, I have my "sister" getting in touch," she says, air quoting the word.

"Whether you have anything to do with Sophie or not is between the two of you. Don't let what Carole said get to you. If you want to message Sophie back, then do it. Even if it's only to ask her not to contact you again if that's what you want."

"I don't know what I want."

I can hear the uncertainty in her voice. It breaks my heart that she's feeling this way. Her tumultuous emotions play out across her face as she sits silently, thinking.

"Do you think perhaps you should sleep on it for tonight? It's best not to make any rash choices that you can't take back."

"Yeah, you're probably right."

She takes a long gulp from her mug and a sort of acceptance crosses her features.

"Do you mind if I go and grab a shower?"

"Like you need to ask, baby. Go, take your time. I'll keep an eye on the kids."

As she stands and places her mug in the sink, she turns and leans down to place a chaste kiss on my lips.

"I love you," I tell her with conviction evident in my voice.

"Ditto."

And with that parting movie quote, she disappears for a shower and some space to think.

I walk into the lounge and grab the second controller for Caleb's game.

"Fancy seeing if you can thrash your old man at Mario Kart?"

"Why do you play when you know you'll lose?" he asks with a laugh.

I love this boy so damn much. He may not share my DNA, but he's my son in every other way conceivable. He's my son where it matters most—my heart.

"I just thought I might stand a chance this time."

Sitting on the couch, I select my character and vehicle, ready for Caleb to beat me like he does every single time. I don't care about winning or losing, it's just a fun way of spending time with my boy.

A short time later, Elise pads into the lounge in her pyjamas and slippers. Her hair is damp, like she hasn't got the energy to dry it.

"Hey, Mum, look at this."

"What's that baby?"

"I beat Dad…again and again!" he boasts, making me chuckle.

"You should give the old man a break; it can't be easy losing to a kid."

A small smile graces her lips and I'm glad she seems to be trying to keep thoughts of Sophie, Carole, Phil, any of them at bay.

"To be honest, I think I should practice more while he's at school."

That makes Caleb laugh which, in turn, makes Elise laugh.

There's a lightness in the air; it feels less oppressive than it did.

We spend the rest of the evening in relative peace. Cassie fell asleep and I took her to bed. Caleb continued to play on his game, leaving me and Elise to sit and watch television in peace. Thankfully, Caleb's games can mostly be played on the gamepad of his Wii-U.

Elise and I watch a couple of episodes of Grey's Anatomy to catch up on what we've missed. Elise once asked me if any of the stuff that happens in the show has happened in real life. I regaled her with stories of a real-life paramedic. Some of the stuff in the show might seem a little unrealistic or done just for shock and awe, but the things I've seen in real life could put the show to shame. The situations people have got themselves into in the years I've been doing my job … well, you have to have a strong stomach at times.

Caleb went to bed an hour ago and Elise and I have been snuggled on the couch under a blanket, watching a film. Elise fell asleep about twenty minutes ago and, rather than watch the rest of the film, I've been watching her sleep; the rhythmic rise and fall of her chest, the way her face looks relaxed, all traces of stress erased from her features. I wish I could carry her to bed without disturbing her. Instead, I turn off the film and gently wake her.

Once we're in our bedroom, I strip down to my boxers and pull the duvet back. I climb into bed whilst Elise brushes her teeth in the en suite. When she returns, she climbs into bed next to me without saying anything. We lie down, and I pull the duvet up over us. Snuggling up behind her, I wrap a protective arm around her waist.

"I love you, baby," I whisper into her ear.

"I love you too, Drew, so very much."

It's not too long before her breathing evens out as she falls asleep. I lie and watch her for a while before allowing myself to drift off to sleep. I can only hope tomorrow brings more clarity to the situation Elise has found herself in.

Chapter Eight

Elise

I wake feeling slightly refreshed. Last night weighed on me so much that it felt like an actual physical ache. This morning I feel like I can deal with it, I need to face it head-on. Sophie is my half-sister and, whether Carole likes it or not, I am going to respond to her and see where it leads.

Drew is still asleep as I get out of bed. I quietly walk into our en suite, strip down and get in the shower.

I'm just about to step out of the shower when Drew walks in. He looks at me and instantly I see hunger flash in his eyes. His gaze sets me on fire as his eyes scour me from head to toe. It feels good to know that, after having two children and putting on weight since the operations on my spine, he still finds me attractive. I've never felt as beautiful as I do under his intense scrutiny.

Moments later, he drops his boxers to the floor. He turns and locks the door before getting into the shower with me. His erection presses against me as he pulls me into him. Warm, soft lips claim mine in a sweet, tender kiss. A hand in the back of my hair and one at the base of my spine, Drew holds me as if I might break. My tongue seeks entry into his mouth and he yields immediately.

The water cascades over us as if to put out the fire we are creating.

***

I'm on my third coffee of the morning when I decide to reply to Sophie. I want to know how she seems to already know I have a son and daughter, amongst other things. I don't know exactly what to say, if I'm honest. I'm not normally stuck for words, but this time I just can't seem to figure out how best to approach the message.

I have a sister and two brothers I never knew anything about. I didn't expect my dad not to move on and have kids with someone after my mum, but I'm struggling to wrap my mind around it. If they feel anything like I do today, then I can understand where they're coming from. Carole accused me of turning their lives upside down and, at first, I said that it was her and Phil's fault for never telling them about me. But now I'm wondering if it isn't at least partly my fault. I mean, I contacted Sophie in the first place.

I thought I had a right to know who my father was. I didn't really think through the possible ramifications for him or his family. Was that selfish of me? Perhaps it was.

Deciding to start with an apology, I compose a message back to Sophie.

Hi Sophie,

Firstly, I'd like to say I'm sorry. Really, truly sorry. I was selfish in my pursuit of my biological dad and didn't think through the possible consequences for your family. I didn't want to hurt you or your brothers. I do hope that you can forgive me.

You asked if I have a son and a daughter. The answer is yes. How did you know about them?

Also, you asked how I know about you as a family. Well, to address that, I went on 192.com one day, just on the spur of the moment, wondering if I could find the right Philip Andrews. I'd looked for him in the past but didn't find him. This time, though, I found a match, a man seemingly the right age. It listed people in his household and that was you, your mum and your brothers.

So, I looked up the names on Facebook and found all except Phil himself. Trust me, if I'd found him, I wouldn't have messaged you. I never meant it to hurt you. Like I said before, I've gone my whole life not knowing who my dad is and I felt I had a right to know. Now, although I feel I still have that right to know, I've also realised the consequences of my actions.

The message your mother sent me was loud and clear. Phil doesn't want to know me. And I'm fine with that. I didn't hold my breath in hope of him wanting to know his long-lost daughter. Turns out I was right. I've made my peace with that.

Until I found you and the boys were in his household on that website, I didn't have a clue that you existed, and I get it if they don't want anything to do with me. But I was wondering if you might maybe want to get to know me. You said you'd always wanted a sister. Now you have one. I won't pressure you. I know you'll need time to get your head around things, just know that I am here if you should choose to keep in touch.

I'm attaching pictures of the kids for you. I've told my husband about you, but not the children. Cassie is far too young to understand and, although Caleb is old enough, I don't know what to tell him.

Anyway, I'll leave you to get your head around things. You can contact me any time and I'll be waiting.

Elise.

After I've sent the message, I realise that what I said was wrong. Well, partly at least. I said I'll be waiting, but, although I'm not putting a time limit on it, I won't wait around forever. I can't. I'm going to give her some time, but I can't wait on tenterhooks for months or more.

I hear Cassie babbling away to her toys in that way that babies do and it makes me smile. She and her brother are my heart. My world would be nothing without them.

Caleb went off to school with his friends this morning and, though the thought plagues my anxiety, I have to believe he'll be okay. He understands how I feel and didn't mind when I set up the tracking app on his phone. That way, I can know where he is at any time.

As I'm brewing more coffee, I also put some bacon in the pan to make my man breakfast. He comes downstairs and straight into the kitchen. The enticing aromas have done their job.

He stops in the doorway and looks over at me. The smile on his lips brings out the cute little dimple I love so much. He's got a gorgeous Hollywood smile and the look in his eyes is appraising as he looks me over from head to toe, noticing I'm wearing just my silk negligée and kimono-style dressing robe.

Pouring us both a coffee, I offer Drew a smile.

"Morning, gorgeous."

"Morning."

He walks over to me, takes both mugs from my hands and puts them on the kitchen island.

Wrapping his arms around me, he nuzzles my neck and the hairs at the nape of my neck stand on end.

"You feeling okay?" he asks quietly.

"Better now."

I turn in his embrace to take my phone from the kitchen counter. I pass it to him and tell him to read the apology I sent to Sophie.

I'm still worried she won't forgive me, worried I have only just found my sister and I might lose her again so soon. But I've reached the decision that I'm not going to let it hold me back. I knew Phil most likely wouldn't want to know me and Carole's message showed me she doesn't care either. I have two brothers that I will likely never get to know. And maybe even Sophie will turn her back on me. But I realised that I'm no worse off than I was before I contacted them. I haven't had them in my life up to now and it hasn't mattered, so not having them around now won't matter either. I have my family: Drew, Caleb and Cassie. They are all I'll ever really need.

"If she doesn't accept your apology, then that's on her. You were the bigger person and apologised—even though I didn't really think you needed to—so, now, if she doesn't take you at your word, that's her problem."

Leave it to Drew to say exactly what's on my mind as well as his.

"I'm not going to think about it anymore. I said I'd wait while she got her head around things, but there's a high probability that she won't manage to get her head around it. She's twenty-six, she's never been told she had an older sister, so I get that it could take a while for her to get used to it. But, honestly, I've resigned myself to the fact that I'm no worse off than I was before I ever contacted any of them. I've never needed them up 'til now, so I'll be fine without them."

"You had to try though, right? You had to see if he was out there, just waiting for you to get in touch. Okay, so now you know he wasn't. You can move on from that and, although I know you won't forget it, you can put it to the back of your mind, knowing that you tried."

"Can we just drop the subject now, please?"

"Of course, baby."

We take our coffees and walk through to the lounge.

***

Work has been hectic. Amanda and I have had one event after another to plan and oversee. Thankfully we haven't had to attend each one, otherwise I'd be even more exhausted than I already am. It's the busiest time of year for event planners and I intend to make the most of it.

I walk into the lounge, kick off my shoes and slump on the couch. Amanda brings Cassie in from the car for me. She came with me today because Drew had work and I didn't have to go out of the office, so she's been keeping me and Amanda on our toes.

I'm sure Amanda would make an amazing mum. She's great with Cassie and Caleb and they seem to love her to bits. If things go well with her and Pryce, then maybe babies are on the cards.

Handing me a steaming mug, Amanda sits down with one of her own. She draws her feet up underneath her and flicks the television on. There's literally nothing on, but mindless TV is probably about all I have the attention span for right now. I am so tired I could fall asleep right where I am.

Drew should be home soon and I can't wait to curl up in his embrace. He's off for the next couple of days, so he'll have Cassie while I go and check out how the plans are coming along for the Christmas ball. We have the layout of the tables and stuff to go over with Pryce. Amanda said that she could do that with him anytime, but I don't want them to have to talk business when they're supposed to be having romantic dates and doing all the things young couples do.

Waking up, I rub my eyes with the heels of my hands. I didn't mean to fall asleep. I was just so comfortable after such a long day.

I look over to Amanda in the chair and notice she's fast asleep. So much for the mindless TV and girly chat.

Looking to my right, I'm greeted with a megawatt smile, complete with sexy dimple. My hubby's home and he didn't wake me when he got in. Ever thoughtful, that man of mine.

"How long have you—"

He puts a finger to his lips and I wince in case I was too loud and woke Amanda up. Looking at her, I see her still fast asleep.

"How long have you been home?" I ask, this time a little quieter.

"Long enough. I fetched Caleb from school. He's upstairs making a start on his homework."

"Why didn't you wake me? What time is it?"

I look at my watch and am startled to see it's long past the time I should have made a start on the tea.

I get up and walk into the kitchen, Drew hot on my heels.

Pulling open cupboards and the fridge, I grab the ingredients for bolognese. Drew slips his arms around me from behind and I turn in his embrace. His lips claim mine in a bruising kiss. His tongue swirls with mine in a frenzied dance and all thoughts are abandoned.

A coughing sound breaks us apart. I look to see Amanda in the doorway and I'm pretty sure my face turns a deep shade of red. She has the nerve to poke her tongue out at me.

"I didn't realise I'd fallen asleep. Why didn't you wake me?"

"She fell asleep too," Drew chimes in before I can respond.

"You're such a snitch, Drew Wright," I say as I elbow him in the ribs.

Amanda laughs as Drew pretends to be wounded. He's such a class clown.

***

Once Amanda left, we had tea and put the kids to bed. We watched a film and then headed to the bedroom. Drew is currently in the shower and I am trying to make myself look sexy.

I pull on a purple negligée that I know is one of his favourites. Sitting on the bed, I wait until I hear the water being turned off, before turning the iPod on quietly.

Drew walks into the room and his eyes roam the length of my body. He drops the towel he was using to dry his hair.

He stalks over to me like a hunter would his prey. His hands take hold of my hips as he leans down to kiss me.

His kiss is anything but soft and tender. I'm sure if I looked in the mirror, my lips would be swollen.

With one hand around my waist, the other comes up behind my neck, bringing us as close as we possibly could be. His arousal presses against my stomach, evident even through the low-slung joggers he put on after his shower.

Edging me slowly backwards, Drew guides me and the edge of the bed bumps the backs of my knees. He lowers me gently, then rests on his forearms above me. Dipping down to claim my lips again, this time he's soft and sweet. He kisses along my jawline and down the side of my neck, trailing feather-light kisses to the swell of my breasts. His right hand comes up to brush my pierced nipple through the satin material still covering me.

A moan of desire bubbles from my lips as he leans down to gently nip it between his teeth, through the material.

My body is coming alive under his tender touch. A blaze of fire begins to burn within, and his kisses are stoking the flames.

Pulling back from me, he gently helps me to sit, then whips the silky material over my head. It lands in a purple puddle somewhere at the side of the bed. He slips out of his joggers and his erection springs free. He strokes his hand over his length a couple of times, then cages me in against the bed; his body covering mine and his arms either side of my head. I don't mind. After all, there are worse places to be trapped than underneath my sexy, muscular husband.

Dipping his head to kiss me, it starts out soft and gentle. Then his tongue probes deeper and I kiss him with as much fervor. A hand slips between my legs and I moan as my back arches off the bed. The sheet is fisted in my hands as I lie there and wait for him to give himself to me.

Desire pools in my abdomen and I'm almost ready to spontaneously combust. It feels like I'm a tank of gas and he's the striking match … a lethal combination.

As he slips another finger inside me, I feel myself explode. My climax rolls through me in waves and I ride out the little aftershocks as my body begins to relax.

Drew rolls to lie beside me and I manoeuvre myself so I'm straddling him. I lean down and claim his lips in a soft, tender kiss. Then he takes hold of my hips and I buck against him for some much-needed friction. My hands roam the planes of his muscular chest and my nails dig in a little, leaving small marks, staking my claim on him.

He reaches down between us and plays with my clit, making me moan in delight. I want him more than I've ever wanted anyone. People always say their current partner is the best lover they've ever had, although that's not always true, but Drew is by far the best lover I have ever had. He's everything I could need; selfless, giving, incredibly sexy and knows exactly which buttons to push.

I reach between us and guide him to where I need him to be. As he slides down inch by delicious inch, I feel myself stretch to accommodate him. He fills me in a physical sense, but emotionally too.

Drew's hands knead my hips as I begin to set a pace with his hips matching me thrust for thrust. An intense craving builds within me and I know from the look in his eyes that he feels it too. His eyes darken to the most intense green, eclipsing the gold flecks I know to be within them. He invokes so much passion within me that it doesn't take long before I feel that free-falling sensation. Drew's hips thrust upwards a few more times before he reaches his own release. Our moans and heavy breathing are all that can be heard.

Chapter Nine

Drew

This morning, I feel great. I've left Elise sleeping, but the kids are in the lounge. Caleb is watching Cassie while I make breakfast. I have to go in to work this afternoon, but I'm going to make the most of our morning together first.

Once Elise wakes, we decide to watch a film with the kids. Caleb chooses Doctor Strange. Typical of him. He's a Marvel kid through and through. It also pleases Elise as she gets to drool over Benedict Cumberbatch.

I'm tired and really wish I didn't have to go to work. I'd rather lounge around all day, spending time with my family.

Arriving at work, I see Danny on the back of the ambulance. I'm early for my shift, so he must have got here even earlier, considering he's cleaning the vehicle and making sure it's stocked.

Our first call of the day is to a man who's been stabbed. What a way to start a shift. We make our way to the scene as quickly as possible, getting the guy, Jason, on the back of the ambulance and to hospital as fast as we can. He's been stabbed in the side. A fight had broken out and he was unlucky enough to get caught up in it.

He says he wasn't one of the people fighting, but he tried to break it up and ended up with a shard of glass sticking out of him. I hate calls like this, especially when people who aren't involved end up getting injured.

On my break, I make my way to Jason's cubicle to check up on him.

I look at him as I pull the curtain aside. He reminds me of a young boy I used to see hanging about over the park when I was a teenager. The boy was a little bit older than me, maybe three or four years. He seemed a bit of an oddball, but he never made trouble. He used to watch me, though, which I found odd.

Jason has the same eyes as the boy. Funnily enough, they are similar to my own. I know lots of people have green eyes, but there's just something about him that seems familiar.

We chat about how he's doing. They want to send him up to a ward, but there aren't any beds free, so he's waiting down here until they manage to locate somewhere for him.

He seems like a nice enough guy. A little scruffily dressed maybe, and a little unkempt, but that doesn't make him a bad guy.

I head back to work, but something Jason said stays on my mind.

"We can't all do so well for ourselves. Loving family, beautiful wife … some of us are just unlucky, I guess."

I don't know what made him say that, but he must mean in general, even though it feels more personal. I guess I'm just taking things to heart today. I need to shake it off and get back to work.

***

We've had a non-stop day today. Danny and I are shattered, but we have another call out just before the end of our shift.

When we arrive, I see Jason. I thought he'd been admitted, but I didn't have time to check, due to how busy we'd been. We don't always check on patients after their admission anyway, but I had meant to; I just got waylaid.

"You again. Mr Perfect," he slurs.

He smells of alcohol and something else. I don't want to take too deep a breath, but I get a whiff of ammonia, like he's soiled himself. This surprises me, based on how he was earlier today. And what does he mean 'Mr Perfect'?

"Jason, what seems to be the problem?"

My tone is friendly, but he sneers at me in response.

Danny takes over from me and asks Jason if he can assess his injuries. I know Danny has taken the reigns because he feels Jason might have something against me. I don't know why he would have a problem with me, but I don't want to make whatever it is worse, so I leave Danny to it.

Jason starts to make a scene and Danny asks him to calm down. He's verbally abusive, so we'd be in our rights to call another ambulance for him and refuse to treat him based on his actions. But I don't want to have to do that.

It doesn't seem like he's bled through the bandage on his side, I can't see any fresh blood. Danny tries to placate him, but Jason starts hurling insults at me about how I'm Mr Perfect with a loving family and the perfect little life. He says it must have been nice to have been brought up by loving parents, to which I almost laugh out loud. He knows nothing of me and my life. My parents were anything but loving. Sure, I have a great life now, but it wasn't always that way.

More insults come my way and Danny shouts to get Jason's attention.

"Listen, buddy, if you don't stop this, we're leaving. Now, I can't see any injuries, so why did you call an ambulance?" he says in a stern voice.

"Because I wanted to see Mr Perfect and tell him what I think of him."

"So, you don't need an ambulance?"

"No. I just wanted to see my brother and there seems to be no other way than to call an ambulance."

"Your brother?" Danny asks, confused.

"Yes, my baby brother Andrew."

What the—? He can't mean me because I don't have any siblings.

"What are you on about, Jason? If you aren't injured, then you don't need us, and we are needed elsewhere."

"Too busy to see his brother, but always got time for others. Typical," he slurs.

"Look, I don't have time for your word games, buddy. We are medical professionals, on call for those who need us. And you don't seem to."

"Oh, I don't *need* anyone, buddy," he says as he points a finger at Danny's chest. "I needed people a long time ago. But I've since learned to stop needing anyone because you can't rely on them. They always let you down. Parents. Friends. Everyone comes and goes."

I don't know what he's going on about but it's obvious he doesn't need medical attention.

"Danny, we have another shout."

"That's it, baby brother, leave me on my own as everyone else always has."

"I think you're confused, Jason. I'm not your brother. I don't have any brothers or sisters. Look, I'm not being funny, but I think you're drunk and you just need to sleep it off."

I begin to walk away but the next words out of his mouth trip me.

"Sleep it off in another shop doorway. Yeah, okay, bro, I'll do that."

No wonder his clothing is shabby if he's sleeping rough. It tugs at my heartstrings that so many people are homeless. I feel sorry for this guy. He doesn't know what he's saying, he's drunk, and he really needs to just sleep it off. But in a shop doorway? That's hardly fair. Then again, life isn't fair. I should know.

Danny and I leave, earning us yet more verbal abuse. Danny calls it in over the radio. We don't really have any choice. He's might be drunk, and he might be homeless, but he doesn't have a medical emergency.

We head back to base and begin to clean the ambulance ready for the next shift. Danny restocks a couple of things we're running low on and I mop the floor.

I'm left in my own head, my thoughts plaguing me. Jason seemed familiar when he first came in, but I know for a fact I don't know him. And I certainly don't have a brother. I am an only child and I am actually truly grateful for that. My parents weren't good enough parents to me, never mind if they'd had another child. He must have me confused with somebody because I would know for a fact if I had a sibling. I'd have had to take care of them when I was younger. Although, Jason is a few years older than me, so maybe he would have had to look after me. But, either way, he's talking rubbish.

How did he know my name though?

Danny and I decide to go for a quick pint after shift, so I pull out my phone and text Elise.

Sitting in the pub, nursing a pint, I am still mulling over the incident with Jason. I tell Danny that the one thing that's really bugging me is the fact he knew my name.

"You introduced yourself as Drew when we arrived on scene after he got stabbed. It's an easy assumption to make, dude. Drew is a shortened name for Andrew, the same as Andy is. Simple."

I scrub my hand over my face. I'm so stupid sometimes. How did I not even think of that? Of course, that's the only explanation that makes sense.

I finish my drink and head to the bar for a Pepsi. I don't drink more than one pint if I'm driving, so I'm on a soft drink until Danny's done with his second pint. I'll drop him off home on my way. He couldn't get his bike to start this morning, so either he gets a taxi, or I give him a lift.

Looking out of the pub window, I see it has started to snow. It's not much and I hope it doesn't stick. A small flurry won't hurt, but Elise hates when it snows. It's more difficult for her to get around since becoming disabled.

***

It's the week before Christmas and I am glad I've got time off in a few days. Caleb's excitement over the festive period is contagious. He's been rocking around the living room to some old Christmas songs since he broke up from school.

I'm back on shift this morning and, thankfully, it's free of snow, unlike the last week. Sitting on the back of the ambulance with a coffee in hand, I see Danny pull up on his bike. He removes his helmet and smiles at me.

He sits down next to me and grabs the coffee I bought him. Strong and black is the way to start the shift when we're here this early in the morning.

We're just finishing when a familiar face comes into view. I'm hoping the only words he has to say are that he's sorry for the way he kicked off. Though I don't really need an apology, I just don't want a row either.

"Drew," he says with a nod, "I wanted to ask if we could talk."

"I'm sorry, Jason, but I'm working."

"It won't take a minute. Please? I shouldn't have kicked off at you, I'm really sorry. I was drunk, though that's no excuse."

"Take five, Drew. Just keep your radio on," Danny says quietly.

I walk away from the ambulance and stand outside. Jason follows, looking remorseful.

"Say what you have to say, Jason."

"I wanted you to know I'm sorry. I really did just want to get to know my brother."

"You must have me confused with someone else, Jason. I'm sorry. I don't have any brothers or sisters."

"That's what you think. Look, I can't prove I'm right, unless we do a DNA test, but we are brothers."

I feel annoyance start to take over. This guy just doesn't know when to stop.

"Your name is Andrew Wright, right?! Your parents were Miriam and James. You grew up on Tinsley Avenue. You used to hang out over the park by St James School."

"How do you know any of that?"

My heart thunders in my chest. How could he know these things? Has he been stalking me or something?

"Like I say, I'm your brother. Miriam and James gave me to a foster family when I was about four years old. I went to St James's School. I used to hang out over the park near there."

"You must be confused, Jason. Like you say, you were fostered around the age of four. You can't possibly know me."

"But I do. I might have been young, but I remembered my way home. I used to run away from my foster parents and they always found me outside Miriam and James's house. I watched you through the window, wondering why they wanted you but not me. As you grew up and started to hang out over the park, I would see you there. I always wanted to talk to you, but I never had the courage."

"Jason, I…" I don't know what to say. Could he be telling the truth? He knows things he shouldn't know.

"Look, I'm sorry to drop this bombshell on you. I didn't intend to. But when I was stabbed, you were there, and I looked at you and saw everything I never had. My first foster family were awful. I was shunted around different families for years. I was always the black sheep. I never had people who loved me, gave a shit about me. Unlike you."

"You think I had a great life with Miriam and James?"

I don't know how much I should share with this stranger. But his face seemed familiar when he was in hospital; there was something about his eyes.

"Well you had them, they were *our* parents, but they didn't want me."

"Trust me, they didn't want me either. Look, Jason, there are things you don't know about Miriam and James. They weren't good parents. It took everything I had not to fall into the care of social services myself."

"So, why weren't you in care if they were that bad?"

His voice sounds full of accusation, like he thinks I'm lying.

I give him the short version of the story, telling him what appalling parents I really had, how I ended up in care until they located my grandparents. I tell him about the drugs and the abuse, the neglect I suffered as a kid. But when I mention Edie and Pops, he gets angry.

"Why the fuck did social services manage to put you with them and not me? Why didn't they locate them when I needed them?"

"I don't have the answers you're looking for, Jason. My parents are dead, my grandparents too. So, I'll never have the answers you need. I'm sorry."

I feel a punch I didn't see him land. My head rocks back and my jaw hurts like hell.

"Motherfucker!" he spits.

"I think you need to leave," Danny says, making me jump.

"And I think I need answers. He's the only one that can give them to me."

"Do you want me to call the police and have you done for assault?" he argues in my defence.

"You need to go, Jason. I won't call the police, just go."

"I deserve answers, Drew. I deserve closure. Okay, our parents were shitty and didn't treat you right. I'm sorry that that happened to you. But our grandparents took you in and not me. Why? Didn't I deserve a loving family too?"

"I'm not saying that, Jason. I'm saying I can't tell you why they didn't take you in. I can't ask them because they died years ago. So what else can I tell you?"

"I don't know but there has to be something!" he shouts in my face.

"Mate, you—" Danny starts.

"Don't 'mate' me. I'm not your mate."

Danny puts his hand on Jason's shoulder.

Jason launches at Danny and tackles him to the ground. I radio the base to call the police, then try to break the two of them up. My jaw takes another right hook, though I think he was aiming for Danny and I just got in the way.

I manage to pull them apart as the police arrive on the scene.

Telling them I don't want to press charges, I look to Danny to see if he wants to. He shakes his head and tells the police he doesn't want to, but he wants them to escort Jason off the premises.

They take him away, but he kicks and punches his way back to me.

"You have every fucking thing I never had. A wife, a home… probably kids too…" he sneers at me.

The policemen grab hold of him and, this time, they put him in cuffs. No doubt they'll arrest him for hitting them.

He's no brother of mine. DNA could prove it beyond doubt, but he is still no blood of mine. If he ever comes near me again, he'll regret it. Okay, part of me feels sorry for the guy. If he really had as rough a life as he described, then I empathise, because I didn't have it easy either. But he could and should have approached me in a better way. Lashing out at me and Danny wasn't going to do him any favours.

***

It's the end of the week, my last shift before Christmas and I'm totally worn out. We've been up to our eyeballs in work—people getting in fights because of daytime drinking. I guess that's just the festive season for you.

We get called to a suspected overdose in a shop doorway in town. Danny and I take the ambulance and get there as fast as we can.

I get out of the ambulance and see a familiar face. I rush to his aid. Searching for a pulse, I find a very shallow one. Danny grabs the stretcher and helps me lift Jason's limp body. We strap him on and wheel it up to the ambulance. Danny sits in the back with him as I drive.

Arriving at the hospital, Danny opens the back door of the ambulance and shakes his head solemnly at me. I can see pity in his eyes.

The doctor pronounces Jason DOA. There was never any hope for him. Now I'll never know whether he was my brother or not. I don't know if I ever would have known anyway, but now that chance has been taken from me.

Danny tries to console me. He says that Jason probably heard a story from someone and claimed it as his own. Either way, we'll never know if he was telling the truth or not.

As I get home, Elise comes out of the kitchen with a coffee in each hand. I take one and sit in the lounge with her. I end up spilling the whole story about Jason and she wraps her arms around me. She holds me tight and whispers over and over that it'll be all right.

Jason won't be all right though. I was angry at him the day he fought with Danny—he's been more like a brother to me than anyone I've ever known—but, after the anger subsided, somewhere in the back of my mind I wondered if I'd see Jason again and if we'd find out for sure if we were related. Now I'll never have answers.

Chapter Ten

Elise

I don't know how to feel. Shock is the most prominent feeling, along with a deep sadness for Drew and the fact that he'll never know whether Jason was his brother.

He came home angry when Jason first confronted him, but I know that, given time, he would have come around to the idea. I probably could have talked him into doing a DNA test, but now that will never happen.

It seems like neither of us will ever know the love of siblings. Sophie got back in contact with me after my last message; she said she didn't see a future as sisters. I was kind of expecting it, but it left a hollow feeling in my gut for a while. She explained that her brothers hadn't taken it well and both had moved out of home. Neither were able to talk to Carole and Phil, never mind live under the same roof.

That left her trying to pick up the pieces and she felt sad that it had torn the family in two. I felt guilty that it was down to me, but I also felt like it was ultimately down to Phil for never telling his children about their eldest sister. He had years to tell them. When they were kids, maybe they were too young, but he could have sat them down as teenagers and addressed the situation. I think he deserves to take the blame for that and so does his wife. That's something I refuse to allow myself to wallow in guilt for.

I know what it's like to think there's a possibility of something and then have it snatched away from you. Drew may have had a brother, but it turned out that Jason overdosed before they could find out.

Drew questioned the fact of him being a junkie like his parents, but he also felt guilty, like it was his fault for the altercation with Jason and that's why he took the drugs.

It's been an intense few days since Jason died. Drew has been up and down. He puts a plastic smile on for the sake of the kids, but I know my husband and I know how he really feels. Our guilt may be for different reasons, but we both feel it nonetheless. I'm hoping we can help each other through it.

With his leave booked from work for Christmas, we begin to decorate the house and erect the tree. We would have done it sooner, but we wanted to do it together as a family while we all had some time off.

For the first time ever, we have a real tree. It was a luxury my parents never bothered with and Drew's parents never bothered to decorate full stop. Christmas might be mainly about the children, but it's nice for us to have something we never had growing up.

Caleb helped decorate the tree and it looks so beautiful. We have handmade ornaments and we have one with Cassie's handprint in as well as one with Caleb's. It's nice to start family traditions. That's another thing we never had growing up, so it's important to make some new traditions with our own family. Something that maybe, one day, they'll be able to do with their children.

Both Caleb and Cassie have a mountain of presents. They've been spoiled rotten. Some people may think we are overcompensating for our own traumatic childhoods, but we know that isn't true. We just love our children and want to give them everything they could ever need, not just for Christmas but for the rest of their lives.

I've bought Drew something special this year. I've been wanting to get him something that really means something, but I didn't know what. Now I've found the perfect gift—a family photoshoot. It may not sound like a lot, but he doesn't have any pictures of himself growing up; there are no albums full of childhood photos like a regular family. And I don't have many pictures of me either, except an album my grandmother gave me. So, in the spirit of making memories, this photoshoot is going to be full of fun and we'll be doing something for us and for our children that was never done for us. In effect, I guess you could say it's a gift for the whole family, but I know Drew will love it. He's a selfless man, says he doesn't need gifts, just my unconditional love and the love of his children. So, I know he'll be overjoyed that we get to do this together.

I'm also planning on using my business contacts to organise a party for Caleb's birthday which isn't too far away. He deserves to have fun with his friends from school, so I have a few ideas I'm going to run by

Drew. Hopefully, it might even help Drew to stop drowning in his guilt. It will give him something else to think about instead.

Putting all my focus back on getting the house ready for Christmas, I get all the ingredients out that we'll need to bake Christmas cookies. No doubt the boys will get into a flour fight, like they did last year. My kitchen ended up such a mess, but I couldn't be mad because Drew and Caleb had so much fun.

I take my cookie cutters from the drawer and lay them out on the kitchen island. With everything ready, I set up Cassie's highchair, so she can sit and watch us. I can't wait until she's old enough to take part.

***

Although he'd already started his annual leave as of today, Drew has been called in this evening because the guy meant to be on shift has phoned in sick. I only hope that the snow we've been having on and off all day doesn't get worse or he could end up being late home tonight. At least he'll be with Danny. That should make it an easy enough shift because they work so well together.

I can't wait for him to get home, so he can start his time off properly and we can snuggle up under a blanket to watch a schmaltzy 'Hallmark' Christmas film. I have a bit of an addiction to the Christmas24 channel at this time of year. I'm just glad Drew indulges my habit without complaint.

Chapter Eleven

Drew

The snow is coming down thicker and faster than I ever remember seeing it. Danny is driving the ambulance with windscreen wipers that seem to be working overtime. It's almost impossible to see with a dark grey sky and a blanket of snow covering every surface possible. Thankfully, Danny's driving is better than a lot of people's. Like me, he's had advanced training in evasive manoeuvres and is more than up to the task, no matter how deep the snow is.

Unfortunately, we've been snowed under at work too—no pun intended. The inclement weather is causing all manner of issues for people. Just yesterday, we had a lovely elderly lady who slipped and broke her ankle just walking down her driveway. Then there was the little boy who didn't realise how deep the snow was and ended up with a sprained wrist after falling into a hole he couldn't have known was there. We've had so many more calls to attend thanks to this slippery white crap falling around us. Don't get me wrong, I have nothing against the snow, so long as it melts away by the next morning, but it doesn't seem to be doing that this week.

Elise has problems walking anywhere due to the nerve damage in her leg, so the snow really doesn't help matters. I worry about her being on her own and risking going out in this weather because if she were to fall there'd be nobody to help her.

Danny pulls up to the house, grabs his kit bag and braces against the cold before we get out of the ambulance and make our way quickly, but carefully, to the doorstep.

"Right this way," says the young blonde woman that answers the door.

She points us in the right direction and we follow her to find our patient. He's lying across the couch with his leg elevated and three young children sitting on the floor next to him.

"Mr Lewis?" I ask as I put my kit bag down.

"That's me," he answers with a grimace on his face.

"What seems to be the problem?"

"He was trying to fix the Christmas lights on the conservatory roof. I told him not to because of the weather, but he brushed my words off and climbed up the ladder anyway," replies the blonde lady, who I assume is Mrs Lewis.

"I slipped and ended up on my ... umm ... backside, with my leg caught in one of the rungs of the ladder. I heard a loud crack and this god-awful pain shot through my calf."

"Have you taken any pain relief, sir?"

"Two paracetamol, but they haven't even taken the edge off it."

I see Danny open his bag to start the patient on something stronger.

"Okay, I'm just going to take a look at the injury, is that okay?"

Mr Lewis nods and seems to brace himself for the pain ahead. I pull on a pair of latex gloves and Mrs Lewis shoos the children out of the way so I can do my job.

Three sad faces look at me and I can see dried tears as well as fresh ones. I feel a twinge in my chest as I think how my children would be if something like this happened to me or their mum.

"Daddy will be okay guys. Let's just give the man room to move around and look at Daddy's leg, okay?" Mrs Lewis says, as she moves the children into the conservatory.

I check over the patient's leg as carefully as I can. It seems like a closed fracture, and we're going to have to stabilise it before taking him to hospital. The ankle is swollen and discoloured from poor circulation due to the awkward angle it's resting at. I'm going to have to give him nitrous oxide to move his foot and get it into a brace.

"Danny, could you grab the brace for Mr Lewis's ankle?"

"Sure thing."

Danny walks back out into the cold and I catch a brief glimpse of thick white flakes falling faster than when we arrived. If we don't leave soon, there's a chance of getting snowed in and that's the last thing we need, especially with such an injury. Mr Lewis is going to be in a lot of pain and we don't want him to have to endure being snowed in at home.

"We have three small children with special needs, though I really hate putting it that way; it's just easier if I do. Anyway, they saw that the lights weren't working properly and got upset. Shea, my wife, she told me just to turn them off, but that upset the kids even more. So, I said I'd get the ladder out. I thought it was just a faulty bulb or something," Mr Lewis says in a rush before he draws another breath of the nitrous oxide.

"I see. It's not really the weather to be having to do such a thing, but you didn't want to upset the children. I get that, it's only natural. I'd be the same with my two."

"It wasn't a smart move, that's for sure."

He takes another deep breath from the gas and air before continuing.

"The children are my world and I'd give anything to make them happy. I just didn't see it ending in a broken leg."

"Here's the brace, Drew. Want me to do it?" Danny asks as he walks back in, shaking the excess snow from his jacket.

"Nah, it's all good, Dan, I'll take that."

I take the brace from him and move to get Mr Lewis's ankle into place.

"Take a big breath on the gas and air, sir. This will be over quickly, don't worry."

Once the ankle is positioned, I do up the straps, causing Mr Lewis to take another deep breath. I can only hope his wife is entertaining the children; I wouldn't want them to see this.

"I'll follow in the car," a small voice says from the doorway.

"No Shea, it's better that you and the children stay here. It's really coming down with force out there and I'd only worry about you getting into an accident. Please, stay here, stay safe. I'll call when I know anything," her husband rushes to placate her before taking another deep breath of pain relief.

"But—"

"Mrs Lewis, he really is right," I butt in. "I know you're worried for him, but if you drive in this weather he'll only worry about you. You don't want to cause everyone more distress than necessary."

Okay, so it's not my place to tell her what to do, but her husband is right. The weather is atrocious and, whether she's the best driver or not, she could get into an accident and then he'd feel so much worse.

"Okay," she concedes. "But you better call the moment you get there. I'll try and get the children to bed."

Mrs Lewis walks into the lounge and kisses the top of her husband's head before returning to the children.

"Bye, Daddy, feel better soon," a blonde-haired, blue-eyed little girl says as she waves.

We slide Mr Lewis onto the stretcher that Danny brought in with the brace. It's not easy when he's roughly six-foot two and bigger built than me or Danny.

Danny pushes the stretcher and I guide the front of it towards the front door.

"Ah … there's a bit of a problem, Dan," I say as I open the door wide, revealing the depth of the snow on the path.

"Shit … I mean, umm … sorry, Mr Lewis."

"We have a shovel …" Mrs Lewis says, appearing behind us suddenly with a large snow shovel.

"Thank you, ma'am."

I take it from her and start to clear a path. It's hard when the snow won't stop coming down. As I shovel it out of the way, a new layer lines the path behind me. We're going to struggle, but we have to do something. We have no choice but to get the patient to hospital.

***

As Danny carefully navigates the road to the closest hospital, I sit with Mr Lewis. He's more relaxed with the gas and air. It has that effect.

"Bet I'm the stupidest injury you've had this festive season," he says quietly.

"The stupidest?"

"Yeah, you know, not very smart to climb a ladder in the snow."

"Well, I'm not here to judge. But, for the record, it wasn't stupid. You were trying to do something for your children. That's part of being a dad."

"You got any?"

"Two. A boy, Caleb and a girl, Cassie. They are my absolute world. Their mother, Elise, she gives me a reason to be happy every day."

"Know what you mean, man. We'd do anything for them, anything in the world. They see us as invincible. Well, mine did until today."

"You'll be back home with them before you know it, Mr Lewis."

"Adam, please. Mr Lewis makes me feel old. The only 'Mr Lewis' in the family is my dad." He air quotes for emphasis.

"Okay, Adam. Well, you'll be back home before they have a chance to miss you too much. Are you all sorted for Christmas?"

"Are we ever really ready?" he asks with a smile.

"Umm … let me think about that and get back to you later."

Adam laughs at my acknowledgment of never being fully ready. That's just the way it is when you have children.

"Umm … Drew … bud, I think we have a problem up ahead."

Looking out of the windscreen, all I can see is how dark it's become since we got to the Lewises' house and how white everything around us is. The headlights don't look as if they can penetrate the depth of it all.

Ten minutes pass and we haven't moved more than a foot. The traffic jam is ridiculous. You'd think sensible people would be wrapped up indoors with a mug of hot cocoa or something. Nobody in their right mind would want to battle travel in this weather. Only, it seems they do.

Adam seems as comfortable as anyone could be in his position. I, on the other hand, am itching to get out of here. I'm not usually claustrophobic, but it feels oppressive in the back of a tin can on wheels in this environment.

Danny is muttering to himself and I'm sure I've heard him swear once or twice. He's not usually easy to wind up, but he seems to be stressing out.

Making idle chit-chat with Adam passes the time, but, when I look at my watch, I'm confounded at how little time has actually passed.

We start to move forward at a snail's pace. Danny seems to relax his posture a little and we're back on the move. I don't want to jinx it, so I go back to talking sport with Adam. He's a Wolves fan and I support West Bromwich Albion, so there's a playful banter as we slowly edge closer to our destination.

***

We're about to pull up to the hospital. It's a mere five minutes away in normal conditions but could take us a lot longer today. It's still coming down ferociously outside and I just hope that Elise and the children are wrapped up warm in bed. I can't wait to slip beneath the covers with her.

Closing my eyes for a moment, I envisage sliding into bed next to Elise's warmth. I wrap myself around her from behind—not to be selfish, I don't do it to make her cold, I do it because she actually likes it. She likes my cold hands on her skin. I imagine her lithe body flexing alongside me as I snuggle in close.

The soft, creamy expanse of her skin and the scent of her fresh out of the shower draws me in closer. If I keep my eyes closed much longer, I may be awkwardly trying to rearrange myself in the downstairs department. But I can't help it. Just a few more seconds with her in my mind's eye …

Elise's beautiful smile is the last thing I see. In the next instant, I hear a huge bang and feel the ambulance catapult through the air.

***

We're at a standstill, but we're overturned. Everything is the wrong way up and I have the biggest headache I ever remember having. Adam has been thrown around and is lying at an awkward angle. I struggle to get into a position to feel for his pulse. His eyes are closed and I'm not sure whether I can see any movement in his chest. If there is any, it's minimal.

I can't hear anything from upfront where Danny is. I'm worried about both my patient and my partner.

Silence. It's absolutely deafening. It's suffocating me. I need to get out of here. But not before I make sure Adam and Danny are okay.

Adam has a thready pulse. You could easily miss it if it weren't for the pressure I'm applying. I listen for sounds of his breathing, but I can barely make that out either.

"Danny," I call out, "Danny."

After a few moments with no answer, I shout once more. It's no good. There's no response from him. I need to find him and assess if he's injured, but Adam is my immediate cause for concern. Still, the need to make sure my friend is okay has my own heart racing faster than the patient's.

I try to move closer to Adam, but my leg feels pretty banged up. Gritting my teeth against the pain, I try to assess the extent of his injuries. An absence of breath sounds, but the fact that he still has a shallow pulse, seems to indicate he could have a tension pneumothorax. I really wish Danny could help me, but I'm guessing whatever the hell happened to us knocked him unconscious.

It's not that I don't know what to do, it's just that I shouldn't attempt it. A tension pneumothorax must be decompressed rapidly with a needle thoracentesis, meaning I haven't got another choice—I need to insert a needle into a space between his ribs to help him breathe. If I don't do this, there's a high chance Adam could die.

I have no idea how long we could be trapped here for. I don't even know if anybody will really be looking for us. I mean, sure, we're on a call-out and when we don't arrive at the hospital, that might have some people questioning our whereabouts. But this snow will indicate a reason for us being late. Will anyone look any further beyond the inclement weather as a reason for our delayed arrival?

I haven't got time to worry about that now though—I have to help Adam.

***

Adam is breathing better now and that gives me cause to be grateful, but, hell, if that wasn't the scariest thing I've done for a while. I've helped women give birth in the ambulance when they've been too far along in their labour to wait to get to hospital. I've attended scenes of accidents and treated all sorts of varying injuries, but I haven't done a needle thoracentesis before—ever.

Now that Adam is more stable, I feel around for my phone. I usually keep it in a zipped pocket on my jacket, but I remember having it in my hand when Adam and I were talking about the football scores.

Looking around the chaos that is the back of the ambulance, I can't spot it in the wreckage. I manoeuvre myself into a position where I can see through to the front of the rig.

Danny isn't anywhere to be seen. What the hell? I pull a small torch from my pocket and shine it into the front. There's no sign of Danny. I begin to panic. Where the hell could he be? He was driving. Something happened that caused us to be in this mess, but Danny should be in the driver's seat.

A frigid wind catches my skin and causes goosebumps to break out. That's when I notice the gaping hole in the windscreen. Fuck! How did I not notice that before? Now that I pay more attention, I can see snow on the dashboard. It looks like that's where Danny went, but how the hell do I get to him?

Trying to stand hurts more than I thought it would. I have to push through. Danny has to be okay. He's my partner, but he's also one of my best friends. I push at the back door, but it won't budge. Whether due to the crash or the snow, I have no idea.

After another fruitless search for my phone, I try to get to the radio in the front. If I can let someone at the base know what's happened, we can get some help for Danny and Adam. I quickly check Adam's pulse and find it's stronger than it was before. He's also breathing better. He won't be for long if we don't get him to the hospital, but, for now, I have to think about how to get us out of here.

***

A banging sound makes my heart skip a beat. It sounds like someone has found us.

I don't know how much time has passed, but the person banging on the back door of the ambulance hasn't given up trying to help me get out. The better news is that he's called for help. The worse news is … well … I can't bring myself to say it until I see the evidence for myself. I need to see it with my own two eyes. For now, I just hope it isn't possible.

Finally, I feel the bitter cold air bite at my skin as the back doors are pulled open. I hear a familiar ringtone and see my phone lying not too far from my feet. I'd given up hope of finding it in this wreck, but jostling stuff around to get the doors open seems to have uncovered it.

Picking it up, I see the beautiful faces of my family light the screen like a beacon of happiness in all this chaos.

"Elise, baby, I can't talk right now."

"Drew, are you okay? I thought you'd be home hours ago."

"I'm okay Elise, there's been an accident and I have to find Danny."

"What do you mean 'find' Danny?"

Just hearing Elise's voice makes me want to cry. The emotions of what's happened come roiling over me in waves. Taking a deep breath, I try and answer her in a steady tone so as not to alarm her more than necessary.

"The accident, baby, it was … bad. The ambulance was flipped over. Danny ended up being thrown through the windscreen. I have to get to him and I have to get our patient to hospital."

The guy who helped open the doors looks at me, empathy written across his features.

"Elise, baby, I have to go. I'll call you when I know more, okay? Don't worry about me. I'm a bit banged up, but I'll be fine. I love you."

"Call me as soon as you can, baby. We love you."

Hanging up the phone is difficult. Just hearing her voice helps keep me grounded. It feels like I would just fly away from it all without her here to keep my feet on the ground. She's my rock.

"I'm a doctor. I was on my way home from a shift when I saw the wreck. I've called for backup. Let me get a look at the patient," says the nameless guy rescuing me.

"I'm Drew, by the way. The patient's name is Adam. I had no choice but to perform a thoracentesis. I know I shouldn't have, under ordinary circumstances, but we were losing him. He'd be dead now, otherwise."

"It's okay, Drew. You did the right thing. Don't worry about repercussions for now. I'm sure they'll see it for what it was—extenuating circumstances."

He climbs into the ambulance and looks over to Adam, lying there, not alert, or awake.

"I'm Chase, by the way," he adds as he sets to work on Adam.

"Would it be okay for me to go and see Danny, doctor?"

"Of course, son. I can handle this."

His sombre tone does nothing to help me prepare for what I'm about to witness.

With much difficulty, I climb from the back of the vehicle. Walking round to the front, I am covered in snow in mere moments. It's difficult to move in snow so deep. I make slow progress, but I need to get to my friend, so I don't stop pushing ahead.

Danny's prone body lies in just a couple of feet ahead of me. My footsteps feel heavy, but not just from the snow. It feels like there is something lodged in my throat, thick and hard to swallow around. The burden of what I know is constricting my heart and I have to stop for a moment to catch my breath.

Looking at the awkward angles of Danny's body, I know there probably wasn't anything I could have done, even if I had managed to get out to tend to him. Knowing I probably couldn't have saved him anyway doesn't help matters at all. My head and heart don't want to accept what they know to be true, but I fear I must.

Settling down on my knees next to the body of my best friend, my whole body feels the pain. Whether it's just from being thrown around in the ambulance, or whether I feel his loss in my bones, I don't know.

Feeling for his pulse is futile, yet I do it anyway. I want there to be a way to save my friend, but his lips are cyanosed, and it isn't just from the snow. His chest is still, no soft rise and fall to show he's breathing. I try to find any sign of life but am at a loss.

I feel a coldness settle over me that has nothing to do with the snow. I'd give anything to hear his laugh one more time, to have got to him in time to hear his voice once more. I feel like a shitty friend for not being able to save him. I should have found a way out instead of remaining trapped in a damn tin can while my friend lay dying, cold and alone in the darkness.

"If it's any consolation, Drew, your friend … he was alive when I arrived on scene. I tended to him first. He knew the end was near. He asked me to tell you what a good friend you are and that you aren't to feel bad. He heard you calling to him and knew you couldn't get out of the ambulance. He knew there was no way you could save him. But he cherished your friendship and the love he had with Ashleigh."

A long sigh escapes me as I scrub my hand over my face.

"Thank you, doctor."

"Chase, please. I'm just Chase right now."

A hand settles on my shoulder and I take comfort in the strength of his grip. I don't even realise I am crying until my vision blurs too much for me to see. I wipe the tears away with the back of my hand, yet more fall in their place.

Chase places a blanket around my shoulders and I draw it around me. My only comfort on this cruel night.

Danny was a good driver, even in a snowstorm. This should never have happened. I get to my feet and walk to the other side of the vehicle to see what crashed into us.

"The driver was dead when I got here," Chase says from behind me, "I checked on him after your friend."

"Danny. His name is—or should I say *was*—Danny."

"I'm sorry for your loss, Drew. I really am."

"How's Adam?"

I walk back round to the back of the ambulance and look in on Adam.

"He's breathing, thanks to your quick thinking. I'm guessing his original injury was a broken leg, seeing as though it's in a brace."

"Yes. He fell from a ladder in the snow. He was trying to please his children as a light on their conservatory had blown. They… they have special needs and were distraught about the lights being out."

I take a deep, calming breath.

"I should contact his wife, Shea; let her know what's happened. I have no idea how long we've been here, but she expected him to call when he got to hospital."

"I found this," Chase says as he hands me a phone.

Taking it from his hand, I scroll through Adam's contact list, grateful that his phone isn't locked. Seeing Shea, I open the contact details before hitting 'Call.'

I take a few deep, steadying breaths. I know she'll be worrying and I don't want to add to that, but needs must.

I dial the number and hear the phone ring three times before a small voice answers.

"Adam? Oh, thank goodness, I've been going out of my mind. Why haven't you called sooner?"

"Mrs Lewis, this is Drew, the paramedic."

"Oh. What's happened, where's Adam? Is he in theatre or something?"

I breathe in through my nose and out through my mouth before answering, hoping that my voice won't wobble.

"Mrs Lewis, are you sitting down?"

"Oh, lord, please don't tell me he's dead. People always tell you to sit down when it's bad news. He only broke his leg, he can't be dead," her words come tumbling out.

"No, he's not dead. Something has happened though. His injuries are more than they were."

"What? How?" her tone has gone up an octave.

I don't break bad news to patients' families. That's not part of my job. But I must tell her what's gone on.

"There was an accident. The snow came thicker and faster than we hoped. There was a truck, it hit the ambulance."

A sharp intake of breath and the sound of her sobs tugs at my heartstrings.

"Adam is okay, Mrs Lewis. He had trouble breathing; I had to perform a small procedure to help him. There's a doctor with us now and he managed to call for help. Help is on its way, I assure you. Adam will be okay, I'm sure of it."

I can't make her a promise I have no idea how to keep, so I don't. It's hard when you can't placate somebody with a lie and yet cannot tell them the full truth either. The truth is, I hope Adam will be okay, but I can't be one hundred percent sure. Nothing is certain.

Hearing an approaching siren, I glance up.

"Mrs Lewis, do you hear that? Help is here. We'll get Adam to the hospital as soon as we can. I'll make sure someone calls you and keeps you updated."

"Thank you. Can you be the one to call me?" she asks with a hopeful tone.

"I'm afraid I can't. I'm a bit banged up from the accident myself. I promise I will get someone to call you. I'll see if my friend Sam is working. If she is, I'll get her to contact you when they know more. She's a good woman, a fantastic nurse. You can trust her."

"Okay."

"For what it's worth, Mrs Lewis, I'm really sorry."

"It's not your fault. It's this weather. It could have happened to the most careful driver. I hope the driver of the truck is okay."

The selfless way she cares makes a lump form in my throat.

"I hope so too."

I can't tell her he's dead. She's already cracking under the pressure. I don't want to be the one to break her.

The sirens draw closer and I see the blue lights penetrate the darkness that blankets us.

"The ambulance crew is here, Mrs Lewis. I promise someone will be in touch soon."

"Thank you. And thank you for helping him. Goodbye."

Her voice cracks as she says goodbye. I hang up and slip her husband's phone into my pocket until we reach the hospital.

***

At the hospital, Chase sits with me in my cubicle. He's finished his shift, but he can obviously sense my desire not to be alone.

"You should call your wife," he says, looking up at me.

"I should."

Slipping my phone out of my pocket, I take a deep breath and dial Elise's number.

Chase leaves and draws the cubicle curtain shut to allow me some semblance of privacy.

***

Elise arrives and, as she steps into my cubicle, I break down in tears. Danny's death hurts my heart. Oh, how I wish I could have done something to help him. Chase explained that he'd been with him as he'd taken his last breath. It was almost like Danny had been hanging on until help arrived, just so he could say goodbye.

"Drew."

Warm arms wrap around me and I pull her in close. Breathing in the scent of her calms my racing heart just a little.

"Oh, baby, I'm so sorry."

"How did you know?"

"I spoke to Sam as I arrived. Shush now," she soothes as she traces her hand up and down my back.

We sit wrapped up in each other for I don't know how long. Her arms are all that's keeping me from falling apart. My best friend gone in an instant. I'm not sure who will inform his family, but I need to call them and tell them how sorry I am.

He was still dating Ashleigh, the girl he met on our trip to Iceland. She'll be torn up. She doted on him. He was talking about proposing on Christmas Day, but now he's been robbed of that chance. He's been denied the pleasure that comes with being a husband and a father. He would have been a great dad. He was so good with my children. He was their pseudo-uncle. How I'm going to break it to them that 'Uncle Danny' is dead, I don't know.

Chapter Twelve

Elise

Drew's grief threatens to overwhelm us both. He'd told me on the phone that Danny was thrown from the ambulance, but I didn't know he was dead until I got to the hospital, where my best friend Sam—a senior nurse—told me.

As soon as I heard there had been an accident, I asked Mrs Short next door if she'd look after the children who were both tucked up in bed. She's such a lovely woman and has such a way with Caleb and Cassie. Of course, having had five children of her own—all of whom are grown and left home now—would be the reason for her ease with them.

Sitting on the bed in Drew's cubicle, the world is at bay outside the curtain. For a moment, I'm tempted to not believe this is all true. I wish this hadn't happened; I wish I could turn back time. But no matter how many wishes I make, none of them will come true. So now I must wish that Drew pulls through his grief and that Danny's family can find some peace.

I wish that I could absolve the guilt I see shining in Drew's sorrowful hazel eyes. I know he wishes he could have done more, but, in truth, he was trapped and couldn't have helped even if he wanted to. But he's wracked with guilt for not being there with his friend at the end.

Drew doesn't say a word, so I keep quiet too, wanting to share his grief and the burden that weighs upon him, albeit silently.

I look over his injuries—minor bruises and contusions for the most part, but they will take him to x-ray his leg soon. He said he stood on it to get to Danny, but he could feel something wasn't right with it.

Sam told me the patient he brought in should be okay and that, if anything, Drew saved his life. But that news will only lighten Drew's heart a little.

I hear a small cough outside the curtain to Drew's cubicle.

"Excuse me," a small voice says.

I draw back the curtain and see a blonde woman, pretty beyond the tears she has shed.

"Hi."

"Hello, I'm Mrs Lewis, but you can call me Shea."

She extends her hand, so I close my own around her soft skin.

"Hi Shea, I'm Elise."

"Your … umm … husband?" She poses the word as a question, unsure whether we're married. "He saved my husband Adam's life."

"Oh, Mrs Lewis," Drew says softly. "How is he?"

"He's out of the woods. They operated on him just now. He had a perforated lung. They tell me you performed the procedure that saved him."

Drew looks her in the eye, a softness in his gaze.

"I did what anyone would have done."

Always humble. That's my husband through and through.

"Not just anyone would have known how to do what you did. They tell me it's tricky but that you noticed his thready pulse and his struggle to breathe. Your actions gave him the extra time he needed until help arrived."

"I'm just glad to have been able to help him. How's his leg doing?"

"It's broken in two places. They tell me it's a wonder that he didn't do more damage. He'll be able to get around on crutches, but he will need it in a cast for six weeks or more. What am I saying? You'd know that. Sorry to ramble."

A blush rushes across her pale skin.

"You're not rambling, Shea. Can I get you a cup of tea? You look like you could use one," I say as I look her over.

She looks dishevelled, her clothes rumpled like she slept in them—and maybe she did before she got the call to come here—and she could probably use something stronger than tea, but I can't offer her anything to steady her nerves. Her hands are trembling slightly—excess adrenaline, I'm sure.

"That would be—" she breaks off as tears roll down her pink cheeks.

"Come on, I was just going to get Drew and myself a coffee anyway. It's right this way."

I turn to make sure she's following me and see her cast a glance back at Drew as she softly draws his curtain closed.

"Your husband, he's amazing. If it weren't for him, my three children wouldn't have a father."

"He's one of a kind, my Drew. I mean, of course, medical professionals all do their job to the best of their abilities—I mean no offence to them—but Drew's special. He's got a heart of solid gold."

We arrive at the little coffee shop and I order two coffees and a tea for Shea. She reaches for her purse but I shoo her away.

"Your money's no good here," I tell her with a smile.

"Thank you."

"Should you be getting back to Adam?" I ask as we walk towards the cubicles.

"He's not awake from the surgery yet. The doctor told me to get myself a drink and he'd come and get me as soon as there was anything more. He said I looked frazzled, like I could use a break. So, I came to find Drew to pay my thanks."

"You're welcome to come and sit with us if you'd like. Drew has to head down for an x-ray soon, so it'll be just me for a while. You'd be keeping me company."

"That would be … nice."

She smiles at me and I can see just how tired she looks. The worry seems to have aged her a good few years. But she'll be able to get back to normality soon enough.

"How are the children?" Drew asks Shea as we return, hot drinks in hand.

"They're being babysat by their Grams. She's the only person they'll sit well for."

"How many children do you have?" I try to keep the conversation light.

"Three. Lily, Jayde and Matty."

"We have two of our own, Caleb and Cassie."

I pull my wallet out of my bag and slip a photo from one of the pockets. Shea smiles wide as she sees my two beautiful angels.

"They're gorgeous. You're incredibly blessed."

"Oh, we are. They are the moon, the stars, the sun, our everything."

I feel a smile of pride tug at my lips at the thought of Caleb and Cassie.

"Here's my three."

Shea hands me a photo and I give her a wide smile.

"You're very blessed yourself."

"We are. They are a handful, but Adam is such a good dad. He's kind, gentle, loving. When we realised they all had learning difficulties, he took it in his stride. It nearly broke me, but Adam is the glue that held us together. He still is."

"I can understand that. We've had our own ups and downs and Drew is the person that keeps us standing strong."

"I'd disagree, baby. I'd say you are the glue that binds this family," Drew says tenderly.

"We'll have to agree to disagree."

Shea laughs and strokes the picture of her children.

"Adam's the same. He says it's me that keeps us together. But it really is him. So many people could run from their responsibilities after finding out how hard their children will find life. But Adam? Pfft! He's the most amazing man I've ever known. He wouldn't run. Not ever. He raises us all up."

"He sounds like a good man."

"The best. He fell off a ladder today because he wanted to keep the children happy."

"Oh?"

"Yeah, we have Christmas lights on the outside of the conservatory. One of the bulbs went, plunging the whole lot into darkness. The children were upset. I said just to leave them off and we'd find a way to distract the children, but he wouldn't hear of it. He grabbed his ladder and a new bulb and went outside in the snow. He fixed the new bulb in place but then lost his footing. His leg was caught in the rung of the ladder and he said he heard a snapping sound. I managed to get him inside and called an ambulance. That's when Drew and his partner came to the rescue."

At the mention of Danny, Drew's face falls. Shea doesn't seem to notice, maybe because he's quickly slipped on a mask, complete with plastic smile.

"I'm so grateful to them both," Shea continues, not noticing the pain it's causing Drew.

"Excuse me, Mrs Lewis?" Sam asks, standing outside the cubicle.

"Yes, that's me."

"Adam is awake and is asking for you. Would you like to come with me?"

"Oh, thank goodness," Shea says, with a smile that touches her eyes this time and lights up her whole face. It seems to transform her appearance and I'm so happy for her.

"Thank you for everything. And thanks for the tea."

"Anytime, Shea. I hope Adam is back on his feet soon. If you need anything in the meantime, let me give you my number."

She hands me her phone and I save my contact information.

"It's saved under Elise Wright. If you and the children need anything at all, just give me a call."

"I couldn't impose on you," she says quietly.

"It's not an imposition; it's an offer of help. I may be disabled and unable to get around as easily as some, but I can cook, and I can bring over my famous lasagne. Anything you need, please, if you're truly stuck—I'm here."

"Thank you."

"I hope Adam is okay. Tell him not to go climbing any more ladders." Drew tries for a light tone, but I can hear the pain in his voice.

"I will," Shea says as she turns to follow Sam.

Chapter Thirteen

Drew

What a couple of weeks it's been since the crash. Yesterday was Danny's funeral. It was one of the hardest days in my life. I said goodbye to one of the best men I knew, one of the best friends I've ever had. My heart broke as I read the eulogy I'd been asked to write. Never in my life did I think I'd have to stand and face a room full of people and tell them what an amazing man Danny was. Silent tears rolled down my cheeks as I read the heartfelt words I'd written in the days before. My voice cracked a little more the further I read. When I sat back down, Elise wrapped me in her warm embrace, soothing me as I cried and my body shook with the force of my grief.

Elise has been my rock through all of this. The guilt I carry like an albatross around my neck threatens to overwhelm me. But Elise is my anchor as I feel adrift at sea. She's there to ground me and keep me going. I've taken some time off work. Partly because I'm injured and partly because I can't face being there without Danny's presence.

Sitting here on the couch with my injured leg raised, I have a blanket draped around me to fight off the chill in the air, but I feel cold to my bones. I've been lucky to never suffer such a loss as an adult until now. The last time I lost anyone was my grandparents. That day will forever live in my memory as the worst day of my life. I know that the only thing in life that is certain is death, but it took Danny too young. It wasn't his time. He had a girlfriend to propose to, babies to make, a bright future full of love and happiness. Fate is cruel to have taken that away from him. At least my grandparents had a long and fulfilled life. They had lived to a decent age and had done a lot with their lives—bringing me up to be the best man they knew how being the biggest thing, in my opinion—so, although I was broken when they died, I knew in my heart that they'd had good lives.

Elise has been working from home, but her assistant Amanda has stepped up and taken over a lot of the responsibilities while Elise has cared for me. I told her to go back to work today because she has the final arrangements to make for the hospital Christmas party—a party Danny won't be a part of. I won't get to see him making an ass of himself as usual. His comedy stylings will be missed this year and every year. There's a hole in everyone's lives where Danny should be.

One thing that makes me feel slightly better is that the woman in charge of the hospital party has said that part of the proceeds will go to a charity Danny felt strongly about. That's another thing that will be missed. He was a real pillar of the community; he was very charity minded and would fundraise on some of our trips abroad. His grandmother had early onset dementia and so he always made sure to raise money for the people that took care of her at the end of her life.

Danny has been in my every thought today, as he has been since it happened. It's hit me harder than I thought it would. I don't know how to shake off the fog that surrounds my mind. I know I need to get my head together, but it's so difficult. If he was still here, he'd tell me to buck up and shut up, as he often did. But then, if he was here, I wouldn't feel like this.

Maggie, Danny's mum, asked me to keep a secret until Christmas, but I don't think I can. It feels like an extra weight on me. I have the ring he was going to give Ashleigh on Christmas Day. Maggie asked me at the hospital to keep hold of it and I swore I would, but now I just need to give it to her. She needs to know how much Danny loved her.

Picking up my phone, I decide to ask the wisest person I know what she thinks.

Drew: Hey baby, I know you're working, but I need some advice.

I see three dots bouncing, meaning she's typing a reply.

Elise: Anything I can do to help, baby, you know that. What's up?

Drew: I want to give Ashleigh the ring. I want to do it now. I can't hold onto it until Christmas. It feels wrong to withhold it from her. I know Maggie asked me to, but it just feels wrong.

Elise: Why not ring Maggie and explain. Give her the ring back and tell her to keep it until Christmas if that's what she wants. Tell her you just can't do it. She'll understand.

Drew: But I don't want to burden her.

Elise: We all have a burden to carry. I know how she felt at the time, and I know you wanted to keep her happy, but it's making you sad. Maggie will understand that, I'm sure.

I know Elise is right, but, still, I feel all kinds of bad for not being able to keep my word. I call Maggie and explain my predicament before I lose the courage.

It turned out Maggie understood better than I thought and she told me to give it to Ashleigh now if I want to. She said she should never have asked me to keep it from her and she apologised for burdening me with it in the first place.

I dial Ashleigh's number and take a few deep breaths as the phone rings. The sadness in her tone as she answers breaks my heart a little more. She agrees to come over, considering I can't drive with my leg in a backslab. It turned out I had a hairline fracture, so I was sent home in half plaster cast, half tubular bandage. They couldn't put a full cast on in case of swelling. Even with half a cast, it's heavy and cumbersome. I can't get around very easily, which makes it hard looking after the kids. Elise even took Cassie with her today so that I could get some rest. She is the most thoughtful, loving woman I've ever known.

I struggle to get up and put some coffee on for when Ashleigh arrives. I had texted Elise about what Maggie said and told her Ashleigh was coming over. She said as long as I was comfortable, that's what matters.

***

Ashleigh looks like she hasn't had a wink of sleep. Her clothes are wrinkled and the bags under her eyes are dark and heavy. My heart aches for her. Sure, when I first met her, all I saw was blonde hair and fake tits, but underneath all the makeup and perfect hair is a down-to-earth and genuine woman.

I don't say anything as I pull the small blue box from my pocket. Handing it over to her, I see the shock in her eyes. She looks between me and the box, not moving a muscle, just her eyes darting around in uncertainty.

"He was going to give you this on Christmas Day."

Trembling hands open the delicate Tiffany box. Tears flow as she looks at the contents. I don't know what to say, so I remain silent instead.

"It's beautiful," she says, so softly I almost don't catch it.

A few deep breaths and then she takes the ring from the box, nearly dropping it because her hands are shaking so much. Sliding it onto her ring finger, she looks down and the tears cascade like a waterfall.

We remain silent for what seems like an eternity but is realistically only a few minutes.

The gorgeous ring shines on her finger as the sunlight catches it through the window. I wish Danny was here to see the light of love shining in Ashleigh's eyes as she admires the last thing he bought her.

"It's so perfect," Ashleigh whispers as she turns her hand this way and that.

"Danny spent weeks searching for the right one. His words were 'Ashleigh is my heart, my soul, my world. She deserves a ring that shows her the depth of my love. It doesn't matter how much or how little it costs, as long as she can see my love for her and hers for me shining in it every time she looks at it.' He wasn't one for words, our Danny, but he loved you with all that he had."

Fresh tears fall from her blue eyes as I remind her of Danny's love for her. The smile on her face says it all. She wanted to be his wife, the mother of his children.

"I haven't told anyone this, Drew, and I'd rather not until it's safe to tell, but…" she places her hand on her stomach and I know what's coming next. "I'm having a baby. I've not long found out, so I don't know how many weeks along I am, hence why I don't want to tell everyone just yet."

"Oh, Ashleigh…" I don't know what to say. Words can't express my feelings.

"At first I thought I'd missed periods due to stress, but I found out the day before the funeral. I told Danny as I stood alone at his grave once everyone had left. I'll tell his parents soon, I promise."

"Don't think about that now. They won't blame you for keeping it to yourself until your first scan. They'll be made up to be grandparents."

"I hope so. This baby is the only part of Danny I have left. I'll tell him or her every day what a wonderful man Danny was."

"Maggie has asked that we scatter his ashes in places he loved. Instead of scattering all his ashes in one place, she wants me to take some and scatter them somewhere. Did she tell you?"

"Yeah, we discussed it. It's what Danny would want."

"It feels weird, if I'm honest. I have a small part of him in a box in my closet. I didn't know where else to keep the box out of the way of the children."

"I get that. I have my box on my mantelpiece. I talk to it every day. It'll be hard to let go, but I know I have to. I'm still thinking of where to scatter him."

We chatted a little longer, making small talk before Ashleigh went home. She hugged me tight and reminded me how much Danny admired me. I got a little choked up and had to discreetly wipe my eyes. I've cried more in the last few days than I have in years.

Chapter Fourteen

Elise

I've found it hard to concentrate on work this past couple of weeks. The funeral was the hardest thing I've ever had to witness Drew go through. They didn't have a wake; they wanted it to be a celebration of Danny's life and what he achieved rather than a mournful day for all concerned. We weren't allowed to wear black; Ashleigh insisted everyone needed to wear bright colours in honour of Danny's bubbly personality. But, despite sharing memories of Danny and laughing at all the tales of things he got up to, there was so much pain in the air that it was palpable. We didn't take the children. Instead our neighbor watched them, because we felt they were too young. Caleb misses Uncle Danny, and sometimes he clings to a toy Danny had bought him last Christmas and talks to him. I've heard him whisper about how hard Daddy finds it without his best friend and that he wants to be strong for him, so he asks Danny to help him find the strength to comfort his dad.

I've done my best to comfort Drew, but, although he's here physically, sometimes he doesn't seem fully present in the moment. He smiles and plays with the children, but the smiles seem forced and the laughter feels hollow. How can I reach him? That's the question that plagues me. I want to give him time, space, whatever he needs. But I also don't want to allow him to withdraw too far into himself. I don't want him to have the same issues as when his grandparents died. I wasn't with him then, but he's told me how he suffered. They were his only real parents because unfortunately, his biological parents weren't there for him. They were drug addicts who beat, abused and neglected him, and eventually died of an overdose.

***

It's the evening of the hospital Christmas Ball and Drew looks handsome in his tuxedo. He's got a pale blue bow-tie to match the colour of my dress. I feel a little like Cinderella, all dressed up in pale blue with accents of silver. We're early to the venue to make sure everything is in place and ready for the festivities.

Amanda is in attendance with Pryce. They seem like a good match. A new couple in the first throes of love. They remind me of how happy Drew and I were until Danny's death. We've always been so happily in love since we first got together and over the two and a half years since. I wouldn't say we've stopped being so in love, but Drew hasn't been as tactile, instead he seems like he's just going through the motions of life and I don't know if I am enough to see him through it.

Looking at my husband, I see a myriad of emotions in his hazel gaze. There's heartache and loss, but there's also a twinkle like he's in there somewhere, waiting to come back to the surface.

Taking his hand, I pull him towards the corridor where it's quiet.

"What's up?" he asks as we stop in the silence of the empty corridor.

"This," I say softly, before slanting my lips over his.

His hands wrap around my waist and he pulls me flush to his chest. His mouth opens to allow my tongue to explore. He tastes of whiskey with a hint of mint mouthwash. His scent envelopes me and it feels good as he kisses me with as much fervour as I kiss him. For a moment suspended in time, he's not grieving and I'm not trying to reach him; we're just Drew and Elise, a happily married couple, in love with each other every bit as much as the very beginning.

A hand reaches up and tugs gently at my wavy hair. I left it down in loose curls, just the way he likes it.

"You are so beautiful," he whispers against my lips. "You look just like a princess."

"I won't leave a glass slipper behind at midnight."

"Slipper or no slipper, I'd always find my way back to you."

My heart somersaults at his words. I didn't think he realised I thought he was lost. Maybe he's fighting to get back to normal. I sure hope so.

"I love you," I reply as I lean in for another kiss.

The second kiss is more tender, it warms me all the way to my soul.

"We'd better get back before I find a supply closet," Drew says as he breaks our kiss.

"Ever the romantic."

I try for an offended tone, but don't quite pull it off, so I nudge him gently in the ribs before taking his hand to head back into the ballroom.

It's hard for Drew to get around in the boot the hospital put him in last week, but it's easier than when he was wearing that awful, heavy backslab. At least the boot is a bit lighter. But I know he can't wait to be unencumbered.

The ballroom is bustling with people when we slip back quietly through the side door. The men all look good in their tuxedos and the women are gorgeous in their ballgowns. Each couple has come in a matching colour, just like Drew's bow-tie and my dress.

Queuing at the bar, we bump into Pryce.

"Doesn't Amanda look amazing?" I ask.

"She's stunning. Inside and out."

"Somebody's got it bad," I add with a wink.

His skin flushes pink and I smile a genuine smile. It feels like all my smiles have been plastic just recently, but I'm genuinely happy for my assistant and friend.

I look over at Amanda and she smiles as she meets my gaze. Her face transforms as it lights up her eyes and I know that she's in love. She says they haven't exchanged those three little words just yet, but I have a feeling tonight might be the night. Even if not tonight, I know it will be soon because she's bursting to tell him. She says she's just scared of being the one to say it first.

***

Drew holds me close as we sway gently to the music. Both being careful of my leg and Drew's broken leg, our dance may look awkward to some, but it's how it feels that matters. And tonight, it feels like he's holding me for the very first time and the butterflies in my tummy take flight. He's even more handsome than when we first met over a decade ago. He doesn't look like he's aged all that much since the tender age of twenty-three. But he has matured and he's over his commitment issues. When we got set up on our blind date by Sam, he wasn't ready for a relationship and yet we both fell head over heels and couldn't control our hearts' desire any more than we could our destiny.

As the song ends, we walk back to our table. Sam and Karl look up as we approach. Sam's been a godsend since Danny's death. She's looked after the children so Drew and I can have some time alone, she's cooked for us, she's really gone the extra mile. A lifelong best friend, she's the one person I know I can turn to. I've confided in her about Drew not being himself and she's given me her usual sage advice. She says I need to gently coax him round, remind him he has a life—children and a wife that need him.

'I'll Be Home For Christmas' begins to play and I don't even realise that tears have fallen until Sam discreetly passes me a napkin. I sniffle and wipe my eyes as I think of Danny, who won't be home for Christmas, now or ever again. His child will grow up with only second-hand accounts of how wonderful a man he was. He or she will never get to experience firsthand how amazing he was and how devoted to Ashleigh he was. He would have made a great dad. Fate can be so cruel.

Sam gently squeezes my arm and gives me a reassuring smile. I excuse myself from the table and go off in search of the ladies' room to check my makeup.

As I close the door behind me, my shoulders slump. I draw in a deep breath and let it out slowly.

Checking my makeup isn't smudged in the mirror, I add a layer of lip gloss to the gorgeous soft pink LipSense lipstick I have on. I touch up my eyeliner and take another deep breath before pulling my shoulders back and heading back to the others.

Approaching the table, I see Drew and Karl are engaged in conversation, but Sam isn't with them.

"I thought you could use this."

I turn to see Sam holding a glass out to me.

"Thanks."

I try to smile but it feels fake, so I take a sip of the prosecco in my hand.

"He needs me to be strong and here I am falling apart at the lyrics of a song," I sigh.

"Babe," she says as she puts an arm around my shoulders, "you are strong. So much stronger than you give yourself credit for. But you're only human, you're fallible, you have feelings. That's not a bad thing."

I try to smile again and this time it feels a little easier.

"I know, but here and now isn't the place to break down."

Sam holds me tighter for a moment before releasing me to walk back to the table. I sit next to my husband and look at his handsome profile. He really is the epitome of everything I need in a man.

Before long, it's time for Seb to do his round as *Secret Santa*—something that Danny was supposed to do. He hands everyone a gift with a "Ho! Ho! Ho!" but the jolly voice is covering for a man as broken as Drew.

Opening my gift, I see a box of chocolate willies. I know it could be from anyone, hence why the sender's identity is secret, but I laugh to myself as I think of them coming from Danny himself. The only reason to think that is because of the museum they went to on their trip to Iceland—the Icelandic Phallological Museum. It's as the name suggests and, as Drew sees the contents of my gift, he laughs a real laugh for the first time since his best friend's death.

"The museum! He told me your gift was a jokey one. Never did know how to be serious, that boy."

"What? Secret Santa is meant to be secret."

"He told me because he didn't know what to get you."

I take the box out of its wrapping, open it and share the contents around the table.

"Here's to Danny," Drew says, holding his chocolate willy aloft.

We giggle and join him in a mock 'cheers' with our own chocolates before eating them.

***

Arriving home to a quiet house, we see our neighbor, Mrs Short, asleep on the settee with the baby monitor next to her. I gently rouse her as Drew goes to check on the children.

I thank Mrs Short, see her to the door and bid her goodnight. Heading to the kitchen, I decide to pour us both a glass of brandy. I don't drink much, but I love cherry brandy and I only had one glass of prosecco tonight before moving on to Pepsi.

I walk to the lounge with the glasses in hand. Drew is sitting with his jacket off, his bow-tie discarded, and the top button of his shirt undone. He looks so masculine and sexy. My thighs involuntarily squeeze together at the thought of him naked.

He takes his glass from me and smiles a genuine smile that lights his eyes.

"He would have loved tonight."

"He was there in spirit," I reply softly, as I squeeze his shoulder gently before sitting next to him.

"He was, I'm sure of it."

We sit in comfortable silence until our glasses are empty.

A soft warmth envelopes my hand and I look down to see Drew's fingers entwined with mine. He gives my hand a gentle squeeze and I return it as I meet his gaze. The look in his eyes is so intense it takes my breath away. I see desire swirling in his irises as his gaze travels from my face down to my cleavage, which Sam said looked—and I quote—sumptuous in this dress, and then sweeps back up to my lips as he leans in and claims them with his.

The kiss is soft, gentle, and full of love until he reaches to draw me closer when it becomes more urgent. Our chests rise and fall with the speed of our breathing, our breaths mingling with each other's. One hand travels the length of my spine before coming to cup my breast in his palm. I gasp as he reaches for both breasts and rubs his thumbs across my nipples. Even through the fabric of the dress I can feel his touch and it sends sparks of desire through me.

Suddenly I feel my dress fall away and I watch the material pool in my lap as the zip is undone by my husband's deft fingers. The sharp intake of breath through his lips tells me all I need to know. He's thinking about how I haven't worn a bra all evening. Faster than I can blink, his hands are roaming my body. I come alive under the touch of his skin on mine. It's like he ignites a fire in my veins. I squeeze my thighs together to try and stop the warmth pooling there, but it's in vain.

Drew's hands burn a trail across my skin as he touches me so gently. He looks at me like it's the first time he's ever seen me. Hunger shines in his eyes and his arousal is obvious. I want to reach out and touch him, but, as I try, he swats my hand away. He wants to focus all his attention on me. His desire is palpable and makes my heart try to break out of my ribcage. I'm sure he must be able to feel it racing as he traces his hand down over my heart. His hand lingers there for a moment before he runs his index finger down the valley between my breasts. Slowly, he cups my breasts in both of his hands before leaning down to take one nipple in his mouth. The sensation burns through me like wildfire. I arch my back and wrap my arms around his neck. I want so much more than what he's giving, but he's taking his time and it's going to drive me crazy.

We haven't been close like this—intimately—since everything with Danny. I know he's struggled with losing his best friend, and I don't blame him at all. All I can do is be here for him and wait for him to come back to me. Tonight feels like a new beginning, maybe.

I'm struggling to tamp my desire, my wish to get Drew right where I want him. I want him inside me right now, but I know that's not going to happen, so I try to relax and enjoy the sensations he's got swirling inside me.

Drew kisses up the valley and over the swell of my breasts, up to the hollow of my throat. Mapping a trail up the side of my neck, he then nips my earlobe between his teeth before suckling it to take away the sting. I'm panting like I've run a marathon and the butterflies in my stomach have morphed into moths, flapping their wings and making me feel like a giddy teenager in the first flushes of love. Even after how long we've been together, Drew still makes me feel this way.

Looking at me with hooded eyes, I see the lust within them. His eyes darken depending on his emotions, so I know just how to read him.

His soft, full lips claim mine in a searing kiss. His tongue urgently swirls with mine, duelling for control. A deep moan reverberates through his chest and he grasps the back of my hair in one hand, pulling me closer. His other arm snakes around my waist and pulls me flush to him. It doesn't feel fair that I am exposed, and he doesn't even have his shirt off. I want skin on skin contact. I'm desperate to feel him set my body ablaze.

As if he reads my mind—or shares the same thought—Drew moves to unbutton his shirt. I pull back slightly so I can see him expose that gorgeous body of his. He's so toned and defined. He's not ripped like some bodybuilder, but he has a six pack, and the sexiest thing about his body is that V shape that drives women wild. I love to run my tongue over it, there's just something so sexy about it.

His shirt falls to the floor and his hot lips are back to claim mine as he undoes his trousers. All too suddenly, his lips leave mine and he helps me to stand so we can discard the rest of the material that separates us.

My dress pools at my feet and Drew helps me step out of it before pushing his trousers down over strong thighs.

"Drew—"

I'm cut off as he puts a finger to my lips.

Stepping out of his trousers, he kicks them to one side and stands before me in just his boxer shorts. I'm only wearing my panties, so there's all but two scraps of material between us.

Putting his arms around me, Drew lowers me slowly, reverently. He looks into my eyes and I see fire.

"I love you," he whispers before going back to worshipping me.

My body shivers in anticipation as he rests above me, held up by his strong arms braced either side of my head. He places a chaste kiss on my lips before he peppers my face and jawline with sweet little kisses. I can feel an electricity crackle in the air. It feels like being in the middle of a storm when the lightning strikes. It's palpable and is driving me crazy. Nothing can save me now. I know that in my heart. Drew and I are intrinsically linked for the rest of our lives.

His fingers play me like a violin and it isn't long before I feel my climax build, almost ready to take me over the edge. I'm at the point of no return as Drew stops and my climax recedes slightly. My breathing is heavy, and I watch Drew's chest, moving fast as he pants. His eyes lock on mine and he slides his fingers through my wet folds to the sweet spot, that little bundle of nerves that is like a detonator button. Suddenly my breathing catches in my chest as my orgasm rips through my body. It crashes in waves, I feel like I could float away, but Drew is my anchor, holding me here in his arms. I feel our bodies slick with sweat. Never have I felt like this before. Not until Drew. I've never had a lover like him. It's like all those relationships before were rehearsals for the 'real thing'.

Drew's lips claim mine in a soul-searing kiss. His tongue duels with mine, but I gladly surrender to him. He staked his claim on my heart the first time we met, but he's since staked a claim on my soul. There's no denying we were meant to be and I'm so glad he changed his mind about not being able to be serious with someone. He didn't want to settle down; he didn't want to chance getting hurt. But now, his heart is in my hands and I intend to cherish it with every fibre of my being. I'll never hurt him, never let him down. I'll keep him safe, just like he does for me.

Looking into his eyes that shine like the rarest gems, I see lust, need, passion and, most of all, love. Reaching down between our bodies, I stroke the length of his shaft from base to tip, rubbing my thumb in the pre-cum I feel there. His breath hitches as I grip him more firmly and stroke him up and down. I want to take my time with him, but I don't want to waste a moment while the children sleep soundly. I guide him so the tip of his cock is aligned with me, then I reach round to grab his gorgeous ass and pull him closer to me. The tip of him slides inside me and I can't help the gasp that bubbles out of my mouth.

Painstakingly slowly, he enters me, filling me inch by inch and I feel myself stretch to accommodate him. I feel almost euphoric. It's a heady feeling when we're connected like this. Our bodies move as one as he begins to build a rhythm. My hips match every thrust of his, my hands cling to him and my nails dig into his ass. I rake them up his spine, making him shiver and momentarily lose his pace. Bringing one hand behind his head, I pull him towards me for a kiss. His tongue gently nudges mine and I revel in the mixture of sensations I'm feeling. His hungry kiss leads to him moving more frantically, chasing my climax before his own. My body climbs higher and my head feels lost in cloud nine—maybe even beyond.

If there's something that's never wrong between us, regardless of anything else going on in our lives, it's our sex life. It's always been beyond amazing, beyond words even.

"Drew—" I pant out as my body nears its undoing.

"Shh, baby. Just let me love you," he replies as he ups his pace, pushing himself to the limit as well as me.

"I'm going to—"

"I know, baby. I know."

My brain barely has time to register his words as my climax tears through me like a tsunami. It crashes in waves over him and it's only mere moments before Drew moans out his own release. I feel my walls tighten around him, milking him for every last drop.

Collapsing beside me, Drew pulls me towards him and tucks me into his side as he slides the blanket over us. We're both breathing heavily, and our bodies are slick with sweat.

My eyes flutter closed and I sigh contentedly, wrapped in Drew's embrace.

"I love you, Elise Wright."

"I love you too, baby."

With those last words, I feel myself drift off to sleep.

Chapter Fifteen

Drew

Last night was amazing. I keep playing it over in my mind as I make breakfast. Caleb is awake already and is playing on his games console while he waits for me to finish cooking. Cassie is still asleep, and I have the baby monitor on the kitchen counter, so I can keep an ear out for when she wakes, leaving Elise to have a well-deserved lie-in.

As the bacon sizzles in the pan, I hum to myself, feeling happy. My iPod is in the dock, playing quietly. As *Tenerife Sea* begins to play, I am reminded of the first dance Elise and I had as husband and wife. I chose the song specifically because of the colour of her eyes. Those gorgeous pools of blue that sparkle in the sunlight … they are one of the most striking things about her. I could drown in the sea within them.

I turn to ask Caleb to set the table ready for breakfast and he jumps up to help. He's such a good kid; I really do love him to bits. I cherish my whole family and know in my heart I could never do anything to hurt them.

I'm on shift later, but I have a day out planned for the four of us first. We're going to the Sea Life Centre because Caleb is addicted to penguins and Elise loves to watch the baby otters being fed. Personally, I love to stand under the glass archway they have. You can watch the fish, sharks, and various other species swim around and above you. It's fascinating to feel surrounded by nature.

Elise pads softly down the stairs as I am plating up the breakfast. There's nothing like a 'full English' to start the day off right. She walks into the room and I stop for a moment, drinking her in. She's still in her pyjamas, her hair has that 'just got out of bed' look, but she is still a sight for sore eyes. If Cassie grows up to look like her mother, I can imagine putting a lock on her bedroom door and not letting her out until she's twenty-five. The over-protective father in me will want to wrap her up in cotton wool and never let her go.

Walking over to the coffee machine, Elise turns it on and pulls two mugs from the cupboard. I walk over and wrap my arms around her from behind, resting my chin on her shoulder.

"Morning, gorgeous."

"Morning," she replies as she yawns and stretches her lithe body.

Turning in my arms, she wraps her arms around my neck. Bringing her face infinitesimally closer to mine, she acts as though she's going to kiss me, but doesn't. Instead, she looks over my shoulder and asks Caleb if he wants a glass of orange juice.

I lean down and kiss her neck instead. I feel her shiver as I nip her earlobe and draw back to ghost a kiss over her lips. She seeks to kiss me back, but I go to the other side of her neck instead. I wrap her hair around my hand and pull gently to expose the hollow of her throat. Kissing my way down her delectable throat, I feel as a low moan threatens to spill from her lips. I quickly move to kiss her full lips; instead of letting her moan escape, I swallow it. The last thing we need is our little PDA to make Caleb feel uncomfortable.

"You're such a tease," she says as we break away.

"You started it, Mrs Wright."

"Well, I can't help it if you're standing there cooking in just a pair of low slung jogging bottoms, looking all sexy."

Cassie begins to stir, making the baby monitor burst to life.

"I'll get her."

I walk to the bottom of the stairs and look back to see Elise putting breakfast out on the table. I watch her for a moment, mesmerised by her beauty. She turns back to the coffee machine and finishes what she started.

I take the stairs two at a time, slip into our room to grab a t-shirt and pull it over my head as I walk to Cassie's room.

"Hey, baby," I say gently as I lift her into my arms.

She's so much like her mother, with the same 'just got out of bed' hairstyle this morning. I chuckle to myself as I take her downstairs and get her situated in her highchair.

Caleb and Elise are at the table, but both have waited for me to return before eating.

***

After the plates are cleared away, Elise goes for a shower and I get myself and Cassie dressed for the day. I hear Elise singing in our en suite. It makes me smile because she has a beautiful voice.

Once we're all ready, we pile into the car and I put on our usual playlist for trips out. We haven't told Caleb where we're going, but he's excited to do something different this weekend.

Arriving outside the Sea Life Centre about forty-five minutes later, I see Caleb's face light up in the rearview mirror. What neither he nor Elise know is that when I bought our tickets I paid extra for Caleb to have a penguin feeding experience. I can't wait to see his face and take some photos.

I grab Cassie's baby carrier from the boot of the car and strap it to my chest. I thought it would make it easier than pushing a pram around all day. I also grab the changing bag I made sure was packed with everything she'd need this morning.

Putting Cassie into the baby carrier, I make sure she's comfortable before going any further.

We walk inside and I present our tickets. I'm given the time for the penguin feeding, but still don't let on to Caleb. I pass Elise the tickets and silently point her in the direction of the time stated. She looks it over and smiles at me, wordlessly. Like me, she knows just how excited Caleb will be when he finds out.

***

I have so many photos on my phone. Caleb had so much fun being so close to his favourite animal and getting to feed them. Elise couldn't stop smiling as she watched, and, while most of the photos are of Caleb, there are a few candid shots of my wife too.

We all had a brilliant day and now it's time to order takeaway for tea. Neither Elise or I feel like cooking. It's been a tiring day, but in such a good way.

Caleb sits at the kitchen island, chatting away about the penguins. He hasn't stopped talking about them all the way home, but I wouldn't have it any other way. It's good to see a smile on his face and hear the excitement in his voice.

I'm going to have to shower and change ready for work right after we've eaten. I haven't been back to work since Danny's death. My boss gave me compassionate leave and I've used it all up now, so it's time to return. I'm not looking forward to being introduced to my new partner. That's one of the reasons I took all the time I was offered instead of returning sooner. I've heard from Matty—who's been temporarily partnered with her until my return—that she's good at her job. According to him, this is her first placement, but she's not as inept as some of the student paramedics we've had come through our doors.

We've had people who are squeamish at the sight of blood and have passed out. Then there have been the ones who know what to do when practicing with Resus Annie—the mannequin used to practice CPR—but have just frozen when it's time to do it on a real person. Sometimes it's just about nerves, but every second counts when you're trying to save a dying patient.

I know I was once just a student paramedic, and I sympathise with them, I really do. But if you aren't cut out for the job, you just have to face facts. But this girl seems to suit the life, so I'll give her a chance. However good she is, though, she isn't Danny. We had this rhythm when we worked together, a synchronicity. Having a partner that you know and trust is of the utmost importance; it's vital to the patients and to saving their lives.

Danny and I worked so well together and I just don't know if anyone can measure up to him. He's the bar that's been set, even if it was unknowingly at the time.

I pull my car up and turn off the engine, then sit for a moment to gather my thoughts. Deep breaths in and out. I steel myself to do what must be done. Danny wouldn't want me to quit my job—which I seriously considered for a day or two—he'd want me to go in there and work with this girl, Ash, and get on with my life. He'll never be forgotten and I hope that, in his last moments, he knew that. I'll never forgive myself for not being there as he took his last breath, but it's of some comfort that Chase happened to pass the scene of the accident and stopped to be with him for a moment.

Chase came to Danny's funeral. He seems like a good guy. I'm surprised I haven't met him before, considering he works at the hospital, but I'm just glad that he was around when someone needed him the most.

Taking another deep breath, I grab the handle and push open the door before I can change my mind. I get out and head over to where the ambulances are parked.

I see Matty and he waves at me with a smile on his face. He's a good guy. We were partnered together for a while after he finished his training.

He's one of the few that didn't flake out. Mostly, we seemed to have a whiny bunch that just couldn't pull it together, but Matty never wavered.

Making my way over to him, I try to seem as though I'm ready to be back here, when the truth is I wish I'd taken longer away. My footsteps falter as I hear the guys laughing. I can distinguish each laugh and identify the person it belongs to. When I realise Danny's isn't amongst them, I am hit smack dab in the chest with a pain so severe it threatens to cripple me.

Finally joining the others, I see Seb, Luke, Matty, Jonas, Boyle—whose name is actually Sam; we refer to him by his surname like we're American or something. Probably because he was born in Connecticut. He only moved over here about four years ago, following in the footsteps of a woman he'd fallen in love with when she was on holiday.

I look up and see a blonde woman. She's got her back turned to me, but as she's the only one I don't know; I know she has to be Ash.

I've been warned she's pregnant so can't do some of the things required of the job, but that's fine by me. I'd rather jump back in and work my ass off to take my mind off my old partner.

Taking a deep breath, I go over to introduce myself to her.

"Hi, Drew," she says as she turns and catches me walking over.

"Ashleigh?"

The shock in my voice must be evident because she smiles at me—a small shy smile.

"How are you?"

Me? How am I? More like how is she and what the hell is she doing here?!

"Umm … good."

I swallow a lump of emotion as I look from her face to her small baby bump.

"I hear we're partners," she says, emotion catching her voice slightly.

"Umm … I guess we must be. I … umm … I didn't know it was you."

"Didn't Matty tell you? He told me he'd texted and told you about me."

"He … umm … he mentioned my new partner was called Ash and that she was pregnant. He didn't say it was you, though. I didn't know you'd qualified as a paramedic. I didn't even know you'd trained as one. Danny … he never mentioned it was what you were studying."

Swallowing hard to try and dislodge the lump that seems to be blocking me from breathing or talking properly, I just stand and look at Ashleigh.

"Yeah, I was training in Bristol originally, because that's where I lived when Danny and I met. Then, when we got more serious, I decided to move here. I can't believe you never knew."

"No, I … I had no idea."

I'm not exactly on form, what with all the humming and stumbling over what I'm trying to say.

"It's okay, Drew," Ashleigh says as she puts a hand on my arm. "I miss him too, you know. More than words can express. And I know this is probably weird for you, working with me and all. But I want to honour Danny's memory. He wanted me to be here eventually anyway. Yeah, okay, I guess he thought he'd be around to see it for himself, but…"

She trails off, a misty look in her eyes.

"It's okay, Ashleigh."

I wrap her in a hug as tears begin to roll down her cheeks. I didn't mean to make her cry. Now I feel bad.

"I'm sorry, Drew," she replies as she pulls away and wipes her tear-stained face with her hand.

"Sorry? What on earth are you sorry for? I'm the one who made you cry, not the other way around."

"Well, technically, thinking about how Danny isn't here made me cry, not you. And I meant I was sorry for crying on you."

"Can we start again?" I ask after a moment of hesitation.

"Sure. That would be good. Hi, I'm Ashleigh, your new partner."

She holds her hand out and I shake it as I chuckle.

"Sorry, I'm not laughing at you. Just the formality of you introducing yourself when I already know you."

A brief moment passes and Ashleigh laughs too. It's not long before we are both bent over laughing.

"Well, that certainly broke the ice," I say as my laughter subsides. "Welcome aboard!"

"It's good to be here, Drew. I never intended to do this without … well, you know, without Danny. But here I am. I hope we can work well together. Danny would have liked that. Well, he wouldn't have liked me stealing his partner, but you know what I mean."

Her words come out in a rush over each other and she stops to breathe.

"Well, Matty says you are a welcome addition to the team here."

"He said that? That's sweet. I've been looking forward to you coming back. I had to get to work and take my mind off my crap for a while. It's nice that they've partnered me with you. I mean, it would have been nicer if Danny was still here and I didn't have to take his place. No, not take his place, that's not right. What I meant was—"

I put a hand on her arm and offer her a warm smile. I know what she means without her having to say it. But all this mentioning Danny isn't what I had in mind. Don't get me wrong, I don't want to forget him. But I've only just arrived on shift and I didn't expect to talk about him straight away.

At that moment, her radio decides to crackle to life with a call from base. Talk about being saved by the bell.

***

It was weird working my first shift with Ash. She seemed to pick up on some of Danny's mannerisms when they were together and certain things she said and did reminded me of my best friend.

He would have loved to see his fiancée being so good at her job. He would have been so proud. I don't believe in God, Heaven or Hell. But if Danny's out there somewhere in the afterlife, wherever it is we go after our life on earth is over, I'd bet he's watching over her.

We had an easy kind of shift and it was a good way of easing us into working together. We don't have the rhythm that Danny and I had—though I seriously doubt I'd ever have that with anyone but him—but we seem to work well together. She knew what I needed when I needed it and seemed to understand that I needed some peace and quiet to get used to my new normal on our first call of the shift.

I am glad to be home. I'm tired, emotionally as well as physically. I need a shower before doing anything else. Letting myself in, I walk into the lounge to see Elise sat reading a book in her favourite recliner.

"Hey, baby," she says softly as she hears me approach and looks up with a smile. "How was work?"

"Weird. Well, at first anyway. You'll never guess who my new partner is."

"Who is it?"

"Ashleigh."

"Ashleigh? Ashleigh who?"

I see her confused expression clear as she realises we only know one person called Ashleigh.

"Oh, my god. Really? I didn't even know she was a paramedic."

"Neither did I. She was training before she got with Danny. I guess it's just coincidence."

"Wow. That's just … wow. How was it, working with her?"

I don't want to get into this conversation right now. I feel drained as it is.

Elise must see something in my expression because she closes the distance between us and takes my face in the palms of her hands. Ghosting a kiss across my lips, she smiles at me. It's bittersweet, but I take comfort in her warmth.

Pulling her to me, I kiss her. She puts up no resistance and I take what she's giving—exactly what I need; warmth, love, affection.

Kissing her until I can't breathe, I break away feeling slightly dizzy. She steals my breath away. Every kiss from her touches every fibre of my being. She warms me from the inside out. She's an addiction that I'll never seek a cure for.

"I'm going for a shower. Care to join me?"

Her beautiful face lights up at my suggestion.

"Sure. The kids are in bed, so why not."

I take her hand, relishing the touch of her small palm enveloped in mine. I snag the baby monitor from the coffee table as we pass, then head for the stairs.

Once safely in our bedroom, I close and lock the door. Caleb shouldn't wake and want to come in, but, if he does, at least this way we'll hear him knocking instead of getting caught out.

I begin to strip, but Elise shakes her head at me and I drop my t-shirt. She takes the material in her hands and slips it off over my head. Her soft hands travel over my abs, down to the V she's so fond of. She slips her hands over the prominent shape and my cock stiffens. The feel of her creamy smooth skin against mine is enough to make me want to shoot my load in my boxers like a teenage boy, but I show some restraint as she explores the planes of my body.

A tension I didn't realise I was feeling ebbs away. Elise undoes my trousers and slides them down over my hips, pulling the waistband of my boxers as she goes. Suddenly my cock springs free and I feel an animalistic urge to claim her right now.

As the material pools at my feet, I kick it aside. I'm naked and standing to attention in front of my not-so-naked wife. I need to rectify that immediately, so I begin by unbuttoning the pyjama top she's wearing. The silky material feels good, but not as good as her bare skin against mine.

Once the material drops down her arms, she tosses it to one side. Then I take the waistband of the silky pyjama bottoms and push it down over her hips. Elise gives me a sly smile as she steps out of them. I don't realise what that smile means until she reaches her hand out and strokes me. All the blood in my body rushes to my stiffening cock.

I take Elise's hand in mine and lead her to the bed. The shower can wait. I'm suddenly not bothered about being clean. I'd rather be dirty. Very dirty.

Chapter Sixteen

Elise

After a few shifts with Ash, Drew seems to be feeling less emotionally drained. At first, he said it took all his energy not to cry. She wasn't who he was expecting to be partnered with and I know he wished he could ask his boss to change it. But he's getting used to it now and isn't coming home so close to breaking down.

That first night, I knew it had made an impact on him, so I'd distracted him the way only a woman knows how. Sex. Amazing, mind-blowing sex. Multiple orgasms had him coming undone before he finally had a shower and fell asleep in my arms.

With each shift, it's like some of the tension drains away and he feels better about working alongside her. He knows it's only until her maternity leave anyway, at which point, he'll get partnered with somebody else, probably Matty.

He said he isn't sure if the bosses put him and Ash together so they could help each other through their grief. He doesn't really want to know, so he hasn't asked.

It's my birthday this weekend, so we're having a few friends round. I've made a list of things we need to get, but top of that list is booze. As long as there's a fridge stocked with cold beers for the lads and some wine for the girls, we should be good. I've decided to invite Ash, so I also have to have plenty of soft drinks, for her and for me. With the amount of tablets I take, due to my disability, I can only have the occasional drink. And with Ash being pregnant, she's abstaining from alcohol altogether.

***

The party is in full swing by mid-evening. Some of the lads from

Drew's work are here, along with Ash, my best friend Sam and her husband Karl, my assistant Amanda and her boyfriend Pryce and several other friends of ours.

My iPod is in its dock, playing some of my favourites; I made a playlist especially. Caleb is awake still, but Cassie is asleep and I have the baby monitor to hand. I've told Caleb he can stay up to have some birthday cake—a cake he and Drew insisted on buying—but then he's got to go to bed. Though how he'll sleep with the sound of so many people in the house, I have no idea.

True to his promise, Caleb lets me tuck him into bed after he's had some cake—and brushed his teeth, of course.

"Night, my sweet boy. Try and get some sleep. Your dad has plans for tomorrow and you wouldn't want to be too tired, would you?"

"No mum. I'm tired anyway."

He gives me a hug and a kiss before I turn and walk to his door.

"Goodnight, sweetheart. Sweet dreams. Love you."

"Love you too, mum."

I slip out of his room and make my way back down to the party. I feel sort of sexy in this dress that Drew bought me. It's unusual to find me in anything other than trousers, but Drew insisted on buying this last week when we saw it in a shop window. What he hasn't seen is the sexy underwear I have on underneath. Nude in colour, it's a lacy balconette bra and G-string. It leaves very little to the imagination. I made sure to pop into Ann Summers during our shopping trip but told Drew to wait outside. I can't wait until everyone has gone home so I can strip off for him. But, for now, I rejoin my husband and our friends in the lounge.

Ashleigh seeks me out moments later. She's wearing a dress that clings to her curvaceous body. She has a figure many women would be jealous of—hell, I'm jealous of her, I just wouldn't want breast implants—and a baby bump most women would be jealous of too, seeing as though it's small but perfectly formed. Not an ounce of "fat" in sight.

She asks me if we can talk for a minute and, seeing that Drew is caught in conversation, I know he won't notice if I'm gone for a few minutes longer. I walk with her into the kitchen and tell her to take a seat at the kitchen island while I grab her a drink.

"I just wanted to ask if you would be godmother to my daughter?" she blurts out when I turn back to face her.

"Me?"

I don't know what to say. We don't know each other very well, but she was my husband's best friend's girlfriend, almost fiancée.

"Yes. I wanted to ask you and Drew, but he's busy talking with the boys, so I thought I'd leave him to it. He seems to need to relax."

"He does?"

"Yeah. I mean, it has to be weird for him, working with me. I thought he knew I was his new partner, I thought Matty had told him. But seeing me that first shift seemed to rock him a little. And ever since he's been tense. I mean, we work well enough together, but it seems like he can't wait for each shift to be over. He never goes out for a drink with the lads after and he's always first out the door."

"He is? I thought he was doing okay. He tells me he's okay. I mean, yeah, sure, the first shift was something of a bolt out of the blue for him. But he told me it feels easier each time."

"Oh, well then I must be getting the wrong vibe. He hasn't said anything. It's just how it feels to me, you know? I guess it could be my hormones making me overthink things."

"He loved Danny. They were like brothers. I mean, you know that. But he's gone, and we can't change that. I'm sure he's still adjusting to having you as his partner."

"It's a big thing for me too. I should have been doing this job *alongside* Danny, not *instead* of him. Nobody can replace him and I'm not trying to. I just hope that Drew can accept working with me. He avoids talking about Danny at all costs."

"I guess men deal with loss differently to women. That's probably all it is. I'm sure in time he'll be able to talk about him without it hurting so much."

"Counselling helped me. I still grieve for him every single day, but I need to carry on for our daughter as well as for myself. Our daughter is precious. She's all I have left of Danny."

I'm not sure talking about Drew behind his back is such a wise idea. He wouldn't want to hear that people think he might not be coping. I believe in him, I always will. But if he were to overhear us, he could misconstrue what's being said.

"Well, if you're sure, then I'd like to be her godmother," I say, to change topic subtly.

"I'm sure."

Ash smiles at me and I can't miss the misty look in her eyes. Soon she'll be giving birth to her daughter, but without her would-be husband. It will be bittersweet. I only hope it doesn't lead to postnatal depression. I know what it's like to suffer from that. It didn't affect my bond with Caleb, but it affected me and Jensen. We argued like mad until I was diagnosed. I guess I was stubborn because I wouldn't admit I had a problem. I kept it all bottled inside and it drove a wedge between the two of us.

This time, with Cassie, I had PND for a while, but I managed to get it under control with medication and some counselling. I can't say I'm fully over it, but I control it rather than letting it control me.

Drew walks into the kitchen and smiles at me. He comes to stand beside me and kisses me on the cheek.

"Hey, what are you girls up to?"

"Actually, I'm glad you're here Drew," Ash says before I have chance to speak. "I wanted to ask you both to be godparents to the baby."

"Oh wow, really? I don't know what to say."

"Say yes, silly. You can't be that shocked that I asked you. I mean, you were Danny's best friend. He'd have asked you if he was still here."

"I'd be delighted."

His tone isn't as sure as his words, but either Ash doesn't notice or just doesn't make a big deal out of it because she smiles widely and thanks him for agreeing.

"You'll be pleased to know, Elise has already agreed."

"She has? Well, that's great."

This conversation is getting a little stale and I don't want to prolong it any further. I don't know what I can say without seeming rude though.

"Well, I'd best be going. Some of us have a shift in the morning!"

"Subtle, Ash, real subtle," Drew replies sarcastically.

"Hey, I'm not the one swapping shifts because I want to spoil my wife."

"Well, you would be if you were married to Elise. She's worth spoiling."

It would seem I don't have to drop hints at a topic change after all. Thank goodness for that.

"Well, I'll leave you both to it. I'll just grab my coat and be on my way."

We walk her to the door, collecting her coat along the way. Once she's in her car and pulling away, I sag against Drew.

"Hey, what's up?"

I don't want to admit the truth that some conversations just leave you feeling drained, so I just shrug nonchalantly. It's not that I don't like Ash, I just don't really know what to say to her. I don't really know her, but we don't seem to really have anything in common.

"Should we call it a night?" he asks as he looks me in the eye.

"No, don't do that. It would seem rude. Let's go and have another drink and then we can think about kicking their asses out, so I can show you what I'm wearing under this dress."

I wink at him and take his hand in mine. He follows me into the lounge where we continue chatting with everyone for another forty-ish minutes before calling it a night. Drew tells everyone we have an early start on my birthday surprise in the morning, so they bid us goodnight and leave us to it.

***

"Comic-Con tickets? Are you kidding me? You told me they were sold out when I asked you about going."

I look at the piece of paper in my hand and realise my husband knows me only too well. He's taking the children and me to Comic-Con for the day. I'm shocked he got tickets considering who's attending this year.

"It was. I just know somebody who knows somebody. They got the tickets for me."

"Well I'd better get dressed then," I say as I go to get out of bed.

"Umm ... no way! Not looking like that, you don't."

"Looking like what?"

He has me questioning whether I have a bird's nest for hair or something.

"All sexy and naked! Get back here and kiss me."

"Yes, sir."

I mock salute him and he tickles me into submission. I can barely breathe through laughing so hard, but in the next instant his lips are on mine and it's like he's the oxygen I need.

He draws me flush to him and pulls my hair back to expose my neck. He growls playfully before nipping his way from my earlobe down to the hollow of my throat. He peppers my throat with little butterfly kisses, delicate and sweet. It makes me shiver as goosebumps break out across my skin. This man could make me come undone with just one touch. Heat begins to build in my abdomen as he puts his one hand under my silky chemise and the other cradles my head as he brushes our lips together. He licks at the seam of my mouth, making me open up to allow his tongue to dance with mine. What starts as a sweet kiss quickly turns urgent and has me panting for breath. His hand tweaks my pierced nipple and I gasp at the same time as I squeeze my thighs together. He knows exactly what he's doing with those deft fingers and drives me wild. My chest rises and falls rapidly with my heavy breathing.

Grasping the edge of my chemise, he pulls it off over my head, leaving the top half of me exposed to the cool, crisp air.

Moments later, he dips to take my nipple in his mouth. His warm lips make me tingle and when he nips it gently between his teeth, my back arches and I have to catch my breath.

Just as Drew has his hand poised to go underneath my sleep shorts, there's a knock at the door. Thank goodness it's locked, and Caleb didn't just walk in on us.

I pull my top back over my head as Drew gets up to open the door.

"Is it time to go yet, Dad?" he asks, his voice still sleepy.

"Not quite, buddy. We should grab some breakfast first. What do you say to bacon sandwiches?"

He guides Caleb out of the door and closes it behind them. Thank goodness for that. I don't really want my son seeing me all flushed and asking why my cheeks are so red. I can feel the heat in them as I scrub a hand over my face.

Getting up, I twist my hair up and grab a clip from my bedside drawer. A quick ten-minute shower should help me get rid of the feelings I'm experiencing.

I put a shower cap over my hair and turn the water on. Washing myself all over, I rest my head against the shower tiles, thinking about what I'd be doing if Caleb hadn't woken up. It's a good job I use a stool in the shower, else my legs might buckle under me like jelly as I think about my sexy husband and those deft fingers of his.

Ten minutes later, I'm showered, dried, dressed and almost ready for the day. I sit at my vanity mirror on the dressing table and apply some makeup. Just a little bit of mascara and my favourite colour LipSense on my lips will do. I straighten my hair and take one last look in the mirror. Happy enough with my reflection, I head downstairs to catch up with the boys.

Walking into the kitchen, I see Cassie strapped into her highchair. We have a dining table in the other room, but most of the time, unless we have guests, we eat at the granite-topped island in the spacious kitchen.

I kiss my baby girl on the top of her head and she beams at me. Her smile could light up even the darkest of rooms.

"Did Dad tell you where we're going today, Mum?" Caleb asks between bites of his bacon sandwich.

Drew places a plate in front of me and I add some ketchup before eating.

"He did, but not until we woke up."

"Isn't he the coolest? I can't wait. Do you know who's going this year?"

I have to think because there are quite a few celebrities—I really hate using that word but can't think of another—attending.

"I know there's a few from Game of Thrones, then there's the gang from Red Dwarf, who I assume you can't wait to meet. Umm … I can't think who else off the top of my head."

"Dad got us a photoshoot with the guys from Red Dwarf. Told you he was the coolest!" he answers as he gets up to put his plate in the dishwasher.

"I also booked Mum a couple of photoshoots too. And we'll have fun seeing people in all sorts of costumes. But I know what you're looking forward to, Caleb. You'll be going to all the stalls that sell Funko Pop! figures, won't you?"

"Umm … does a bear poop in the woods, Dad?"

I crack up laughing. Caleb is addicted to those pop figures. He has a whole shelving unit in his bedroom full of them. If he buys any more, I'm not sure where he'll put them. But, then, I can't say anything about his addiction because I have some rare 'Chase edition' ones like Pennywise from IT and Buddy from the Christmas movie 'Elf'. I also have the Hogwarts Express and all the Harry Potter characters, so I guess we're as bad as each other.

Drew creases with laughter and ruffles Caleb's hair.

"So, are we ready to go?" Drew asks.

"I have to get Cassie ready and what about your breakfast?"

"I've had mine as I was cooking for the two of you, babe. And Cassie is dressed; her changing bag is good to go. We just have to put her pram in the boot of the car and we're ready."

"Oh, well then, let me just grab my shoes and we'll get moving."

I can't wait to see who Drew set up photoshoots for me with. I'm as excited as a teenager. I can tell Caleb is excited too by the way he's bouncing on the balls of his feet as Drew gets Cassie out of her highchair. What can I say—we're nerds in this house! I don't care who calls me a nerd or geek. I might be in my thirties, but I still love Disney, I even have a couple of Disney tattoos. I also love Marvel and DC, but if asked to choose between the two, I'd say Marvel. I have an Ironman tattoo on the back of my left calf. It's Ironman's torso, but then, like a reflection, underneath him is Ultron, Tony Stark's creation. Oh boy did Caleb and I love that movie. We're really excited about the next Avengers movie because we've seen the trailer for it and it looks awesome.

"Come on, slowcoach," Drew says, breaking me out of my thoughts.

"I'm coming."

I grab my coat and slip my shoes on. Thank goodness I only wear flat shoes anyway because I have a feeling my feet are going to be tired after today.

***

What a day! I can't believe how much fun we've had. And how much money we've spent. It's a damn good job that event planning pays me a good wage. I had photoshoots with the cast from Game of Thrones and I have autographed photos of them all. We also met the guys from Red Dwarf and had photos with them. Caleb looks so happy in each shot. He has a grin that split his face from ear to ear.

We're weighed down by bags containing all sorts. Pop! figures for me and Caleb, graphic novels, books from a couple of lovely authors that were in 'Author Corner,' a new thing for Birmingham's Comic-Con. We also have a Batman cookie jar like the one featured in one of our favourite shows, Big Bang Theory. And so much other stuff that I am already rearranging the house in my head in order to fit it all in.

It was good to see Drew with a smile on his face. After recent events, it's good to know he can still smile. Today was a good surprise and I'm touched that he thought to do this for Caleb and me. He's not quite as nerdy as the two of us, but I think we're slowly converting him.

"Danny John-Jules was hilarious, Dad. Don't you think?" Caleb pipes up from the back of the car.

"Almost as funny as Robert Llewellyn," Drew teases.

He knows full well that Cat is Caleb's favourite character.

"No way, Danny was funnier!"

"Now, now, boys, stop arguing!" I tease.

"Well, I wouldn't argue if Dad wasn't wrong," Caleb says, eyeing me in the rearview mirror and bobbing his tongue out at me.

I laugh and both boys burst out laughing along with me.

As we arrive home, we close the door behind us and the boys take the bags into the lounge. I bring in the small carrier bag that I'm carrying. Neither of my boys know what's in it. The contents are a secret. I bought Caleb all the 'Penguins of Madagascar' Pop! figures because he loves the movie, but also because he's a penguin addict. I'm putting them aside for his birthday, though, so he can't see them today.

I slip into the kitchen and hide the bag inside the pantry. Deciding to cook tea, I get out the ingredients for bolognese. Caleb doesn't like spaghetti, so I always do it with tagliatelle.

I turn my iPod on quietly and start chopping onions and mushrooms. I sing quietly to myself as Depeche Mode play.

"It seems a good moment to give you your last present," Drew says from the door, startling me and nearly making me cut my finger.

"I thought today was my last present?"

"Turns out I lied," he responds with a smirk.

"Where are the children?"

"In the lounge. I asked Caleb to keep an eye on Cassie while I came in here."

"So, what's this present then?"

I'm impatient at the best of times, but especially when it comes to birthday or Christmas presents.

Drew passes me an envelope. I wipe my hands on a tea towel and take it from him. I eagerly open the envelope, desperate to see what's inside.

"Depeche Mode tickets?" I squeal like the fangirl I am.

"Well, I won't be able to hear them now you've burst my eardrums," he replies with a wicked grin.

I take my apron off and pull Drew into a hug.

"I take it you're it happy?' he whispers, his breath making goosebumps spread across my skin.

"Happy? Try ecstatic!"

Drew knows I was meant to see them with Jensen, but when he

broke it off I ended up selling the tickets. I was devastated. Since Jensen introduced me to DM, I've been wanting to see Dave Gahan in the flesh. He's sex personified.

"Well, I'm glad. I wouldn't have wanted to sell the tickets because you didn't like them anymore."

His laugh is infectious and soon I'm laughing with him.

"I'll pour us some wine as you're cooking. Is there anything I can do to help?"

Bless his heart for trying but I don't like having people in the kitchen as I cook. I don't know whether it's a woman thing or just a me thing. I just don't like people getting under my feet. I like to cook solo. No exceptions, not even for Christmas dinner.

I shoo him away, so he grabs a bottle of wine and two glasses. He doesn't have work until tomorrow. It'll be nice to spend an evening together as a family.

"I'll leave you to it then."

He places a glass beside me and I continue cooking. Smithfield begin to play on my iPod and I sing along to 'Hey Whiskey'.

* * *

We enjoy a meal as a family and Drew tucks Cassie into bed as I read Caleb some of his favourite book; *Harry Potter and the Prisoner of Azkaban*. We usually take it in turns to read chapters. I love snuggling with my baby boy and reading together.

After we finish a chapter, I go back downstairs. Drew has poured us some more wine and I snuggle up next to him as he grabs the DVD remote. *The Best of Me* begins to play and I relax into Drew's embrace.

When the movie is over, Drew takes my hand, snags the baby monitor from the coffee table and leads me to the bottom of the stairs. He always makes sure to be careful with me as I walk up the stairs, in case my leg gives way or something. Even though I've walked a lot today, it's not actually too bad.

Drew locks the door and goes to plug my iPod into the dock in our room. 'The Only One That Gets Me' by Charles Kelley begins to play and I smile. Drew says that this song could have been written for me. He says I'm the only one who puts him back together when things go wrong.

As Charles's honey-like voice sings softly in the background, Drew takes me in his arms and gently sways to the music. I inhale the scent of his cologne and something unidentifiable that just smells like Drew.

It's a heady mix and I move my head from his shoulder so I'm looking him in the eye. My lips slant over his and he cedes control to me. I take what I want from him in a breathtaking kiss. My head feels giddy and my heart feels full.

I want to finish what we started this morning. With that in mind, I take the edge of his t-shirt in my hands and lift it. He raises his arms and I throw the material over onto the chair by the bed.

Once he's standing before me in just his jeans, I can't help but stare at the planes of his body. The contours of his sculpted torso are something I will never get bored of looking at. I let my hands roam gently before undoing his jeans. I slip them down over his hips and they pool at his feet. He steps out of them and kicks them to one side. As he stands before me in just his boxers, a kaleidoscope of butterflies takes flight inside me.

Taking his hand, I guide him to the end of the bed and he sits down in front of me. I change the song to 'Earned It' by The Weeknd. Drew's eyes roam my body as I move to the sensual beat.

I begin to strip my top away from my skin and Drew's eyes follow me hungrily. I throw it on the chair with his and move my hands to undo my jeans. I shimmy them down over my hips and let them fall to my feet, carefully stepping out of them and kicking them to one side.

Standing in front of Drew in just my underwear, I sway to the beat of the song. I roam my hands over my body and see Drew fighting his urge to reach out and touch me.

Slowly, I drop the straps of my bra down one arm, then the other. I unclasp it from behind and drop it to the floor. Drew's eyes are drawn to my breasts; I know he's focussing on the piercing he loves so much.

I walk closer to him, yet still he doesn't reach out to touch me. I take his hands in mine and place them on my hips as I move them in time with the song. I plant my feet shoulder width apart for stability and I watch as Drew's eyes drink me in. Looking down, I see his erection standing proud, covered only by his boxers. I smile at him and hope it looks as salacious as it feels.

No words are spoken as Drew is hypnotised by my body. I slide a hand down the front of my lacy panties and his smile transforms as he watches me begin to play with myself. He shows some restraint as he doesn't move his hands from my hips.

"Drew ... panties," I breathe out as I touch myself.

He takes the sides in his hands and pulls my panties down my legs.

His breathing catches as he sees what I'm doing. One finger slips inside as my thumb teases my clit.

Drew zones in on my hand and I remove it. He captures my wrist in his hand and draws it to his mouth. He licks my juices from my fingers before letting my hand go.

I discard my panties and stand before him completely naked. He's still seated and wearing his boxers. That has to change. I push him so he's lying on his back, then I pull at the waistband. He lifts his hips, so I can remove them with ease. When his erection springs free, my tongue darts out to wet my dry lips. I see Drew watching me intently, so I discard his boxers and then grab a pillow for my knees. I place it on the floor, so I can kneel more comfortably, then I take his shaft in my hand. His breath catches and his gaze is filled with lust as he watches me lick him from base to tip.

Working him slowly with my hand and mouth, I make use of my tongue bar and the way it turns him on. As my pace increases, so does his heavy breathing. He's panting and moaning and I know it won't be long before he explodes. I get a thrill from just the thought of it.

Drew moves to rest up on his elbows, to watch me. I feel his hand grab my hair and sweep it out of the way, so he can see my mouth in action.

A few moments later, he drops back down to the bed as his orgasm rolls through him. My name is a whisper on his lips.

I'm wet just through turning my husband on. I need him inside me like nothing I've ever needed before. I've always enjoyed sex, but I have a healthier sex life with my husband than any previous partners. And I know women say, "Oh he's the best I've ever had," even when they don't mean it, just because they happen to be their current partner. But Drew really is the best lover I've ever had. I couldn't want anything more than what he gives me.

I move to lie on the bed next to him, but before I can settle down with him, he's up and holding himself above me. He leans down and claims my lips in a hot, passionate kiss. A moan reverberates through my chest and I dig my nails into his back.

Moving to kiss along my jawbone and down to the hollow of my throat, Drew's touch elicits a feeling inside me—the butterflies are back in full force. A feeling of warmth spreads throughout me as he slowly takes my pierced nipple between his lips. He licks and sucks, making me tingle all the way to my toes.

Sliding slowly down my body, he places a trail of kisses down to my navel, then to my pelvic bone as he gradually pushes my legs wider apart. His thumb rubs over my clit and my legs quiver. Far too slowly, he dips down to run his tongue over my wet folds.

I grip the sheets in my hands and my back arches off the bed as he circles my clit with his tongue.

"Drew."

I can't form coherent words; my thoughts are a jumble as these feelings flow through me. He knows what I want. He knows I need more than he's giving me. But he also enjoys taking his time.

My chest rises and falls rapidly as I move up onto my elbows to watch him.

I moan in delight as he slides one finger inside me, searching for that sweet spot. Falling back to the bed, I lose myself in the sensuality of the moment. I feel hypnotised, rooted to the spot.

Slipping a second finger inside, Drew hooks them and hits my G-spot over and over.

Pleasure begins to build inside me, and I know it won't be too much longer before I reach my climax. My legs are quivering and sweat slickens my skin.

Drew uses his tongue on my clit and I can feel myself about to explode.

"Come for me, baby."

His words are a command I can't ignore, and my body lets go. My orgasm rolls through me, taking me over the edge into the abyss.

My eyes flutter closed and I am lost at sea.

Chapter Seventeen

Drew

Elise has been looking at cheap flights to Iceland for the last couple of weeks and today I've finally booked them.

We talked about going together, but ultimately decided I would go on my own. I have some of Danny's ashes in a small sealed box. I wanted to go somewhere I knew he loved and chose Reykjavik—the place we last travelled to together—where I can watch the Aurora Borealis as I scatter them.

I have to carry the box in my hand luggage and have had to ask Danny's mother for a certified copy of his death certificate. That wasn't an easy thing to do, but, ultimately, she understood why I needed it.

I'm leaving tomorrow, flying from Birmingham Airport to Reykjavik. I'm staying at a place called The Capital Inn, just two and half miles from where I can see the Northern Lights. It's a cheap little room for two nights before I fly back to the UK.

Elise has helped me pack. She wishes she could be there for me, but it's next to impossible with two young children. Caleb wants to say goodbye to Uncle Danny, so I've promised I'll text him when I'm ready and he'll light a candle back at home and whisper a prayer as I scatter Danny's ashes. It was the best compromise we could come to given the circumstances.

My passport and ticket are in my hand luggage. I'm just dreading the thought of going alone to say goodbye to my best friend. But it's also something I feel I *need* to do alone.

A couple of days ago, Ash asked if she could come with me. But that felt weird and I had to say no. There's no way I want to go to another country in the company of another woman for two nights, whether she's my best friend's fiancée or not. Elise thinks that Ash has been flirting with me, but I know she isn't because she loved Danny. The thought that she's flirting with me is absurd. Still, I can't go with her. She's free to go where she likes to scatter his ashes, of course, but there's no way we can go on a trip together.

Ash was a little upset, but she understood when I said I needed to say goodbye to Danny on my own. We said goodbye together at the funeral, but now we need to do things in our own way to gain a sense of closure. His death was senseless, avoidable if it weren't for the snow on that fateful night. I'm still harbouring anger and regret. I couldn't help save my best friend. He was going to be a father and now his daughter will grow up without him. People tell me not blame myself, but I can't help it.

Elise thinks I should see a grief counsellor when I return. She says I'm up and down; my head and heart are all over the place. She's right about that, I guess. One minute I'm doing okay, the next I'm giving in to the bitterness that eats away at me. But that doesn't mean I'm agreeing to see a counsellor. Sure, Ash feels like seeing one has helped her, but I'm not her. I deal with things in my own way. I always have.

I'm off work tonight and won't be back for a few days. My flight is at nine o'clock tomorrow morning, so I'm taking a taxi to the airport. For now, I'm just going to do what I can, and I'll deal with how I feel when I I'm back. I'm hoping that finally saying goodbye to him may rid me of some of this pent-up emotion. I'll just have to wait and see.

***

The flight took just over four and a half hours, with a stop in Glasgow. There's no time difference between me and Elise back at home, so I called to let her know I'd landed. I'm off to find somewhere to eat now, having not wanted to eat aeroplane food.

I find a little café called Café Babalú. It's a quirky little place and the food is nice. I'm sitting with a mug of coffee, looking out of the window at the passers-by going about their day. Danny's ashes remain in my hand luggage. They had to x-ray the box at both airports on my departure and arrival. The lady in Birmingham was kind as I explained what it contained, but the bloke in Reykjavik was a little brusque. Still, he allowed the box to come through as I had the necessary paperwork. I don't really care what others think though, to be fair. I'm here for good reasons and I don't need to explain that to anyone else. It's no-one's business but my own.

Checking in at the hotel, I am given my key and I walk off in the direction they told me I'd find my room.

It's small, but cosy. It only has to suffice for two nights and as long as it has a bed to rest my weary head I'll be fine.

I didn't want to jump on a plane, scatter the ashes and then go straight home. That's why I'm here for two nights, because I want to be able to take my time, not have to rush back to the airport for a flight home.

I pull out my phone and dial Elise's number. I feel the need to hear her voice. I haven't been travelling since we got together, and it feels weird not to be with her and the children. I miss them already.

She doesn't answer, so assume she's busy at work. I'll call back later. Instead, I pull up my music and select a song that reminds me of her. As Charles Kelley's voice belts out 'The Only One Who Gets Me' I begin to sing along. I must admit, he's not my normal choice of music, but I did like Lady Antebellum before Elise and I got together, although I only owned one of their albums. Elise, however, owns them all. She also has Charles's solo album, *The Driver*, which I admit I now listen to often.

This song reminds me of my wife because she really is the only person who has ever understood me. She gets me in a way nobody ever has before. At first, that was quite a scary thought, but the longer we've been together, the more natural it feels. She's amazing. She has always been my rock.

Elise thought that no man would ever see past her disability, her walking stick, to the woman underneath. She had her heart torn viciously to shreds by Jensen when he upped and left without telling her why. Deep down, she knew he left because he couldn't cope with a disabled partner. He's an asshole. as is anyone else who can't see how amazing Elise is.

I knew Elise before she became disabled. We had what was meant to be a no-strings arrangement, but it didn't feel like that at the time and it certainly didn't feel like it when she stopped seeing me or returning my calls or texts. It tore my heart out. It was then that I realised I had fallen in love with her.

Then we didn't see each other for over a decade and I had a couple of failed relationships. One of those relationships got to the point where I was going to sell the apartment I lived in and buy somewhere with her. But, while I had been getting ready to do that, she admitted she'd fallen in love with someone else and didn't know how to tell me. So I ended up staying in the apartment and resolved myself to being single. That was fine by me.

I went travelling a lot and, looking back, I can see that was a coping mechanism. A defence built to prevent myself from getting into relationships. It was a good coping strategy until Elise blind-sided me.

Her best friend Sam was a nurse at the hospital I had just started working for. We became friends and she insisted on setting me up on a blind date. I didn't really want to, but she wouldn't stop pestering me. I went on the date to shut her up, but I ended up with something more than I bargained for. I found love.

The blind date was with my ex, Elise Swanson. The most beautiful redhead I had ever seen in my life. Her dyed red hair was lustrous and wild. It totally went with her feisty personality. Walking into that bar, I saw her sitting before me, a vision of beauty. Part of me wanted to run the hell away, as far as my legs could carry me. But the bigger part—my heart—wanted to stay exactly where I was.

From the moment I saw her with her walking stick in the bar, when she explained her disability, I felt inexplicably drawn to her. Her disability was never a problem for me; it wasn't an obstacle to overcome. It was just a part of her. She won my heart and I won her love. She's the most loving person I've ever met. How can I explain what she means to me? There aren't enough words. All I know is that if this is love, then I've never truly been in love before. I've never felt like this about anyone. My love for her is all-consuming. She's my love, my life, mother to my children and my wife.

I never believed in marriage until then. I didn't see the point of a piece of paper and a ring. But Elise breathed meaning into my life. She breathed love into my heart, into my soul and she made me believe in *happily ever after*.

Sitting here in my small room, I close my eyes and picture Elise's face. Her gorgeous blue eyes, creamy smooth skin, her full lips … oh how I love it when those lips are pressed against mine. She steals my breath every single time. Being with Elise is something I find hard to describe. I feel the electricity tingle from the tips of my fingers to the tips of my toes. Making love to her is like being in the middle of a storm. The electric charge builds, you feel it all around you and then, suddenly, the lightning strikes and the crackling in the air is at its most intense.

I open my eyes and look down at my phone on the tabletop. I pick it up and scroll through photos of me and my gorgeous family. Caleb and Cassie are the two most wonderful children. Like marriage, I didn't think I wanted children, but Elise changed my feelings on that too. I couldn't be without her and she came as a package deal with Caleb. I took on the role of a friend to him and, eventually, I took on the role of his father. I couldn't have been prouder. Every time he calls me 'Dad,' I still feel that pride beam within. When Cassie came along, our family was complete.

It's crazy how things happened. Suddenly, I'd gone from being a single man who was anti-marriage, anti-relationship, anti-pretty much everything, to being a husband and father. My perception of the world got totally spun on its axis and I wouldn't change a moment of it.

***

Standing here this evening, I am surrounded by natural beauty at its best. The Aurora Borealis is mesmerising. The hues of green, pink, purple, blue ... it's magical as the colours blend into each other in the night sky. But it's bittersweet. The only reason I'm standing here this evening is because my best friend is no longer with us. I'm here to scatter his ashes, the last remaining part of him. Well, when his daughter is born, she'll carry part of him with her, not only in her DNA, but in her heart. But this box in my pocket weighs heavy on my heart, because I'm saying goodbye to Danny.

Looking up at the sky, I whisper a small prayer. I'm not religious and nor was Danny, really. It's not a prayer to God; it's a prayer to Danny. I want to wish him well on his journey to whatever lies beyond us—be it Heaven, an afterlife, whatever people want to call it—I hope that, wherever his soul ends up, he's happy.

As I open the box, I notice my hands shaking. I remove the lid, take out the bag and unseal it. Pouring some of his ashes into my palm, I close my eyes.

"Danny, you were my best friend. You were like a brother to me. We lost you too soon. There are so many things you'll never get to experience and that makes me sad. Your daughter will never know her father. Sure, she'll have people surrounding her, talking about their memories of you, but she won't have *you*. You won't be around to complain about changing dirty nappies or to experience all of her firsts—words, teeth, steps, boyfriend. You won't be there to walk her down the aisle with tears in your eyes. But I hope that, wherever you are, you are watching over her as she grows. I am sure she'll grow up to be someone her daddy would be proud of.

You were such a good man. Everyone who met you loved you. Ashleigh proved that. The two of you hit it off right here in Iceland, and while Seb, Luke and I thought it would only be a holiday fling, you proved us all wrong there, didn't you pal?! You were going to marry that girl and have your own little family. My best buddy Danny was all grown up. Taking responsibility and shit was never your style until you settled down with Ash. I guess that's why you and I hit it off; I was the same. But Elise tamed me, like Ash did you.

As I stand here, saying my last goodbye to you, I realise that you might be gone, but you will never be forgotten. Be free, my friend. Be happy, wherever you may be. I'll always miss you and I will tell my goddaughter-to-be—your beautiful daughter—what an amazing man her father was. If she ever needs anything, I'll do my best to be there. Goodbye Danny. Rest in peace, buddy."

I let his ashes slip through my fingers before emptying the rest of the bag, allowing the contents to fly away on the gentle breeze.

Wrapping my scarf around me a little tighter, I stand and watch the myriad of colours in the sky as they mix into each other. I never got to see this on my first trip here with the boys. It really is stunning and, under any other circumstances, I would want to share such awe-inspiring beauty with Elise. But this is something I felt I needed to do alone.

I don't know how long I've been standing here, but there's a feeling that's settled into my bones. I feel at peace for the first time since Danny passed.

My mind drifts back to a moment in my past where I felt like this.

The funeral director turned to me and handed me a box. It was light in weight, but it felt heavy on my heart. Edie and Pops had asked to be cremated, that was their final wish. Edie had passed first, her remains were cremated and the box remains on a shelf back at home. Now I'm holding Pops's remains in a box, just as I did with her. I've chosen a place to scatter them both together, a place that was special to them in life.

My heart feels lodged in my throat as I walk back to the car. I feel like I can't swallow around it. My palms are clammy and my eyes are sore. I spent the entire service crying. After my parents had abandoned me in life and then overdosed and died, Edie and Pops were the closest thing to parents I ever had. In fact, they were what real parents should be, instead of what I ended up with. Always having to look after myself because my parents were junkies; that was a hard life to have been handed. But when Edie and Pops took me in when I was fifteen, I learned what real love and affection was. Now that they're gone, I don't know what I'm going to do.

Three weeks pass me by before I am willing and able to scatter my grandparents' remains. I feel stronger than I did in the beginning. It almost feels like they're still guiding me from whatever afterlife awaits us after we pass.

The surroundings are beautiful. They were right when they told me just how stunning this place was. I knew it was special to them; that's why I chose to scatter them here.

As I watch their final remains float away on the gentle breeze, I feel a calmness settle over me. My heart no longer feels so heavy. It's like I was Atlas, holding the weight of the world, but now that weight has been lifted as I tell my grandparents just how much I love them and will always miss them.

A voice breaks my reverie. I open my eyes, only now realising I had closed them.

"Drew, it really is you. I can't believe it."

I look at the woman in front of me and am immediately angry. I don't know why, but I can't help the anger coursing through my veins.

"Ash. What are you doing here?"

"Saying goodbye to Danny. What are you doing here?"

I look at her blonde hair and fake tits and think she's the stereotypical dumb blonde. I know she's not a complete airhead, because she makes a good paramedic, but, in this moment, she couldn't be more stupid. I told her where I was going to scatter Danny's ashes and I had also told her when. So, the only thing that can explain her being here is not coincidence, that's for sure.

"I've just scattered Danny's ashes. What do you think I'm doing here?"

I can't help the blunt tone that coats my words.

"Oh. I'm sorry, I didn't mean to … well, I didn't mean to interrupt. I … umm … I …"

Her eyes shine with unshed tears and I want to take back the harshness in my tone, but I can't. She doesn't say anything more and I want to comfort her, knowing it's hard for her too. But what has me so angry is that she knew I was coming here and she knew I'd said I needed to do it alone. She'd asked me about going somewhere together to scatter Danny and I had said no. But now she's here. She's trying to force something I didn't want.

"I'm just going to leave, Ash. I think that's best. I'm sorry if I upset you. I'll see you back in England."

"Please … don't go."

Her quiet voice is almost lost on the breeze.

"I can't stay, Ash. I'm sorry. This was something I needed to do alone, and I did. Now you need to do the same."

I turn to walk in the direction of my hotel but a hand lands on my arm.

"Please, Drew. I can't be alone when I say goodbye to him."

"Then you shouldn't have come here alone. You should have scattered him elsewhere, had your family around you."

Again, my tone is blunt. I should care, but my head is scrambled. I thought she'd understood when I told her I needed to do this alone. I didn't think she'd up and follow me. Is it really too much to ask to be left alone?

She stands there, her mouth opening and closing, but no words coming out. She looks like I've slapped her in the face or something.

Guilt stabs at my heart. As much as I am angry at Ashleigh for following me, I can't blame her for not wanting to be alone. I can blame her for putting me in this situation in the first place, but I don't want to make her feel worse by lashing out, by asking her why she came her on purpose, when she knew I would be here.

I want to turn on my heel and walk away, but I can't. I'm annoyed at Ashleigh for forcing my hand in this situation, but I can't leave her alone if she really doesn't want to be. Okay, so she shouldn't have come out to Iceland if she knew she didn't want to be alone. She followed me so she wouldn't have to be. I'm pissed off that she's done this, but how heartless would I have to be to walk away now?

There's a time and place to bring up how angry I am with her, but here and now isn't it. She's lost her partner; she's lost in her own grief. Grieving for a man that she loved, but also for the father her daughter will never have. Maybe it wasn't her intention to encroach on my grief. Perhaps she didn't come here to piss me off at all. That could just be in my mind. It's more than possible that she genuinely wanted to be able to say goodbye to Danny with me by her side and, although she knew that wasn't what I wanted, she felt that she couldn't do it any other way.

Either way, now is not the time to be having that discussion.

I swallow down the lump in my throat and try for a tone of voice less blunt than I have been so far.

"I'm sorry, Ash. Saying my goodbyes to Danny was … well, emotional. I shouldn't lash out at you."

She looks at me with wet eyes and a tearstained face. It tugs my heartstrings. I hate seeing people upset.

"If you want, we can say goodbye to him together."

I place my arm around her shoulders and she sags against me in what feels like relief.

"Thank you, Drew," she whispers.

***

Helping Ash say goodbye to Danny was hard. Easier than I expected, maybe, but still difficult. She was emotional, as you would expect. She cried. A lot. She also talked a lot about what he would be missing out on, and that felt like a red-hot knife to my heart.

My heart went out to her and their unborn daughter. It almost made my own grief feel insignificant in comparison, but, as she reminded me, my grief is just as real as hers, even if it is different. She told me that how I feel isn't any less important or significant, just because of the difference in my relationship with Danny compared to hers.

Everyone's grief is incomparable. It manifests differently for everyone and everyone has a right to feel it in whatever way is right for them.

We ended up going to a small restaurant nearby, talking, eating and drinking until we realised how late it was.

I came back to my room at the inn and sent Elise a message to let her know that I was okay and that I would talk to her in the morning. She replied saying she hadn't wanted to bombard me with texts; she wanted to leave me to say my goodbyes and knew I'd contact her when I was feeling less overwhelmed.

After telling her briefly about Ash turning up, Elise had expressed her concern at how she had even come to be here. I couldn't answer that. The only person able to do that is Ash. But Elise agreed with me that it wasn't the right time or place to be grilling her about it.

The only reason I'd even told Elise was because we don't keep secrets from each other or tell each other lies. And after her saying she thought Ash was flirting with me, part of me hadn't wanted to tell her about tonight because I thought she'd fly off the handle, assuming more so that Ash had an unhealthy interest in me. But I couldn't not tell her. She'd find out when I got home anyway, no doubt. More than that though, I just couldn't justify lying to my wife, not for any reason.

Maybe Elise is right; maybe Ash does have an unhealthy kind of attachment to me. Perhaps she came here to Iceland to be closer to me. But, honestly, that just sounds daft to me. She was in love with my best friend; there's no way she would now be interested in me, having not long lost him. It's not even about having 'only just' lost him either. Ash can't be attracted to me. At all. For any reason. Ever. It's just … unimaginable, inconceivable to me.

Chapter Eighteen

Elise

Drew just texted to say his flight has landed and he'll be getting a taxi home. I can't wait to have him back where he belongs. I know he had to go out there alone to say goodbye to Danny, but we haven't been apart this long since we were married. In fact, longer than that, we haven't spent this long apart since his last trip to Iceland—the one he cut short to come home to me.

When he told me Ashleigh had turned up, I wasn't all that surprised. She'd previously asked Drew about scattering Danny's ashes together, to which he'd said no. He wanted to be alone to say goodbye to his best friend, something I could totally understand and respect, but it seems she couldn't.

I've noticed her sniffing around him in the past, noticed she has an interest in him that isn't purely platonic. I haven't mentioned it to anyone, except to say to Drew I think she's keen on him. He dismissed it out of hand, saying she was with his best friend and wasn't interested in him. He assured me that even if *she* was interested, *he* wasn't. It's not him that I don't trust. Some women don't care that the man they are sniffing around is married and Ashleigh strikes me as one of those.

I mean, sure, she was with Danny; she's even having his baby now. I know that she cared about Danny. But I also know what it looks like when a woman is flirting. I know what's on her mind when she looks at my husband in that way. The way that he doesn't seem to pick up on. He's oblivious to it because he doesn't *want* to believe it. He doesn't want it to be true.

After Danny died, she was distraught, as anyone would be after the death of someone they love. But since she's been assigned as Drew's partner at work she's been sniffing around him again like a dog on heat.

I don't want to say anything to her, mostly because I don't want to stir up a hornet's nest. Yet, that doesn't mean I *won't* say something to her if she was to try and take it further.

Sure, I know that hormones can play a part in being horny. When I was pregnant with both of my children, I was even hornier than normal. But she looked at Drew that way when she wasn't pregnant, when her own boyfriend was still alive. Both men were oblivious to the fact and I didn't bring it up, because some things are better left unsaid.

Her turning up in Iceland is another story though. Drew still thinks it's nothing, but I know it's not. He told me he ended up comforting her last night after being with her while she scattered Danny's ashes. I'm not jealous at all—I actually feel rather sorry for her in a way—but if she's followed him to Iceland, how much further is she willing to go?

Drew said he felt awful because he snapped at her. He was angry she'd followed him when he'd made it explicitly clear he wanted to be alone. But, even through his anger, he felt sorry for her because she was grieving the husband she'd never have, the father their child would never know. He said he couldn't bring himself to leave her on her own. And, after scattering his ashes, they'd gone for something to eat. I'm fine with all of that; thankfully I'm not a jealous woman. But if she tries to take it any further when they get back to the UK and back to working together, that's when I'll have to put my foot down with her.

I'm really looking forward to Drew getting home. I've been looking at trips we could take together as a family. I've almost decided on a place, but I want to run it by Drew before I book it. It's in Rovaniemi, Lapland. I thought we could do something totally out of the ordinary. We'd be staying in a glass igloo. Caleb would be sure to get a kick out of it. We've seen adverts on television for these kinds of trips and I've always thought they're too expensive and I can't take time off work because I've been trying to build the business up.

But now the business is doing well. Amanda is an amazing assistant and can totally do without me for a few days. As for the money, it's not exactly a problem anymore. I make enough money now that Memories Made is successful.

"Hey, gorgeous, I'm home," Drew calls as he closes the front door.

I wish I could run and throw myself in his arms, but my damn leg impedes me. So, I'll settle for walking into the hallway and wrapping my arms around his neck.

Burying my head in his neck, I inhale the scent of him. It strikes me how much I've missed that while he was away.

Drew cradles the back of my head with one hand and the other rests gently on my hip. I lean back to look at him and he smiles at me. I am instantly warmed all over as his eyes look into mine and I see the glimmer of hunger in his gaze.

He slants his lips over mine and a kaleidoscope of butterflies take flight in my stomach. Hell, they might even be moths, they feel that big and flutter their wings so strongly.

Deepening the kiss, Drew takes what I have to give, and I am only too willing to give him all of me.

Thankfully, Caleb is at school and Cassie is napping. That gives me time to welcome my husband home in style.

***

After making love, we lie wrapped up in each other, a tangle of limbs. My heartrate is finally slowing down to a normal rhythm. Our bodies are still slick with a light sheen of sweat and I decide to take a shower before Cassie wakes from her nap. I'm surprised she's not awake already, but I'm going to take advantage of her being asleep.

As I walk into our en suite, I feel Drew's eyes burning holes into me. Casting a glance over my shoulder, I see him looking at my ass like a total pervert. He's like a horny teenager that's just seen his first naked woman in the flesh. His gaze sends goose bumps across my skin and my heart skips a beat. Under his intense scrutiny, I feel attractive, sexy and happy in my own skin. That's something I didn't feel after Jensen left me. I felt like my disability made me unattractive. I'd put on weight since I couldn't exercise due to the nature of my nerve damage and spine issues, so I felt fat and frumpy. But Drew makes me feel like a goddess, worthy of being worshipped by him.

I turn on the water in the shower and wait for it to warm up. As I'm waiting, I feel Drew's hands on my hips. A smile forms on my lips as his hands slip around my waist and he draws me flush to his body. Feeling the start of his erection pressing against me from behind sends shivers through me. I felt sated only moments ago, but now I'm feeling like I could forego the shower and take my handsome husband back to bed.

Drew reaches around me and turns the water off. It seems he's had the same idea as me.

I turn in his embrace and his lips slant over mine in a hot, sensual kiss. I put one hand on his chest as the other reaches to play with the hair at the nape of his neck. I deepen the kiss and feel his impressive erection grow larger.

Drew breaks our kiss and leans down to put one arm behind my knees. Before I have time to complain, he literally sweeps me off my feet and carries me back to our bed.

He lies me down gently, reverently, before covering my body with his. Leaning on his forearms, he holds himself above me and leans down to claim my lips once more.

His kiss is dizzying, breathtaking, fuelled with lust and unrestrained passion. My eyes are closed and I revel in his intoxicating kiss. I could gladly lose myself in him forever. Something beautiful happens inside me as he hypnotises me. My nails dig into his shoulders and a deep moan reverberates through my chest. The emptiness I felt inside me while he was away now feels filled with him. He completes me in a way nobody else ever has. When we found each other again, it was as if the broken part of my soul called to the brokenness inside him. It was only losing myself in him that made me rediscover who I am. And I think the same could be said for Drew.

There were a thousand reasons why I didn't want to open up, to put my heart on the line, opening myself up to rejection—again. But Drew silenced each and every one of them. The emptiness inside me faded and over time, disappeared completely as our relationship progressed.

I'd been abandoned, left adrift at sea, then I met Drew and he became my anchor. I'd thought being a disabled single mom would put men off, but it didn't have that effect on him. If anything, it had the opposite effect, like he wanted to show me how much I can be loved and cared for.

He wanted to show me that I'm desirable, just like he's proving as he kisses his way down the valley between my breasts. He cups each breast in his hands and rubs his thumb over the piercing in the left one. They instantly pebble and there's a feeling that begins to take hold in my abdomen.

My hands grip the sheets beneath me as he kisses down to the apex of my thighs. He breathes lightly across my core and my body tingles in response. My insides tighten and my heart beats wildly in my chest, making it feel like it wants to break free of its constraints.

"I love you, Elise Wright."

If my senses weren't so heightened, I might have missed his

declaration, but instead a smile spreads across my face as he touches and kisses me.

I writhe on the bed as Drew slips his fingers through my wet folds before circling my clit with his tongue. I feel light-headed as pleasure courses through my veins.

Drew's tongue delves straight to my core and a moan of pleasure escapes my lips. A low growl comes from Drew as he pushes one finger inside me. My body contracts around it as he hooks it to hit my G-spot.

Adding another finger, Drew stretches me, and the sensation is heady. It's as though we haven't already made love once today. My body responds to his touch just as easily as it did earlier.

"Come for me, baby."

His words fuel the fire burning within me and it's almost as if my body was waiting for his permission to let go. Moments later, my orgasm rolls like a tidal wave. My back arches from the bed as small aftershocks ripple through me.

The muscles within me that were coiled only moments ago now feel relaxed but even more sensitive to his touch.

Taking advantage of my heightened response to his touch, Drew crawls back up over my body and dips his head to kiss me. His tongue dances with mine, tasting of my climax. A purr of satisfaction escapes me as he aligns himself with me and pushes inside.

Slowly, he stretches me to accommodate him. The slight burn in my muscles is proof of the pleasure-pain theory. A little pain actually heightens the pleasure I feel.

Filling me completely, Drew waits a moment before beginning to move inside me. His pace is slow, and my body begs for more. Desire sings in my veins as he builds a more fulfilling rhythm.

Dipping his head toward me once more, Drew nips at my bottom lip, before soothing the sting with kiss. His tongue demands entry, duelling with mine for dominance over the kiss. I willingly allow him to take the lead.

My hands grip his hips as he pushes in and out of my body. I clench my walls around him, taking everything that he has to give.

Breaking the kiss, Drew pulls back to look into my eyes. I see lust, hunger, and love in his gaze. His love for me is unquantifiable, just the same as mine is for him.

Pushing me closer and closer to another climax, Drew's body is slick with perspiration. I drag my nails up his spine and then back down as he shudders under my touch. Gripping his ass, I pull him closer to me. Matching his body thrust for thrust, I can feel a warmth building in my abdomen and I have to try to hold it at bay.

"Drew," I whisper.

His eyes find mine and I shudder beneath his scrutiny.

"Let me fuck you."

His eyes sparkle at my request.

Slowly, he carefully manoeuvres us so that he is beneath me. I like the view from here. I can see his glorious abs and his handsome face.

I begin to move, and I watch his facial features transform into a face-splitting grin. I don't hold back as I rock my hips back and forth. Squeezing my walls around him at the same time has the desired effect. His pupils dilate, and his fingers dig into my flesh. My breathing becomes erratic as I move us closer to the ultimate goal of our combined climax.

Drew thrusts his hips to match my movements and it isn't long before we're both shouting out our pleasure. My body folds in on his and he wraps his arms around me, kissing the top of my hair as he does so.

Chapter Nineteen

Drew

Things have been good since I got home from Iceland. Elise and I are in a good place and I feel more relaxed and at peace with things than I did straight after Danny died. We've spent time talking about how I felt back then. It almost felt like I'd lost a limb instead of a best friend. But now, Elise is helping me feel whole again.

The more we've talked, the more I've been experiencing flashbacks—but not in a bad way—to a time gone by long ago. I thought I was over the death of my parents and my grandparents, but Elise has helped me see that talking about things, sharing parts of my past instead of keeping them locked away, actually helps.

Grief is a funny thing and it affects you in ways that you don't necessarily notice. It affected my ability to fully connect to another person. It wasn't until Elise came along that I even thought about putting my heart back out there. I feared rejection because it felt like I had some kind of reverse Midas touch, where everything I touched fell apart instead of turning to gold. But I touched Elise and we didn't fall apart. In fact, she helped me become whole again. It took time, but we got there. *She* got us there. I have my wife to thank for so many things, but, most of all, for teaching me to love again. Showing me how to love someone wholeheartedly, unconditionally, Elise managed to make me feel things I'd thought I'd long since lost the ability to feel.

We've been talking about taking the children to Lapland and it's given me something to look forward to. Aside from that, I've been putting my focus into my work and looking towards the future instead of living in the past.

I've worked several shifts with Ash since coming home, the first of which she spent apologising profusely for the whole Iceland thing. I forgave her because there's not much else I can do. There's no point holding a grudge and there's nothing that can be done to go back and change it, so I accepted her apology and we agreed on a fresh slate.

But I've still felt a little weird around her. You can choose to accept someone's apology, but you can't choose exactly when you'll forget about it. So, I'm just trying my hardest not to make each shift uncomfortable.

Ash is due to leave for her maternity leave soon and I've been told my new partner will be Matty. He's a great guy; I've worked with him before when Danny had annual leave. We work well together and to be honest, bad as it might sound, I am looking forward to Ash taking leave.

I'm working the night shift tonight, so Elise, the children and I, spent the day together. We curled up and watched movies. Caleb picked one; it was one of the newer Star Wars ones. In all honesty, I didn't think very much of it—you just can't beat the originals in my book—but Caleb enjoyed it and he can't wait for *The Last Jedi* to come out on DVD so he can make me watch that too. He enjoyed it at the cinema with Elise one evening when I was at work.

Elise picked the second movie. Being anything except your typical girl, she chose *The Crow*. We'd decided it was time to introduce Caleb to a classic. He loved it, which didn't surprise me at all. I then decided we should watch *The Goonies* or *Beetlejuice* but left it to Elise and Caleb to decide which one of the two. They chose *Beetlejuice*. I have to admit, it was funny when we all sat there singing along when Lydia started floating and dancing in the air to 'Jump in the Line'.

I'm still humming the song as I pull up at work and kill the engine. I look at the bay where several ambulances are parked and see Seb, Luke, Matty and Ash. It hits me that Danny should be laughing and joking with them all.

Ash leaves to have their daughter later this month and he should be here holding her hand. I briefly wonder who she's asked to be her birthing partner now that her fiancé isn't going to be there. She doesn't seem to have many real friends around here. Before meeting Danny, her life was in Bristol and it was their whirlwind romance that made her move over here. But perhaps one of them, or maybe her mother, intends to come and stay for the birth. All I really know is Ash said she wants to work right until the last possible minute because she wants to take her mind off things. She said the longer she has at home alone, the more she'll stress herself out by thinking of all the things that will never be. I feel sorry for her and wish there was something Elise or I could do to help. Ash said us agreeing to be godparents is enough, but it doesn't feel like it.

I might still feel a bit weird around her, but she's having my best friend's baby. I wish I could do something to ease the pain she's carrying around.

***

We've just got back to base after our first call-out and Ash is restocking the ambulance with supplies. It wasn't a nice call-out at all. A guy had been in a fight—seemingly with his best friend, over a girl—and had a massive head wound where he'd been hit by his assailant with a glass bottle. The bottle had smashed and caused a deep laceration. But that wasn't his only injury. He had what looked like a dislocated jaw, his one eye was bruised and swollen, and the poor bloke was covered in blood. It had been an awful sight to behold. Ashleigh had nearly lost the contents of her stomach as she inspected the head wound. I can't say I blame her. It was one of the worst I'd come across in months.

My radio crackles to life with a call to a guy who is in severe pain with his back. I notify Ash and we jump in the ambulance, buckle up and head towards the address we've been given.

We pull up outside the house and the front door is open. A woman is standing on the porch waiting for us.

"Please, it's my husband, help him."

I look at the woman who must be in her sixties; her face is etched with worry.

We head inside to find our patient on all fours on the floor in the hallway. I kneel beside him and see his features contorted in pain.

"Sir, can you tell me your name?"

"Maxwell, but call me Max."

"And what seems to be the problem, Max?"

"There was a spasm in my back a little while ago and, all of a sudden, I'm on the floor in agony."

"Have you had any painkillers, Max?"

"No."

"And do you have any underlying issues that could have caused your injuries today?"

"No."

"On a scale of one to ten, how would you rate the pain, Max?"

His face contorts in pain before he answers.

"Ten."

He grimaces as another wave of pain washes over him. He's still on all fours on the floor and I want to get him onto a stretcher and to the hospital as quickly as we can. I can't help but feel sorry for him. I had a slipped disc some time ago and I know how he must be feeling. People can be flippant and dismiss back pain, but, as Elise can attest to, sometimes it's the worst kind of pain. Goodness knows she had two operations and she's still in pain every single day.

"We can give you paracetamol one of two ways, Max. The choice is yours. We can give it to you in tablet form, or through an intravenous drip. I'll be honest and say the IV acts quicker and gets to the source of the pain fast."

"I'll take that one then, son, if you don't mind!"

I look up to see Ash comforting Max's wife, but I know she's listened to every word because she immediately starts to set up the cannula for the drip. Once everything is set up, the IV starts to do its job.

"Max, would you say that's taken the edge off the pain at all?"

"A little."

"And how would you rate the pain on a scale of one to ten now?"

"Nine."

"Right, okay. We're going to help you onto a stretcher and get you to the hospital, okay?"

He just nods.

Ash hands me the Entonox and I instruct Max how to use it. It may just take the edge off the pain a little more.

After managing to get Max onto a stretcher and into the back of the ambulance, Ash walks up with her arm around Max's wife. She settles her in the seat next to Max before shutting the doors. I get in the front, ready to pull away when Ash gives me the okay.

We're driving to the hospital and I hear quiet chatter in the back between Ash and Lily. She seems very upset for her husband and he keeps trying to reassure her, as does Ash, that he'll be okay.

Hearing a loud noise in the back, I shout back to make sure things are okay.

"I think you're going to have to drive faster, young man. This young lady's waters have just broken," Lily says in a rush.

It's too early. Ash can't be having her baby now. She's not due for another six weeks. Shit!

I turn the siren on and put my foot down a little harder.

Ash sounds like she's in pain and I hear Lily trying to calm her. I am navigating the roads, weaving in and out of traffic as best I can.

A few minutes later, we pull up at the hospital and I shout to one of the porters to grab a wheelchair. He looks confused because he sees our patient is on a stretcher, but he doesn't question me. Bringing it out as quickly as he can, he steers the wheelchair in our direction.

I help Ash into it and ask the porter to take her into hospital. I wheel the stretcher in and see Lily holding Ash's hand.

I have no idea who to call to come to Ash's side while she's in labour. I don't know any of her friends or family. I book Max in and, once I know he's handed over and in good hands, I go to Ash's side.

I slip my phone out and send a text to Elise. She replies, suggesting I call Danny's mum, Maggie.

Pulling up her number, I press call and wait for her to answer. When she picks up, I relay the situation to her and she says she'll get to the hospital as quickly as she can.

I don't know what to do with myself. Do I wait with Ash until Maggie arrives? What help can I actually be to her? I don't know, but I know I have to try.

I find her on the maternity ward and watch as staff bustle around her. I'm not sure she'll want me here, but she'll welcome a familiar face at this point, surely?!

"Oh, Drew," she says as she spots me, "I'm so glad you're here. I'm so scared. They're telling me they're going to have to deliver her. It's too soon, she can't be coming now. I've got six weeks left."

The pain in her voice isn't merely physical. She's worried about her daughter being premature and the problems that will accompany that. I walk to her side and sit in the chair next to her bed. She reaches out for my hand and I can't deny her that small comfort.

"Maggie's on her way. I didn't know who else to call."

"My mum was meant to be my birthing partner. She was coming to stay in a few weeks' time. But she won't be able to get here from Bristol in time now."

"You should call her."

Ash screams in pain and her whole body seems to contort.

"Where's your phone? I'll call her."

"My … my pocket …"

Another wave of pain hits her, making her shout out in distress. Her contractions seem close together, meaning she could be delivering her daughter any time soon.

She digs around in her pocket and hands me her phone. I call the number on the screen and wait for her to answer, hoping it doesn't go to voicemail. Realising I don't even know her name, I cover the bottom of the phone with my hand and quickly ask Ash.

"Hello, Ashleigh, sweetheart. How are you?" Ellen says.

"Umm … Hello, Ellen. My name is Drew. I'm calling because Ash is in hospital. Her waters have broken and they're telling her they'll have to deliver the baby."

"Now?" she asks, shock evident in her voice.

"Yes, I'm afraid so. Can you get here?"

"No, I don't drive, and her father is out of town for work this week."

"Oh…" I don't know what to say because I don't want to alarm Ash.

Ash cries out in pain and I hear her mother's cry of anguish down the phone.

"My baby, my baby girl … Oh my goodness."

"I can pick you up from a train station, if that helps."

"You would? That would be good, thank you. I'll look at train times now. Thank you, Drew."

"I'm with her for now and Danny's mother is on her way, she won't be alone, I assure you."

"I'll call when I know when my train will arrive. It's around two and a half hours from Bristol Temple Meads station. Do you think she'll be able to hold on that long?"

I don't know how to answer that. I'm not sure there's a timeframe for premature babies. It could happen faster than she'd like. I decide a small white lie of omission won't hurt. It would only distress her further to be blunt at this point.

"It's possible, Ellen. I'm only a paramedic and I've never delivered a premature baby."

"Okay, well, I'll head to the station now. I'll call when I know more."

"Ash is in good hands, Ellen. I promise you that."

We say our goodbyes just as Ash cries out again. I'm not sure if it's actually a contraction or if she's just in pain.

"We're going to give baby corticosteroids, Ashleigh," a voice to my right says.

I look up and see a midwife.

"Steroids? What?" Ash asks.

"It's to help baby's lungs and internal organs develop, Ashleigh. Baby is only thirty-four weeks, so although we'd like to delay labour if we could, it seems baby has other ideas and is coming ahead of schedule whether we like it or not."

"Drew?"

My name sounds more like a question at this point.

"Ash, I can't tell you what to do or not do. It sounds like a good idea if it's going to help baby's internal organs develop."

"Danielle. Her name is Danielle, not *baby*," she mutters unhappily.

"Sorry, Ash, I didn't know. Look, anything that helps Danielle is a good thing, right?"

She debates it with the midwife until another cry of pain seizes her.

"Okay."

She sounds resigned. I wish I could comfort her, but I don't know how. It feels weird being here. If it was Elise, I still wouldn't know what to do, but at least I'd be able to comfort her. I don't know Ash well enough to know what would be of any comfort.

"Ashleigh, darling."

I look up as Maggie's voice startles me.

"Hello Drew. Ashleigh, how are you doing, sweetie?"

"Oh Maggie, I'm so frightened."

Maggie settles down on the opposite side of Ash. Taking her hand, she strokes her thumb gently over the back of her knuckles.

"Darling, everything will be okay."

"They are about to give Danielle steroids."

"Corticosteroids to help her lungs and internal organs develop," I add.

"Well, anything that helps our little darling is a good thing, yes?"

Maggie looks at Ashleigh with such love. I know in her heart she wishes her son was here to witness his daughter's birth. It must be bittersweet for her. For Ash too.

I explain that Ellen is on her way and that I'll be fetching her from the train station, but it will be at least a couple of hours before she's here. I look at my watch and realise that I haven't let the base know that I'm here with Ash.

As I walk from the cubicle, I call the base and Yvonne says she was notified when Ash was taken into hospital. Turns out Ash had the forethought to use her radio while I was handing our last patient over.

I tell Yvonne I'm intending to pick Ellen up and she tells me to take the rest of the day off as she already has cover on their way in. I'm relieved for Ash's sake that I don't have to rush back off to work. There's nobody else that could fetch her mother. Sure, she could probably get a taxi, but that doesn't sit right with me.

***

Ellen was flustered and a lot less calm than Maggie was when she arrived. But I managed to calm her down before she got to the hospital. When I took her to the maternity ward, I left her my number and told her to call me if they needed anything. There wasn't any reason for me to stick around. I felt out of place, so I left them to it and came home.

I told Elise everything as soon as I got home. The feeling at home is quite solemn and it feels like it's suffocating me. It's made me realise how much I miss Danny. I decide to take a shower and try to clear my head.

Danielle had already been born when I dropped Ellen at the hospital. She was in an incubator on the neonatal ward. She was so tiny, weighing in at six pounds and eleven ounces. I saw the photograph they'd left with Ash. She wasn't able to go to visit her daughter until the doctor had examined her and given her the all clear. I saw it written on her face how hard that was, but they were working as quickly as they could to reunite mother and baby.

I turn on the shower and wait for the water to warm up. I strip off and step into the steamy shower cubicle. The water beats down on me like bullets, relaxing my muscles, and I just stand here letting it rain down on me.

Letting my mind relax too, I begin to feel a little more normal. It's natural to miss Danny, but that doesn't mean it's not hard for all concerned.

I step out of the shower, wrap a towel around my waist and swipe my hand over the mirror in front of me. I stand and shave before brushing my teeth and drying myself off fully.

I slip into a pair of slouchy jogging bottoms and a clean t-shirt. Feeling more human than I did a few minutes ago, I head downstairs and switch the coffee machine on. I could do with a strong cup of black coffee.

Feeling a pair of arms wrap round me from behind, a smile forms on my lips.

"Hey, baby."

"Hey, you okay?"

There's unmistakable worry in her voice. I want to comfort her, to let her know I'm okay. Turning in her embrace, I catch her gaze. I could get lost in the ocean that is her beautiful blue eyes.

"I'm good. It's not me we need to worry about."

"That's not true."

She snuggles closer into my chest, so close that not even a breath could get between us. Her warm body feels good against mine and I let out a breath I didn't know I'd been holding.

"It's true enough, baby. I'll be fine. It's little Danielle who needs everyone's focus right now."

"Danielle? A fitting tribute to her father, but also a stark reminder that he's not here."

She speaks my internal thoughts without knowing it. I don't trust my voice, so I don't say anything.

I turn back to the coffee machine and make myself a black coffee, as strong as possible. I make Elise her favourite hazelnut cappuccino and carry them into the lounge. I don't want to talk about Danny, Ash, Danielle … I just want to relax in my favourite recliner or snuggle up beside my wife for a little while. I don't want to do anything or say anything, I just want to be.

Chapter Twenty

Elise

Six months later…

Danielle looks up at me with eyes that look so much like her father's. She's so beautiful. I'm babysitting while Ash gets some rest. She was discharged from hospital and had to wait two weeks for her daughter to come home. I recognised the signs of postnatal depression because I had suffered from it after both of my children were born. Luckily for me, it didn't affect my bond with my children, but Ash is really struggling.

I don't think it's just the PND that's bothering her. I think having Danielle has compounded her feelings about missing Danny.

Her GP diagnosed postnatal depression and put her on anti-depressants. He also arranged for her to see a counsellor, partly for the PND and partly for grief counselling. I'm not really sure whether it's helping her or not. It's been six months and it doesn't feel like she's any better than before.

I have the day off work, so I'm able to lend a hand. I've taken Danielle home with me and Cassie for a little while. Drew is working a two 'til ten shift so I have the whole day to myself. I'm sitting cradling Danielle as she drinks from her bottle. Ash couldn't get her to latch on to breastfeed and, honestly, I don't think she wanted to breastfeed her anyway. She may have done if Danny was still here, if they were a family of three. But the PND is affecting her in a multitude of ways, so Moira—the health visitor at the mum and baby clinic—had suggested she be bottle fed. There wasn't really anything else to be done. We couldn't exactly force Ash to do something she didn't want to do.

As I settle Danielle in the Moses basket, I look down at her and see a picture of pure innocence. Many people would say things like 'I don't know how her mother could just turn her back on her' or 'she should appreciate what she's got', but that's where I'm different to them. I know my PND didn't affect my bond with my children, but I still know how it feels to suffer from it. Many people don't even know the signs of postnatal depression; I know I didn't the first time around. I didn't know that the reason I was so irritable, the reason I kept arguing with Jensen, the reason pretty much any little thing could set me off; all of that was due to the PND. Thankfully, I got it diagnosed and was on the road to recovery, but that wasn't until Caleb was thirteen months old, so I had over a year where I was suffering without knowing why.

I don't think enough people understand the effect something like this can have on a person. Mental health is still such a taboo subject. I wish it were easier to get people to open up and talk about it. I wish there was something I could do to reach Ash, but it seems like everything I try is in vain. The only thing I can do right now is look after Danielle when I can.

Ash's parents want her to move back to be with them, let them help her, let them babysit their grandchild. But she's cut them all off. She's told them that none of them are welcome here. I'm guessing it's because she just wants to be left alone. Not because she doesn't love her family, but maybe because she doesn't know how to explain it to them.

Her parents are in their sixties now, so they couldn't have Danielle full time anyway. It would be too much for them. And Ash doesn't have any siblings, so there's nobody back home to help on a regular basis.

I'm lucky in the fact that I work for myself and I have an amazing assistant, Amanda. I can work from my office at home while Danielle sleeps. It's what I did with Cassie when she came along. Amanda covers a lot of our appointments when it comes to meeting clients or scouting venues, but we try to schedule stuff like that around the days where I have the baby. It's easy enough to catch up with Amanda via FaceTime and she comes over to fill me in and show me pictures of a potential venue, so I can sign off on it.

I decide to get some tidying up done while Danielle sleeps and Cassie plays quietly in her playpen.

***

Relaxing with a cup of coffee after getting some housework done, I look at the clock and realise it will soon be time to take Danielle home.

I don't know how Ash will be when I drop her off and that worries me. She's alone and obviously isn't up to the task of taking care of herself, never mind her daughter. It worries me that if something doesn't change soon, social services may decide to place Danielle with a temporary foster carer. If it were up to me, I wouldn't allow that to happen, but her health visitors are increasingly worried about her and her ability to be a mother.

All too soon, I find myself packing up Danielle's things and calling a taxi. I grab Cassie's coat and bundle both girls up warm.

The taxi ride over to Ash's house has me feeling on edge. It comes to something when you find yourself not wanting to hand someone else's daughter back to them.

As I knock on the door, it seems nobody wants to answer, so I slip my phone out of my pocket and dial Ash's number. I can hear her ringtone through the door, but she doesn't answer. I'm guessing she's asleep, so I root around for the spare key she gave me. My handbag is a bottomless pit, so it takes a few moments to locate it.

Walking into the house, I'm met with silence. I put Cassie down in the playpen in the lounge and lay Danielle down in her Moses basket. I'm guessing Ash is sleeping, so I quietly walk up the stairs to wake her. If it were up to me, I'd let her sleep, but I have to get back to fetch Caleb from his friend's house. He asked if he could go to Jake's to play on his new games console after school and it's almost time to pick him up.

Upstairs is just as quiet as it is downstairs. It's eerie. I'm pretty sure you could hear a pin drop.

I push Ash's bedroom door open and I slip inside. I walk over to her bed, put my hand on her shoulder and shake her lightly to rouse her.

Her skin feels clammy and she isn't coming around. Looking at her more closely, I am paralysed by fear. She's lying on her stomach, head turned to the side away from me. I have to look over her to see her eyes. They are open and look glassy. My blood runs cold through my veins as I feel for a pulse.

My heart pounds painfully against my ribs as I realise I can't find one. My brain tells me to dial 999, but my body feel like it's cemented in place.

I pull my phone from my pocket and, with shaky hands, I dial the number. They ask me if there are any tablets she's likely to have taken, so I look around the bedside cabinet and the floor.

I notice something I didn't see when I came in: a glass of water knocked over on the floor and a couple of boxes of her anti-depressants. It takes my brain a moment to realise that she shouldn't have more than one packet in a month, so she must have stashed last month's tablets instead of taking them. Does that count as premeditation? Did she know she was going to do this? Or is it just as simple as not wanting to take her meds? I remember how foggy it feels when you first take them; maybe she hated feeling like that.

There are also a couple of empty packets of paracetamol lying not too far away.

I don't know what to do. The girls are downstairs and yet I can't leave Ashleigh's side. I'm hoping to God that there's a shallow pulse that I just can't feel, or that I'm doing it wrong. But, in the back of my mind, I know that Drew taught me how to check thoroughly.

It hits me that Danielle could well be an orphan. Pain strikes my heart like a red-hot poker and I collapse in a heap by the side of the bed.

Chapter Twenty-One

Drew

It's been a busy shift, but now we've been called to a suspected overdose and I know that my day isn't about to get any calmer.

Matty drives us to the address the base gave us. Something about it tickles the back of my mind, but, having been so rushed off my feet all day, I don't know what it is. Matty took over driving because he could tell how exhausted I was and how much I desperately needed a break. I could kill for a cup of strong, black coffee right now. But that will have to wait.

We have our blues and twos on, forcing all traffic on the road to move aside for us. We were told that the patient doesn't seem to have a pulse after taking what looks to be an overdose of anti-depressants and paracetamol. But the person with them could just not be able to feel it. I hope to God that's the case.

Pulling up outside the house, I realise with a jolt that I do know the address, and for good reason. It's Ash's house. That means Ash is the suspected overdose. Holy fuck!

I scramble to get the gear from the back of the ambulance and race up the front path and to the doorstep. I knock on the door, but there's no answer. I hear a baby cry and it hits me that that means Danielle is in the house. I have to gain entry no matter what. I don't have time to wait for the police; I have to get in there now. That baby girl is on her own and her mother is dying, if not dead. They can punish me for breaking the door down later if they want, but I am getting in there now.

"Matty, on my three, we kick this door down. Ready?"

"Ready."

"One ... two ..."

I'm interrupted by the door opening. Standing there is Elise. Tears streaming down her face, her eyes sad and hollow.

"She's upstairs, first room on the right."

The emptiness in her voice tells me all I need to know.

Matty and I rush upstairs and I am winded as I cross the threshold of the room and see a lifeless Ash in front of me. It's obvious that she's gone. The pallor of her skin, the glassy look in her eyes … I feel for a pulse, but there's nothing.

We do everything we can to try and resuscitate her, but our efforts are in vain. Ashleigh is dead. There's no helping her now.

I try to swallow around the lump in my throat. It feels like I'm not getting enough air. I rush to the bathroom and make it just in time before throwing up. After I've emptied what little contents were in my stomach, I flush the chain and stand on wobbly legs.

Walking out of the bathroom, I see Elise in Matty's arms. She looks like she's barely holding up. My heart breaks into a thousand pieces, each one sharp and lethal. Not only is my best friend dead, but now his fiancée is too. Danielle is left an orphan and my wife was the one to find the body. There's only once in my life I can ever remember feeling like this.

From what I can see, the room is a pigsty, nothing unusual there. But something feels off about it. It's like there's something in the air, telling me not to venture further. There's an awful smell and it makes me want to crack a window open. Whatever they've done this time, it's left to me to tidy up after them as usual or leave them to their own devices, something I've had to do far too often because of their mood swings.

My parents are strung out junkies. There's no denying it. I've spent too much of my life looking out for myself when it should have been their job. I love my parents, but the older I've gotten, the more I've realised just what kind of people they are. My dad wouldn't dare hit me now I'm of an age to stand up for myself. Well, when he's high, he might still occasionally try and take me on, but he always ends up worse off.

There have been times in my life where he's hit me and I should have gone to the hospital. But I knew never to get anyone else involved. From a young age, I knew that my parents weren't like everybody else's and I knew that, if I involved the police or doctors, I'd get taken away from them. No matter how many times my dad hit me, though, I always forgave him. He's my father after all.

As for my mum, well she's a little firecracker when she gets going. She'll pummel my chest, spit in my face, yank my hair—which I've since learned to keep cut short—slap me, anything she can to hurt me. But she isn't as bad as my dad. Sometimes, she's less far-gone than he is, meaning she keeps an eye out for me. She makes him hit her instead of me. There have been times when she's ended up with broken fingers from where he's grabbed her hand and pushed her fingers back too far, beyond their breaking point. She never lets me involve paramedics and so I know how to splint and wrap them for her.

Today, the air feels like it might suffocate me. So, I move further into the room to open a window or two.

I see drug paraphernalia strewn around every available surface. It seems they haven't bothered to clean up for a day or two. What a surprise!

Looking over at my father, I see him slumped in his favourite, ratty looking, wingback chair. The pallor of his skin looks weird, but then that could just be because the curtains are closed.

I walk over to the window, draw the curtains and crack the window open as wide as it will go. The breeze feels less stifling than the house, so I take in a couple of deep breaths before turning back to the carnage in the lounge.

My mother is lying on the three-seater couch, track marks visible on her outstretched arm. A syringe has fallen from her hand and the tourniquet is still tied around her arm. Typical. She takes a hit and then passes out. Just what I fucking need. I'm trying to study for my exams. I don't need this shit. I'm not meant to be the adult in this house. I'm not meant to be the parent here, they are. But they're both too strung out—both now and all too frequently—to be decent parents.

I can't actually remember a time in my life when they were responsible adults. I can't wait until I'm eighteen and I can move out of this hell-hole. I want a place of my own. A place I can actually call home. This house that we live in, this isn't home; it's a temporary hell of my parents' making.

I reach over to untie the tourniquet from her arm and feel cold, clammy skin under my fingers. I look at her face. It's lax and looks just like she's asleep. Something in the back of my mind tells me that's not true, but I don't want to believe it.

I feel for her pulse, but it's undetectable. I call her name, but there's no response. Not even a flutter of her eyelashes. I slap her round the face—gently, but hard enough to rouse her—but that gets me no response either. Peeling her eyelids open, I see cold, glassy eyes looking back at me. Her pupils are dilated, and her gaze is as dead as a doll's.

I turn to check my father over. He might be strung out, but he usually knows how to rouse her when she's passed out.

Calling his name gets me no response, so I slap him, harder than I did my mother—partly because he needs it and partly because he's a motherfucker who deserves it for getting my mother hooked on drugs. Still no response.

Checking his wrist for a pulse, I spend ages waiting. Sick of the lack of response from him, I walk to the kitchen on shaky legs and pour a glass of cold water. I'm not sure whether you technically 'should' do what I'm planning to do to a junkie, but I don't care. I'm ninety-nine percent sure my mother is dead and it's all his fault.

Back in front of him in the lounge, I pour the cold water over his head. No response.

I scream into the oppressing air around me. I'm frustrated beyond belief. How could they do this? Did they purposefully overdose, or did they take another hit without a thought to the consequences as per usual?

Pulling myself from my thoughts, I grab hold of the landline telephone. There's no dial tone. We've been cut off. Again.

I know they have a phone because they call their dealer with it. But now I have to search two dead bodies to find it.

I think my father's most likely to have control of it. I slip my hand in his pocket and am met by the bulge of a wallet, albeit an empty one. I know that because it always is. I have had to resort to stealing money from my parents when they are passed out, just so that I can put some electric on the meter, or gas to keep the house warm. Usually, I forego the luxury of warmth in favour of food. It all depends how much or how little money they have and how likely they are to notice it's missing.

I push my hand into his other pocket and am able to retrieve a phone. I press the home button to unlock the screen, but it doesn't come to life. The battery must be dead. I see the plug in the socket by his chair, so I connect and wait for it to charge enough to make a call.

Resigned to the fact that my parents are gone, I call 999 and solemnly relay the information to the person on the other end. She says they'll send an ambulance—there might be a pulse too weak for me to detect. But I know that they need a coroner, not a paramedic.

"Drew ... buddy ... Drew ... snap out of it, dude, please."

The urgency in the voice pulls me back to the present where a shiver runs throughout my entire body.

Ashleigh is dead. Her daughter, an orphan. What the hell?! Why did this have to happen?

I shake my head, trying to clear the fogginess that remains in my thoughts.

"Elise, baby …"

She falls into my arms and her body collapses to the floor. I curl myself around her and hold her as she cries.

"I called it in," Matty says, his voice sombre.

"The children …"

"Are fine with me for a minute," he breaks in, "Just comfort your wife. The children will be fine with Uncle Matty. Right?!"

I nod my head and pull Elise tighter against me. I know I have a job to do, but my wife needs me, and nothing will bring Ash back now.

Chapter Twenty-Two

Elise

Ash's death has hit me hard. Drew has been so supportive, but it's tearing me up inside. I don't know what to say or do, how to feel. My brain feels scrambled. My heart feels like it can't take any more.

We may not have been the best of friends. We may not have been the closest. But that doesn't mean her death is any easier to take. There are so many factors that make it painful: Danny's death, Ash's death, Danielle becoming an orphan, social services taking her away in an effort to place her with a foster carer.

Unfortunately, there's a shortage of foster carers. So many children slip through the cracks because of the lack of people able to take them on. So, Drew and I have discussed it and we've decided to apply to be foster carers in the hope of bringing her home with us. The biggest obstacle in our way is the time it takes. It's somewhere between four and six months to complete the assessment. There's also the fact that I'm disabled. It shouldn't necessarily prevent me from being accepted as a foster carer—or so we've been told—but it feels like something else in our way. Then there's the fact that we have to have a spare bedroom, as any child you foster has to have a room separate from your biological children. We've decided that, if it comes to it, we'll turn my home office into a bedroom. I don't really need it now that we have an office in town and, when I work from home, it's all based on my laptop anyway, so I don't need a whole room to work from.

Today is Ash's funeral. Her parents took care of organising some of it, but they wanted input from Maggie—Danny's mother—and from us. I organised the music and the flowers, although I can't be one hundred percent sure it's what she would have chosen for herself. It was a heartbreaking task, but Ash deserves the best send-off we can give her. Her will is being read in a couple of days, while her parents are still in town. Drew and I have been called to the solicitors' office too, although I don't know why, and they won't tell us until we are all there.

I have Drew's suit jacket draped around my shoulders as I look out over the people gathered to say goodbye to Ashleigh. I don't know most of them, but Maggie is here, seeing as though Ash would have been her daughter-in-law.

Social services said Danielle was too young to attend. On one hand, I agree that she shouldn't have to attend her mother's funeral, but on the other hand, she'll never get to say goodbye. But then she's too young to say anything right now, never mind understanding what's happening here. It doesn't stop me missing her though. I loved the time I got to spend with that little girl, even though it wasn't under the best circumstances.

***

The day passed by in a blur. One minute we're standing at the graveside and the next we're sitting in Maggie's house for the wake. She wanted to feel like she was contributing towards the funeral so, when Ash's parents couldn't decide where to hold the wake, she offered up her house.

The sideboards contain photos of Danny, Ash and baby Danielle. Their smiling, happy faces are bittersweet today. Poor Danny never got to hold his daughter in his arms. She never got to know who he was, and now she won't ever know her mother either.

My heart is broken into a million pieces; the shards feel like they could rip me open. As a woman who lost her mother many years ago—although she didn't die, we had a major falling out that will never be repaired—I know how it feels to grow up without parents. I never knew my real dad. He and my mum never had a conventional relationship and, according to her, the last time he saw me was a couple of months before my first birthday. My stepdad was … well, he was abusive. A control freak who sexually abused me for years, telling me that, if I ever told anyone, I'd regret it when he started hurting my family. So, I kept my mouth shut for years. When I finally told someone what was going on, I lost every family member except my grandmother and my aunt. They all believed him instead of me. So much for family.

When I grew up, I swore I'd be a better parent than they were. I'd like to believe I've kept my promise. But I can't help but feel like someone should be looking out for Danielle. She still hasn't been found a place to live. Ash's parents feel like they are too old to look after her. And Maggie feels the same way. They're only in their sixties, but they say they feel like she should be looked after by someone younger and more able to cope with a newborn baby. Truth be told, they've all been rallying around the idea of me and Drew taking Danielle on. But I don't feel like that's going to happen. Drew tells me I'm too hard on myself, but I feel like she's more likely to go to a family where both parents are able-bodied instead of one of them being disabled. I don't feel my disability holds me back, nor does it hinder my ability to be a mother. However, I feel like social services would view me as okay with my biological children, but maybe not with a foster child. I don't know, maybe I am being too hard on myself. Or maybe it's just the grief talking.

Chapter Twenty-Three

Drew

Two days after the funeral, we're sitting in a smart, highly polished solicitor's office. The bookshelves all look like they're lined with law books, some new looking and some worn with time.

The solicitor is sitting in front of us, horn-rimmed glasses perched on his nose. He seems pretty old-school.

As the words leave his lips, I'm sure I misheard him. Us? Seriously? I mean, it's what we wanted. We've been working to try and make it happen. But, in all honesty, we thought she'd be settled with another family before we even got through the application process. Now, here I sit, Elise squeezing my hand so hard I'm sure she's going to break a bone. The thing we didn't expect to happen is about to become a reality.

When my best friend died, I felt strangely lost at sea. But Elise was my anchor and held me fast while everything happened around us. Then, when Ash gave birth to Danielle, it felt like that hole in my heart from the loss of Danny was filled a little with the birth of his daughter. But Ash's postnatal depression was worse than any of us thought possible and she took her own life. We'll never know whether she meant to die or if it was a cry for help and she thought someone would find her in time.

Having to bury two people in such a short space of time has taken its toll on everyone involved. Maggie is lost to her grief. She looks like she's living in a bubble. Ash's parents are the same. They've just lost their daughter and they are having a hard time dealing with it. Then add losing their granddaughter to that and their grief is at an all-time high.

But now … now she's about to be settled in a family that will love, care and provide for her for the rest of her life. Instead of being a father of two, it'll be three. Of course, I won't take the place of her biological father, but at least this way she'll be with people that loved her father, people that knew him and her mother and can give her memories of them to cherish. We'll never let her forget her wonderful parents.

It turns out, Ash left a will—that's obviously why we're at the solicitor's office in the first place—and it seems she stipulated that she wanted us to take Danielle in, if something should happen to her.

I would never have wished for anything like this to happen, never in my worst nightmares did I imagine both Danny and Ash being gone so young. But I will honour her final wishes and be a good role model to their little girl.

Elise looks at me with unshed tears in her eyes. The solicitor finishes reading the will, which I failed to hear another word of. Then we're all on our feet and Elise rushes into my arms. Her head nestles in the crook of my neck and I feel her hot tears soaking into my shirt. I wrap my arms around her, holding her tight just like she's done for me so many times before. I'll be her anchor in the storm.

"We need to—" She chokes up before she can say anything else.

I soothe her, running my hands through her hair. Kissing the top of her head, I reach to take her hand and walk her outside into the fresh air.

"We have to give that little girl everything, Drew. We made a promise as her godparents to be there for her. We never knew this was a possibility, but we have to stand by our word."

"I know, baby, and we will."

We walk over to a bench and take a seat. The air is crisp, the sky is clear, and it would otherwise be a beautiful day if it weren't for the circumstances.

"I never wanted this, Drew. I wish it hadn't come to this."

"I know that sweetheart. But we have to make the best of it for the sake of that little girl."

"Can we do this? I mean, Cassie is only little and now we'll have a baby to look after too."

"We've been over this a thousand times, baby. It'll be hard emotionally, but we can cope. We have each other. That little girl has nobody and could have ended up with complete strangers that didn't know her parents. Which would be the better outcome?"

"Us. God knows we have the love to give her. And we'll never let her forget her mummy and daddy, never. I just—"

"It'll be okay, Elise. Honestly. You're right; we'll never let her forget them. We'll bring her up to know that her parents would have given everything for her."

"I'm scared."

If we've had this conversation once, we've had it a thousand times. She's scared that we'll mess it up. Being pseudo-parents to someone else's child is different than being parents to your own children. You're scared you'll get it wrong. Scared that they won't be the person they were meant to be because they aren't being brought up by their own parents. But if I know one thing, it's this: regardless of blood, family is what you make of it. I wasn't brought up by my real parents, they weren't present for my childhood. I always had to make excuses at school for why they couldn't come to parents evening and stuff like that.

Then one day, when I was fifteen, I was taken in by my wonderful grandparents. They made me the man I am today. Did they do a bad job of it because I wasn't theirs? Am I not the man I was meant to be because they brought me up instead of my parents? No, if you ask me, I am exactly who I was meant to be. And Danielle will be too.

We can give that girl a loving home, a good environment to grow up in. We are good people and we'd never hurt her, just like we wouldn't hurt Caleb and Cassie.

"I'm scared too," I admit quietly, "but that doesn't mean we can't provide a good, stable, loving environment for that little girl."

"You're right. I know you are. I just can't help the thoughts that swirl around my head."

"And you're going to think the same in the future too. There's no stopping that. But being scared doesn't make us incapable, does it?"

"No."

As the word falls from her lips, I see a couple walking towards us, pushing a pushchair. They look a little out of place, dressed in suits, looking stuffy and more than a little uncomfortable.

"Mr and Mrs Wright?" the woman asks.

"Yes."

"We're from social services."

That explains the suits in this weather.

I look into the pram and see Danielle. She's dressed in a little pink dress with a bow on her head. Her blonde hair is slightly curly, and she looks adorable.

We walk with them towards another office. Once we get there, they offer us a drink and we both settle on a strong black coffee.

They go over some of the details of us having Danielle. It turns out Ash made the will a week before she died. If anything suggests she took her life on purpose … I won't finish that thought.

Elise sits with Danielle on her lap. She coos at her just like she did Cassie when she was born. She might question her abilities, but I don't. She's an amazing mother. She's an even more amazing wife and I couldn't be prouder.

I look at my wife and I know we can do this. We can be good parents to Danielle. We can make Danny and Ashleigh proud. She'll always know where she came from and how amazing her parents were. We'll show her pictures and tell her stories. Sure, that's nowhere near as good as growing up with her real parents, but there's no other option now that they are both gone.

I know Elise is scared that we'll make mistakes, but being scared is better than being apathetic about it all. I'd rather she feels something instead of feeling numb. I'll admit, I'm scared too. I'm scared I won't be as good a dad as Danny would have been. But I'm not scared about Elise's abilities. I will never question her ability to be a brilliant mother.

Sitting down next to them, I flash Elise a small grin and she hands Danielle over to me. Just like with Cassie, I'm scared that I'll break her. Why is it that for women it's natural to hold a baby, but with us guys, we feel nervous? Like, the palms of my hands are clammy, and my heart is pounding against my ribcage.

Looking down at her, I see beautiful blue eyes looking up at me. She really is beautiful. She has her mum's nose and her dad's eyes. A constant reminder of the place she came from, and not in a bad way.

Chapter Twenty-Four

Elise

Three weeks later...

We've been packing for hours. Maggie asked Drew and me if we would mind helping pack up the house where Danny and Ash lived. It's being put on the market and the money will be held in trust for Danielle. Some of the stuff is going into storage, but a few bits and pieces are coming home with us.

Danielle's cot is already at our house, in my old office, which has now been decorated in pink and purple. Her wardrobe, chest of drawers, changing table and a few other things are coming home with us today. Plus all the clothes Ash bought her, the bottle steriliser, and tons of nappies and wipes that Ash must have stocked up on well in advance. Her stuffed animal collection in the hammock on the wall will be hung up in her bedroom back at ours too.

It feels bittersweet. We're packing up the contents of her nursery here and taking it elsewhere. That feels wrong. But, at the same time, I know that her living with us will be the best thing in the long run. Both sets of grandparents agree and they are supporting us in any way they can.

Drew and I have discussed adopting Danielle officially, but she's not our daughter, she's Danny and Ash's. She deserves to keep her own surname and to know where she came from. Although Drew is still saying we could adopt her, just to make it legal, and she can keep her surname if that's what I want. It's hard to think about the future, but will she get made fun of at school because we're all Wrights and she isn't? Kids can be cruel over the smallest of things, so ... I guess we still have time to discuss it further.

Drew is moving the furniture into a van we've hired. Matty from work is helping him with the heavy lifting. I'm just packing clothes and stuff into boxes because I can't do any of the lifting. It feels like we're intruding in their home, but Maggie keeps assuring me we're doing the right thing. She's such a good woman. I don't know how she's keeping it together. I think she's like swan; calm and serene on the surface, but paddling like crazy beneath, just to stay afloat.

"Let's get this dresser on the van and then we'll take this lot to storage before coming back for another vanload," Drew says to Matty.

As they move the dresser, I see an envelope fall to the floor. I walk to pick it up and see *Danielle* written across it in Ash's handwriting. It feels like it has a bit of weight to it, more than just a piece of paper. I hold it in shaky hands and walk back to sit on the bed.

"Drew," I call, as I hear him coming back upstairs.

He walks into the bedroom and I hand him the envelope. He looks at it with a myriad of emotions in the depths of his eyes.

"What do we do with it?"

"You took the words right out of my mouth. I don't know whether to open it or not. It's obviously something important, but Danielle can't read it herself, so do we read it or not?"

Maggie comes back into the bedroom and Drew shows it to her.

"You are her guardians now, you should open it and then keep it safe for Danielle in the future," she says.

With shaking hands, I open the envelope and see three rings as well as a piece of paper. I tip them onto the bed and subconsciously move my hand to cover my mouth. It's Danny and Ash's wedding rings and Ash's engagement ring.

I pick them up and place them in the palm of my hand. Looking at them there, I feel tears sting the back of my eyes. We'd wondered where their rings were before their funerals and had turned the place upside down looking for them. Now it's obvious why we didn't find them.

Drew takes the piece of paper from the envelope and begins to read aloud:

My Dearest Danielle,
If you are reading this, then you know that I am gone. I never meant to do this, to feel this way, but I was trapped in a vicious cycle and had to break it. I'm so deeply sorry for the effect this will have had on you. I didn't want to leave you, my beautiful girl, but I didn't know what else to do. This may make no sense at all to you right now, in fact, it may

never make sense, and for that I am so truly sorry.

You were the sunshine in my day, the brightest thing in my life for six months. Your daddy had passed away before I gave birth to you and I was stuck in a depression so deep, I couldn't drag myself out. Please, never question whether you were worth my love, because you were. You deserved all my love and my undivided attention, but depression is a horrible disease.

You see, my darling, if I'm being completely honest here—which I'm trying desperately to be—I had something called bipolar. I struggled with my mental health before I met your daddy. He did his best to make me happy every day we shared together. We had highs and lows, like any couple, but he was an amazing man who gave me reason to smile. I could list a million reasons why I loved your daddy and that still wouldn't be enough words to express how much love I had for him. I loved him completely with all my heart and soul. We had talked about having children together. It was going to be amazing. Sadly, your daddy had an accident at work and he passed away before you were born. He never got to see his beautiful angel and that made my postnatal depression worse. I'm not trying to make excuses here, you just need to know everything, so you know how much we loved and wanted you.

When he passed away, my struggles with my bipolar got worse. I stopped taking my meds, which, looking back, I know I shouldn't have done.

I slipped deeper into depression and couldn't find my way back out. I missed your daddy so deeply and I wanted to be with him. I know that my actions will have hurt you as well as my family, but I couldn't cope with being a mum without Danny by my side. I went to counselling and tried my hardest to overcome my problems. They prescribed medication which I started taking. But they cast a sort of fog over everything. My days were so foggy, and I couldn't cope being a single parent. You are worth so much better than me, Danielle. You deserve a life full of love, laughter, the joy of having siblings to play with.

Please know that I struggled with this. I didn't just wake up one day thinking I wanted to die and made a rash decision. Maybe that makes it worse, for you to hear that it wasn't spontaneous. You need to know, I struggled with the idea of leaving you, but ultimately, I felt you'd be better off with Elise and Drew. I made them your godparents at your christening, now I've made a stipulation in my will that they are to be your guardians. I don't want you falling through the cracks in the system with social services. You deserve an amazing family and, trust me, Elise and Drew are a wonderful couple. They're amazing parents to Caleb and Cassie and now they will be to you too.

I've put my engagement ring in this envelope for you when you are older, plus mine and Daddy's wedding rings, so that you have something that meant a lot to both of us. There are also albums full of photos of us in your room. I hope whoever clears out the house finds them in your wardrobe and takes care of them until you are old enough to look through them.

The house is to be put on the market and sold. The money from the sale is to be put into a trust for you when you turn eighteen. I know no amount of money will bring Daddy or me back, but it will fund your way through college and whatever you want to do in your life.

Please, I implore you, don't be angry with me. I don't expect your immediate forgiveness for leaving you, but I hope, one day, you'll see that I felt there was no other option for me. I loved your daddy so much that it left me with a broken heart when he died.

My love for you didn't diminish, but I couldn't be the mother you deserved. I'm broken, Danielle. So truly broken that nothing and no-one can fix me.

I hope that one day, with the love and care Elise and Drew can provide you, you will understand my actions.

I know Elise and Drew will never replace your mummy and daddy, but I know they'll love you like their own daughter. They have such good hearts and they will give you everything I never could.

If there's one thing I want you to know and remember most of all, it's that I love you, so very much. Wherever you are, whatever you are doing, Daddy and I will be together watching over you.

My hope for my beautiful baby girl is that you grow up to be as beautiful on the inside as you are on the outside. I want you to have a good heart, to empathise with people in pain, to love unconditionally and to just be you.

Whilst a life without your mummy and daddy isn't what we planned for, I want you to see that you are loved, without condition. You are loved beyond what any words can express. My darling girl, you will grow up knowing a love so deep and true because of Elise, Drew and your grandparents.

One day, you'll grow up and get married to a good man, have children of your own and love them with every fibre of your being. When that happens, Daddy and I will be so pleased. We'll always be there with you, like guardian angels, protecting you from harm. We may have left you in this life, but, my darling, we'll all be together in the next life—that I solemnly promise you.

With all the love in my heart,

Mummy.

The tears roll down my cheeks and I leave them there. I never knew Ash had bipolar and I didn't know how much she struggled. I wish I'd known, then we could have done more to help her. But we will help her now by loving her daughter and bringing her up to know she is cherished. I'll keep this letter somewhere safe, along with the rings, until Danielle is older. Drew and I will decide when she is mature enough to handle the words on the page.

I can't help but grieve for Ash. We may not have been the closest of friends, I didn't know her all that long really, but my heart breaks knowing that she felt there was no other option on the table for her.

Drew sits next to me and wraps his arms around me. Maggie is sitting on the floor, where she crumpled as Drew read the letter. There's so much heartache in this room that it's stifling. I need air. I need to get outside now. I can feel the start of a panic attack beginning to grip me.

I grab my walking stick and make my way downstairs. Once I reach the bottom step, I reach for the front door and pull it open. Standing here on the doorstep, I try to calm myself. I try to think of something to take my mind off the panic buzzing around my mind.

"Baby?" Drew's voice comes from behind me.

I turn, and he rushes towards me. Taking me in his arms, he whispers soothing words in my ear. I sob into his chest, but my tears aren't for me. They are for a life unfulfilled. Two lives, actually: Ash and Danny.

As my breathing becomes more erratic, Drew pulls back and talks to me. He makes me recite a series of numbers and colours, thus making my mind concentrate on that instead of the panic. I feel it ebbing away slowly.

Taking deep breaths in through my mouth and out through my nose, I begin to feel calmer.

"Elise?" Drew whispers softly.

"I'm okay," I reply, swallowing down the lump in my throat.

"We can go home and come back tomorrow."

"No, we need to do this now, else I'll come back and feel this way all over again."

"I can take you home with the girls and come back to finish the packing."

"No, Drew. Honestly, I want to get this done now."

"There was another envelope, Maggie found it. It's addressed to us. I didn't know if you wanted to read it or not."

He pulls a folded envelope from his pocket. I take it from him and open it.

"Have you read it?"

"No. I wanted to wait for you."

I take a deep breath and unfold the paper.

Dear Elise and Drew,

By the time you read this, I'll be gone. Please know I never meant for things to happen this way. I've written a letter to Danielle that I would appreciate you keeping safe for her to read one day when she's older. It explains how I struggled with bipolar as well as the depression I sank into after losing Danny. Drew, you probably never noticed when we were working together, I tried my hardest to suppress it. I flirted, I put a plastic smile on my face, I hid the real me from the world. But when I had Danielle and was diagnosed with postnatal depression, there was no more hiding it. I was too exhausted emotionally to be able to hide it anymore.

I'm sure by now you know that I left a will with my solicitor and I'm sure they've told you I wanted you to be Danielle's guardians. I'm sorry to burden you, but you were the epitome of the perfect parents, something I could never be. I wanted Danielle to know what it's like to be loved and cherished, to have all the things I could never give her without Danny by my side.

I hope you have read—or will read—my letter to Danielle. I'm emotionally worn out, too much so to rewrite everything in this letter that I told her. So please, if you haven't already, read that letter. It should go a little way to explaining my actions. I wish things hadn't had to happen this way. I wish Danny hadn't died. I wish that I could have been a good mum without him. I just didn't know how. I didn't know how to look after myself, let alone a baby.

Maybe suicide seems like the coward's way out to you, but I hope you won't always think that way about me. I tried to be brave, I just couldn't pull through. I'm so sorry. Please try and forgive me. I don't expect you to forgive me now, but in time. Please know that I didn't arrive at this decision lightly.

Look after my baby girl. Give her all the love I can't. In the end, I hope you, like me, will see that this is for the best.

Ash.

Again, tears roll down my face. The sadness threatens to overwhelm me. I wish like hell we could have done something to save this from happening. I don't think Ash was a coward, regardless of her words or her actions. I think she was a woman who was sinking without us noticing and I feel guilty for allowing her feelings to swallow her whole.

Drew wraps his arms around me once more and whispers how much he loves me.

I know we can be good parents to Danielle, I just wish we didn't have to be. It isn't a burden to look after her, I don't agree with that part of Ash's letter at all. She's not a burden; she's a beautiful little girl who deserves the world. I know Drew and I will do our best to give it to her.

***

After the house is empty, I stand with the key in the door. I take one last deep breath and turn it in the lock. My heart feels heavy and my bones feel weary and tired. I can't wait to get home and cuddle up with Drew and the children. The only good thing to come of today is the chance to close one chapter and move on to the next, whatever that may hold in store for us all.

Chapter Twenty-Five

Drew

A few months later…

It's Danielle's first birthday and we are celebrating with both sets of her grandparents. They've been a godsend these past few months. They've helped us see that Danielle is in a good place now, with us. We decided to allow her the choice in the future as to whether we adopt her or not. We'll always tell her about her parents and how wonderful they were. But she'll know that we love her like one of our own too.

We bought her a locket that some people may see as a bit morbid, but we don't think so. It's a special locket that holds part of the ashes of her parents. Initially we were going to buy one for Ash and one for Danny, but in the end, we decided to combine them because then they are together, always. It's being kept in a special jewellery box along with her mum's engagement ring and both wedding rings.

The house sold quickly and the trust fund was set up for Danielle. It's enough to see her through college, university and then some, if that's what she chooses to do.

She's such a happy baby, we couldn't wish for more at this point. We treat her just the same as we do Caleb and Cassie.

It was a bit awkward trying to explain to Caleb about the situation without getting into the details of Ash's death. He's a mature kid, but he doesn't have to know every little detail. All he knows is that we are Danielle's guardians and he loves her like another sister. Cassie is playful and happy to have another little girl to play with. She can't say Danielle, so she calls her Elle.

We're having a family party at home for Elle. Elise made sandwiches and other buffet style food. Maggie made a cake in the shape of the

Disney castle. She runs her own bakery, so we knew she could pull it off. It looks beautiful as the centrepiece for the table.

There are tons of presents. I think we all went a little overboard. People would probably say we're spoiling her, but we don't care. She's happy and that's all that matters.

Life has thrown a lot our way, but our coping strategy is much better than my old one of travelling and not getting attached. Our way of coping is to hold strong as a family. We are all in this together after all.

Maggie and Ash's parents didn't know what to expect about being allowed to see Elle, but we've allowed them the same access as Danny and Ash would have done. They see her regularly and they lavish her with love and attention. That's probably why she's such a happy baby.

Maggie lights the candles on the cake and we all sing 'Happy Birthday'. We try to get Elle to blow the candles out, but she blows bubbles instead, so Elise helps her do it.

I sit with Elle on my knee as Elise cuts the cake and hands pieces to everyone. Elle likes trying to feed herself, so, when Elise hands me a plate, she makes a grab for it. She ends up with it all over her hands and face and Maggie takes a photo of her to add to the family album we're keeping for her for when she's older.

***

After everyone else is gone, Elise sits down with the children while I tidy up. She's exhausted after today, so I gave her strict instructions not to help me. Caleb bags up all the wrapping paper strewn everywhere while Elise plays with the girls.

I'm making lasagne for tea. Standing here in the kitchen with my iPod in the dock, I sing along as I chop the onions. 'When You're Gone' by Smithfield comes on and I sing a little louder.

It's been a bittersweet day, but I know that, if there is any type of afterlife, then Danny and Ash are up there, watching over their beautiful little girl.

As the lasagne cooks in the oven, I sit in the lounge watching my little family. Caleb is playing on his games console and Elise is playing princesses with Elle and Cassie. They look so happy and it makes my heart swell with love and pride.

Of all I've learned in this life, one thing is clear: home is not a place, it's a feeling. A feeling of contentment, love, joy … it's not a physical place that exists within your heart.

This is my home. My wife, three beautiful children. What else could a man need? The answer to that is … nothing. I don't need anything else in this life or the next. I have everything I could have ever dreamed of.

I know when I was younger I stayed away from women, from the idea of commitment. I didn't believe in instalove or any of that. But now? Oh, how life has changed my mind. Elise Swanson walked back into my life and I knew that I'd met my match. She's a fiery little spitfire, a beautiful woman on the inside and out. She makes my heart beat faster just looking at her. There's nothing I wouldn't give for her. The day we got back together was one of the best days of my life, except for my wedding day, the day I adopted Caleb and the day Cassie was born.

Loving this beautiful woman, trusting her with my heart is the best decision I ever made. She holds my heart in the palm of her hand and I know she'll never break it. In turn, I will never break hers. We made a commitment for life and that is exactly what I'm going to give her. I'll never break her heart, I'll try my best to never make her cry and, if I do, I'll always make it up to her.

Until my dying day, I will look after Elise and the children. They'll never want for anything while there is breath in my body.

The End

About the author

Keren is a bookworm whose bookshelves groan under the weight of her obsession, but she believes there's always room for "one more book."

She lives in the UK with her son and when she isn't reading or writing, she's nurturing the reader and writer in him as he's currently writing his own book.

Keren loves to connect with her readers. You can reach out to her on social media. She loves to talk anything books, movies and TV.

Her other obsessions include Disney, Marvel, and she's a Potterhead for life.

Also by Keren Hughes

SAFE

In every way Elise is a survivor.

As a child, she was abused by the first man she trusted completely.

As a teenager, she was manipulated mentally and physically by a man, to the point that she could not see just how bad their relationship was. She ended up too scared to stay, but even more scared to leave.

Having suffered for years at the hands of men she trusted, she met Jensen. Finally, she felt that she had someone good in her life. Their relationship was all too brief, and when it ended she built a wall around her heart. How could she ever trust a man again?

Elise; a single, disabled mum. It was all too clear that men could not see past her disability. Forsaking the love of men, she concentrated on her son, Caleb. It was the one thing she knew she could do right. Her love for Caleb was beyond measure. He was her whole world. However, Elise's best friend Sam had other ideas, and set her up on a blind date with an extremely hot paramedic.

With so much hurt in the past, she was not sure if she was strong enough to face rejection again. Could she truly open her heart again to another? Could Elise finally find her safe haven in his arms, or would he just add another scar to her soul?

Coming soon from Keren Hughes

Secret Santa

Being born and raised in the town of Snowflake has its perks for Aneurin Mackenzie, she's seen it all; businesses booming and the town flourishing. Sadly, she's also seen it torn to shreds by a previous Mayor.

Then, in comes cocky, arrogant, filthy rich Preston Wolfric III with his "fresh ideas" to bring business back to this small town. He wants to turn Snowflake around, bringing it to the 21st century.
However, Nye will not let her town be changed without a fight.

He's a big city alpha male, she's a small town girl with no desire to change. She plans to run him out of town but what she doesn't count on is that cocky jerk making his way under her skin, seeping into her veins.

She didn't realise how devastatingly handsome he is. He didn't realise what he needed was right in front of him.
What will happen when Preston and Nye's worlds collide? Will there be sparks or will it become a fire that lays waste to everything they thought they knew?

Do opposites really attract?

A big city, filthy rich CEO and a country girl. What could go wrong?

More of our titles

Cowboys in Charge by Starla Kaye
Her Cowboy's Way by Starla Kaye
Punished by Richard Savage, Nadia Nautalia & Starla Kaye
Accidental Affair by Leslie McKelvey
Right Place, Right Time by Leslie McKelvey
Her Sister's Keeper by Leslie McKelvey
Playing for Keeps by Glenda Horsfall
Playing By His Rules by Glenda Horsfall
The Stir of Echo by Susan Gabriel
Rally Fever by Crea Jones
Behind The Clouds by Jan Selbourne
Trusting Love Again by Starla Kaye
Runaway Heart by Leslie McKelvey
The Otherling by Heather M. Walker
First Submission - Anthology
These Eyes So Green by Deborah Kelsey
Dark Awakening by Karlene Cameron
The Reclaiming of Charlotte Moss by Heather M. Walker
Ryann's Revenge by Rai Karr & Breanna Hayse
The Postman's Daughter by Sally Anne Palmer
Final Kill by Leslie McKelvey
Killer Secrets by Zia Westfield
Crossover, Texas by Freia Hooper-Bradford
The King's Blade by L.J. Dare
Uniform Desire - Anthology
Safe by Keren Hughes
Finishing the Game by M.K. Smith
Out of the Shadows by Gabriella Hewitt
A Woman's Secret by C.L. Koch
Her Lover's Face by Patricia Elliott
Love Times Infinity by K.L. Ramsey
Naval Maneuvers by Dee S. Knight
Love's Patient Journey by K.L. Ramsey
Perilous Love by Jan Selbourne
Patrick by Callie Carmen
Love's Design by K.L. Ramsey
The Brute and I by Suzanne Smith
Love's Promise by K.L. Ramsey

www.ingramcontent.com/pod-product-compliance
Lightning Source LLC
Chambersburg PA
CBHW031337170626
46807CB00002B/745